CALL IT HORSES

CALL IT HORSES

— A NOVEL —

JESSIE VAN EERDEN

2580 Craig Rd.
Ann Arbor, MI 48103
www.dzancbooks.org

Library of Congress Catalogue-in-Publication Data Available Upon Request

ISBN: 978-0983740599
First paperback edition: October 2024
Interior design by Michelle Dotter
Cover by Matthew Revert

Printed in the United States of America

10 9 8 7 6 5 4 3 2 1

in memory of my great-aunt Unabelle Boggs

On a notepad from the dollar store I write you. A red star explodes around the *only one dollar* on the cover. There is a break in the cold weather, as if the earth were taking a gasp, all the frozen grass gone to mud. It's a fissure to step into, or a point of stillness. A letter to you may become a channel, or chute, and could dislodge the thing lodged in me. At various times I have written you scraps on receipts and Denny's napkins and her untendered prescriptions. *Dear Ruth.* And in my childhood there were those three years of letters from you and to you, the language always on fire. My thoughts shift like water when I picture these pages in your hands. The mud will freeze again, after this respite from winter. In this liminal mud—I can almost see its steam—something does begin.

I write you about the dead. I write you to stay alive and, after all this time, I write you, still, to become myself.

Do you think regions and landscapes can body forth what's inside a person? I think that. Here in the steaming quick thaw. Back then, before we left, Mave and I could smell our minds rotting in the awful lush of West Virginia mountain summer, the damp sponge of dirt. We were wringing wet, like cats up from the creek; our breathing was gagged with sphagnum moss and fetid swamp weed. And the humid fog of funerals had left a yellowing film on our skin. We had to go, you understand. We had to make it as far as we could.

If there are indeed regions inside a person, she and I longed for the inner desert region, to meet its physical correlative in the bear grass and prickly pear and quartz and juniper. The smoke of red rock. We longed for an unchoked landscape. I did not know then what the third party longed for—Nan, sitting backseat like a viper. The atlas barreled us forward to cut through our mountains slogged shut with old skunk cabbage and October leaf rot, toward the horse fields beautifully fenced in Kentucky and the Tennessee trees from which ticks would fall into our hair. We would detour to Memphis since Mave, at age seventy, had never seen Memphis, nor had I. Across the blue ribbon of the Mississippi, the atlas held out Arkansas, Oklahoma, Texas in their blocky territories, then the New Mexico line dotted down across Interstate 40 and there was Tucumcari, which I love to say aloud, probably a Comanche word for *ambush*, vocalized and transcribed and retranscribed. The bright line of I-40 would pull us into places dried out, nearer the sun. It would not be your Sinai Desert, Ruth, or your ancient manuscripts studied on sabbaticals, but it's what we could manage.

I promised Mave we would make it to the desert, but I'll tell you now we made it only to the dry windy Texas plains. We didn't speak when we left. Only the fading hydrangeas spoke their goodbye, without any urgency. On the bypass, our tongues loosened.

"How long?" Mave asked.

"Maybe three days," I said.

"Portable oxygen has a shelf life." She deflected her ache onto the highway signs. When she would speak to you, did she also always deflect away?

The car was a blue Oldsmobile, not in good shape, but its metal seemed lighter for its lightness in color. The car belonged to Nan, but she was demoted to the backseat as a condition of our bringing her along. We floated upon the asphalt, and when the earth flattened the least bit, we tried to give ourselves to the road. Two of us were wives—Nan and me. I thirty-six and she somewhere in her mid-twenties.

On a rough-lumber table with a vinyl tablecloth, I write this to you. Dear Ruth, can you feel the unfolding of our disaster? I should write each word as carefully and detailed as a hieroglyph. I should choose sensibly, what bird to mean *soul*, what horse to mean *I'm falling fast through time.* Each word precious. You taught me that, in the letters you wrote me from your desk in Northampton, which I always pictured as dark wood, wide, strewn with books and, at the corner, a vase of tulips. What promise did you see in me? Anyway, I do think it's something else—after the words—that might be precious. Once language slips through the sieve, maybe something remains. Maybe a heart beating.

I WANTED THE DESERT SCRUB TO SHOW ME, FINALLY, whether I was incapable of love, whether I lived too hermetically—"She is too private," said Mother to Mave when I was a child. The desert dust I would sit down in would body forth my arid solitude. That was the idea.

"I'll thatch you a roof for your hermit hut," Mave once said to me, neither kindly nor unkindly.

"On the road," she crooned in the blue car. "I love automatic windows. I want to be windblown. How about you, Nan?"

Nan sat wounded and further woundable in my rearview, perhaps less viper and more nude bird except for her huge mass of hair flying up and out and over. Black eye radiant at its yellowing edge.

She reached up in great transgression to tune the radio, so we all discovered together it was busted. Her arm was a war zone.

"God, he did a number on you," said Mave.

Nan said nothing audible.

I pictured upon the windshield the squint of Dillon's dim eyes, his longing to fly jets, stealth bombers, and how he'd braided yarn into my black hair as if a little boy though he hadn't been a little boy then. But we had been young, pliable. This was now the detailed work of my Dillon—Nan's arms of bruises, Nan his wife.

"By what star do you guide your life, Nannette?" asked Mave, slipping the cotton ball out from under the oxygen tubing above her ear to scratch.

"By what?"

"It's okay, you don't have to talk. Lewd little beast."

I said, "Mave. Stop." But I didn't mean it.

"He called me a little whore," Nan said very small.

"We should make nametags," Mave said.

"That's enough," I said.

"Little Whore, Little Gypsy Moth Hair. In your little apricot shift." She replaced the yellow cotton ball.

I heard Ellis shake his floppy ears to get a flea out, then settle, probably with his chin on Nan's sumptuous leg. Ellis was my husband's dog but somehow his dense houndbody had found itself in the blue car. There were smudges of nose and tongue on the right-side window of the backseat. I'll bring him back, Clay, I'd said to myself.

"Give us the right names in your book," Mave said to me.

"There is no book," I said.

"What book?" asked Nan.

It was 1990. October. The Saturday world outside of Nan's rusty Olds, which was really Dillon's rusty Olds, was all gray dawn and asphalt and trees thinning then thickening back up just when I started to breathe. None of us had ever seen the desert. When Nan drifted off and flattened her hair against the window, I studied her in the other mirror.

"Still jealous?" Mave asked me. "You could've been his punching bag. You dodged a bullet, as they say." Nan's pretty lips parted in her sleep.

I admit to you, Ruth, the word *jealous* didn't touch the hem. I wanted to carve out her stomach and insert myself up through her skeletal system. Rip out her spine like a brittle fish's, and as I did so, it would sound as though I were running a stick over a xylophone.

"Not really," I said.

Was it her loveliness that stung me, in comparison with my weighted hair and dark gaunt face? No, I think it was her forthrightness, her ease. I understood her to be hurt and groping after something—that I understood—but not her ease.

Some time passed, or it didn't pass. Instead time swelled Mave's lungs, squeezing out the rightful air, her death imminent even from the start, though I wouldn't admit it. Some silence fell. Time and silence were the big actors now, calling all the shots. When we were about twenty miles out of Caudell, West Virginia on 119 South, away from the smell of swamp and green and the baled alfalfa, Nan roused and wiped her mouth.

The first time I'd ever seen this girl, I mistakenly thought she'd held a dead baby, and I unmistakenly thought she was starved and stuck.

"Are we ever going back?" Nan asked, as though she had been dreaming about where she'd unpack her suitcase of silk things, her one spare dress, her makeup and her filthy pictures, and, beneath those pictures, her secret beautiful ones. "Or are we going to stay out there?"

Nobody answered.

Mave told me once I needed to write a book, and I said, "Beginning where?"

"At the beginning, Frankie," she said.

"The beginning of what?"

"Time."

We cracked up.

"Start when we slimed out of the sea," she said. "Or in your hopeless cosmology, when the god-turtle surfaced and somebody said, 'Let there be a city on top of her great shell.'" Mave's strong lips somehow like a vise, as if when opened, there would be mercy, reprieve. But more often, there was brusqueness. More often than that, obfuscation.

"Begin before words begin," she said. "Write the chaos and the anthem." She told me I only had to create something to come back to. Get a little traction, hang a little meat out there for myself. Then go mop my many floors with Murphy Oil Soap and do something with my heavy drapery of hair, then come back to it. She wanted me to write it for her, maybe because she'd given up on her own work years before.

I once wrote you sheaves, Ruth. I wrote letters to say everything, and sometimes to not say anything but only to shape the day with my hands, to make sure it happened, as surely as the scuff on the porch floor when I pulled the screen door open. For a brief time, I wrote you daily in my sprawling child hand. When I received your letters about the life inside words, about hieroglyphs of peregrine and bread, about flowers, you rendered back to me myself in a more whole form, which I saw the way an animal sees water up ahead, through the trees. I am unable to write a book for Mave. I can only write to you, about her: the chaos and the anthem.

Why did she and Nan and I load into the beat-up blue car and head west that October in 1990? I'll go back about a year and a half before that, to a night in early spring, 1989, to say what happened. Beginning in the fertile dark of Mave's dining room—your Mave, your love and one-time student, and my Mave, my aunt and guardian. Here, nameless, fusty cells divided in a Petri dish of dark. *Begin before words.*

That spring night, I walked from my house to Mave's through our break in the fence to retrieve her from where she sat on the unmopped dining room floor with no lights on. The overhead was burnt out. I picked over cardboard and books by feel and found a sweater to pull over her foul sleepshirt. She went all deadweight, exaggerated, and let me strongarm her to the concrete slab of front porch glommed with old TVs and encyclopedias and potato skins growing hair. Debris born from porch light, as though uttered by it.

Her mind itched, she would've said if I had asked. Drink is a good scratch. This was one of her bad days.

I propped her up in the patio chair. I had not come for her as much as for myself. I got a Pilsner from her fridge and split it into two pint jars. She situated thickly into the chair and took a sip to ease herself from hangover, and she smelled my uncertainty, ripe as her odor.

"What's Miranda think?" she asked, as if we were in the middle of a conversation, which I suppose we always were—a dense forest of it. Mave had called me on the phone because she hadn't been able to get up off the floor, her body able as ever, breath strong at that time, legs all muscle, but mentally immovable from her pool of large unwashed shirt. Healthy as a horse, she'd say if I asked, but as she raised the Ball jar to her lips I saw that she'd scraped her knuckles somehow.

"Why does it matter what Miranda thinks?" I said. "What do you think?"

Mave rubbed her dirty shirt and sweater against her tired breasts not strapped down by their compression bra. She surveyed the moods available and settled on the one in which she knew Aunt Miranda would have been the better mother to me after their sister, my mother Margot, had died. So: the deflection. Go ask Miranda.

The porch light stretched far enough to show where a clan of crocus had unsutured the ground. Near that, a tight peony bud shivered at the ghost of a bird. I looked over toward my empty house in which I'd lived my entire life, first with my parents, then as an orphan, with Mave as my guardian but we stayed in our separate houses, which everyone found strange. My window lights ever within sight through our break in the barbed wire and the wild rose. I could smell the grass trying to remember itself in thaw, the blades stretching toward the notion of summer. About a mile out on the ridge, the lights of the bronze plant glowed a dome over the town. I wanted Mave to sleep then wake up. Only once had I found her with a handgun nearby, her Browning pistol. Only once had I raised my head terrified that she'd used it.

I scanned the porch—an old butter churn, the three TVs with burned-out picture tubes, the potato peelings in a Shop 'n Save produce box. A gun could disappear in so much junk. "Miranda says I'll think myself into the grave. And she says I'm thirty-five with no kids, I'm a part-time janitor, and the State Road has benefits."

"The State does have benefits."

What Miranda said was that if I didn't marry Clay Good I'd end up like Mave. When I was a child, what Miranda said was, "My sister is very bright, but can't you see that it has done her in?" Miranda's eyes teary, her housedress neat and trim, and her mantle as wife and mother of four bowing her back but also relieving her of any doubt, of any discernible restlessness.

"And she thinks his gospel band sounds professional," I said. "The Good News Boys, like a cassette tape."

"Christ." Mave laughed. I felt some danger pass. We sat for a while, setting our pint jars on top of the never-used electric butter churn missing a part, then I rinsed them in the kitchen and filled them with water and she drank hers. The doubt, the restlessness, was all she and I knew. Moths flitted to the light without hazard. I stepped down off the porch to snap off two purple crocuses for her and put them in my jar on the churn.

I had peered out through the kitchen curtains in Clay's mother's house, eyes peeled for the sarvisberry, but there was only bud-green, mostly brown and black, and Clay saying that's where his mother Lottie's trailer would go. He'd stood a few feet away from me, a head taller than I, smelling of blacktop and work gloves. His gaze gentle. In the corner of the kitchen sat his guitar case with a sticker on it that said *I Am the First and the Last* with the name of the Baptist youth camp underneath. His hound Ellis slept beside it. Clay's band had a song about The Great I Am, the First and the Last. Alpha and Omega. I wondered what lay between the First and Last, in the middle, and how cramped was the bookended space, or how vast? Lottie's trailer would go right there and block my mind's route to the woods.

"You think I should marry him?" I asked Mave.

"Who am I to say?" She squared her shoulders. "You even want a kid?"

I didn't answer. Lottie's curtains were muslin, homemade. They muffled things. A child was a muffled idea to me then, with no real legs or arms or fever.

"Inconsequential is what I think," Mave said. "You should write your book."

"Yeah?"

"Yeah."

"A book about what?"

She never said. She mused, flicked through her file-cabinet mind and internal shelving where miniature versions of all your books sat, passages flagged and memorized, and where her memories of you stayed sealed. Her thoughts telescoped. My mind shrank from hers sometimes, and sometimes kept pace. I told her Lottie would move into a trailer he would put in back, by the woods.

"But it's her house. She's lived there a century."

"I know." I lit a cigarette and offered, but she said no. "Since when?"

"Since I got the patch." She slipped off one natty sweater sleeve and showed me the flesh-colored bandage on her upper arm. "It makes me dream in blue. I'm just doing it for Miranda. They said I'm overdue for everything, the tit microwave, the butt scope, some pelvic spelunking. I said I'd check my schedule." She rubbed below her breasts where the daily indentations probably never left the skin. Her mannish body filling the oversized cotton tee.

Mave's aloneness was a bleached bone tended and preserved and shining. My own was a bone beginning to whiten. We didn't speak of it. And about you, Ruth—we never spoke of you. She hoarded privacy. Had she not raised me up to be the same? You raised yourself up, she'd say, defensive. I grew up strange and thin, independent but tucked into her body, somehow curved to it, adopting her seclusion. Once, I asked her to make me look pretty. She braided my hair at night, while it was wet. In the morning it looked like it had gotten caught in a machine. We cracked up.

On a few occasions, when she was almost blackout drunk, she did talk about you, still cryptically, but I could piece together a scene or a moment. I knew some kind of accident had left your leg unusable, a thing you dragged, such that your travel to the Sinai to study ancient texts was already a memory when you met Mave. But you loved to dance in private. I gathered this from one of her tirades that had her waltzing in her dining room, kicking trash left and right, chip bags and cellophane casings, singing scraps of Billie Holiday off-key. There was a tall empty room in your house on Aldrich Street with only a tapestry tacked to one wall with red elephants and trees on it. Apparently, you kept a record player on the floor and danced only when Mave was not there, but once, she found you dancing, awkwardly with your bum leg, making and unmaking an invisible bowl with your arms, as if dancing in ceremony around a fire, and at the door she startled you so badly you pulled into the tapestry and wrapped yourself up. She laughed; you hid like a child. I loved picturing you like that, hearing the record play, encountering a Mave unwrecked.

On the concrete porch I toed the XYZ encyclopedia at the bottom of the stack, leaned into one of the three cedar posts holding up the porch roof. I twisted my thick black hair into a tail, careful with the cigarette. I'd canned beets that morning, from the Route 9 Market, just to smell them, though it was not their season, my seeds barely in the ground. These were Mexican beets. The smell of beets canning is hot, a bitter-dirt smell you taste—you might not know that smell, as you surely do not know my chemical janitorial odor, my clapboard house, my circumscribed Caudell life so opposite your New England life as I've always imagined it, infused with a vast foreign air.

I'll describe this place for you since you never came here, this place that grew your Mave, like a tuber. Two stoplights, a Shop 'n Save and Dairy Delite and Citgo and a primary school that was once the high school—now kids are bussed to Monroeville for the county's consolidated high school. A motel and feed store on the end of town near the Route 9 Market where, besides beets, you can get bagged corn nuts and boxes of Skoal in bulk. There's a bank, a community center, there's the complex of steel and concrete and loading docks that makes up LaFaber Bronze, where most people still work. The churches are scattered satellites, also the homes, hunkered between small fields of alfalfa or timothy or weeds and outlined in a black mold from the swamp that edges Caudell and destabilizes the soil for building out any farther. Then the woods, the limestone caves—one as tall as a train—the creek Heather Run, its banks lined with small sycamores and laurel. The places I could walk blind.

My hands still glowed faintly beet pink in the porch light, darker at the cuticles. My question about Clay's proposal was really: How rabid was I for life? And what had love to do with that? And would I become a gray bird of a thing like Lottie in that kitchen with muslin curtains, or would I dance in some private ceremony to a record player and cocoon myself in a tapestry to be unwound and unwound? The front of my body, in denim shirt and work jeans, felt open and closed at once, all my inner folds restless.

"The sex will taste like Dimetapp," I said.

"God, Frankie. Do it or don't. It's inconsequential." Gruff, her gray head electric, in that shirt and sweater. As if she'd walked out of a psych ward.

Aunt Miranda had said a few hours earlier what no one else would say: that Stew, who ran a body shop at his house and played in Clay's band and who, she could see, drew me magnetically, already had a wife. And that Dillon—my first love, my only love, from my youth—was not coming back. At that, I'd recoiled my not-young head and looked away from Miranda's stooped body. I'd left her a pint of beets without another word.

Now, I admitted it to myself, speaking toward the alfalfa grass that bordered Mave's lot on the other side, a wide field of it. "Dillon's been gone years."

Next to the defunct churn, a mud dauber stirred heavily around its pan-flute nest of mud long molded by the female mouths. "Go to sleep, you lazy bastard," Mave said to it.

Stew and I had always been nothing—simply a flash of heat—and Dillon a blur across ten years, though I could conjure the water's edge, of course. Always. Lilies and saplings of spruce, the wetlands people fear for their blurred boundary, the shallow waters lapping, and skin everywhere. The tall Train Cave and the small fire we built and our fiercely moving then slowing shadows. And our silence, our deeper chests keeping distance.

"I'm serious," Mave said, "everything's blue. Put that in your book."

"There is no book."

"PBS aired a special on your Holy Mary, on weeping Mary statues across the world. Our Lady of Lima, Our Lady of Sicily and Syracuse, of the Sacred Heart in Platina, Brazil. They said when her statue cried tears of honey or drops of oil she could heal people. But if the pope says hoax, it's hoax. Catholics are mystifying. Like the pope was even there to see it—he doesn't exactly live local to Brazil. I started dreaming about a blue Mary bawling her eyes out and me trying to catch her tears from across the world, in a kind of urn. Fucking wild. Her skin and hair and everything—blue like a Smurf."

I laughed a small laugh.

She said, "I dreamed my shitbox car turned into a blue Mercedes."

I stood to go.

"You watch those bugs rising up out of the alfalfa. They love salt, they'll feed on your sweat."

"I don't know what to do," I said.

"I'm serious about that book."

"I didn't even finish high school. I'm a goddamn janitor at the bronze plant."

"And I've got a master's degree in linguistics and drive a school bus. So what? You're bright. When you were little, you said, Mave, read my book, and you showed me that kitten diary that locked. Remember that? You'd copied out the entire Book of Revelation from Margot's Bible, and I thought, My god, you're misled but, you know, you'll come into your own. She thought it too."

And there you were, Ruth—*she* referred to you, not my mother Margot. Oblique reference.

"Do I marry Clay or not?"

"And you pulled your red wagon across town and people said, What are you hauling in there? And you said, God's body. As if that were obvious cargo, like a stuffed panda."

"You don't believe in God." I stood near her thickness and gray head. I bent down toward her, my hair outspread and inky. She had been my guardian, my teacher when I'd dropped out of school, my cumbersome fellowship. She had filled me full of the table scraps from her graduate studies after washing up back here, bereft.

"It doesn't matter if you get married. Men and women come. Their bodies list over to the left then topple. You know that."

"I still have to say yes or no."

"Write a damn book. Look for more, Frankie." She waved her hand in a hocus-pocus motion over the yellowed encyclopedia stack as though to transform it into that *more.*

A tip of a rabbit ear antenna snagged my shirt as I turned to go.

She said, "I read this line from Rukeyser today, in her *Collected.* 'Do I move toward form? Do I use all my fears?' That's a good line. You have to use all of it, everything."

Some other sound flanked us, maybe the clucking of a whitetail, and then the shuffling of grass. It was night in earnest. I looked back at her profile, her face that had always radiated for me a godlessness and nerve, a sadness, a sickly humor, a mystification. And something close to love but not quite. She went skeletal on the side hidden from light, a little caved in, a face for the night bugs to feed on.

I studied the three ruined TVs she had burned up trying to stay alive. I thought, yes, wash up, throw on jeans, can your beets, and write your book. These are my instructions. Become part of the world and move out into it.

These were our ragged selves in that almost-summer, Ruth. Buzzed and on edge, pressed between a First and a Last.

"You going to be okay tonight?" I asked her.

"Sure," she said. "Why wouldn't I be?"

I PULLED NAN'S OLDSMOBILE INTO THE EXXON LOT, as if steering a sailboat. This was the last turnoff before the on-ramp to 79 southbound. Almost noon and I would go grim after noon, lose the morning's sharp edges. I thought maybe I'd lose my nerve. The plan had been to leave before dawn so we could watch the sky pink up, but there'd been the vehicle complication, then the Nan complication. Nan who, in my rearview mirror, was now trying to French twist her hair with only a few bobby pins.

"Even I know that can't work," said Mave, turned around to watch.

"I can't go in there looking like this," said Nan.

"Piss on the seat then. It's your leather." Mave opened the car door and collected the portable oxygen tank, like a sack lunch. She'd grown used to it, and I didn't like that. "You're in self-serve," she told me. "I'll give them a twenty inside." She hoisted her dense-barrel torso up and out of the car. I saw her take one breath through blades and halt.

"Just hang on, and I'll help you," I said.

She slammed the ton-heavy door.

Nan rolled down the back window. "Will you get me some pork rinds?"

"No, I will not." Mave didn't turn. "We're bound for the desert, little hussy. Prepare to eat your wild honey and locusts."

"What?"

"Don't touch my pain pills."

Nan unfettered her hair and sulked. Left alone with her, I needed to do something with my hands, pump the gas, check the oil. I double-checked for a paper bag stowed in the glove box in case my nerves hit and I hyperventilated, but then I remembered this was not my pickup. Breath constricted just slightly in my asthmatic chest and I was out the door.

Seeking the fuel tank, I took in the heft of the car, probably a decade old. Pale blue, a rim of rust, boxy windows, long nose. An Oldsmobile Royale, the once-bright silver *Royale* stamped near the tank. I lifted the nozzle, selected the grade. I was all narrowness—I was often thus. I willed myself to look upon the waify woman in the backseat as though she were a benign fern. My eyes scanned, scanned, then followed the price ticking upward, steadily, and my chest widened back out. I could picture an entity inside me, elbowing for room. I begged like Saint Augustine—Come, God, insinuate your spaciousness into my narrow channel. Make me all lake and expansive alfalfa field. Make me all desert sky.

Nan abandoned her hair project and slunk off to the service station. I didn't watch her walk more than a few feline steps in her black ballet shoes. Men whistled, men blew. Fine, I was at sixteen forty-nine, sixteen fifty.

I skipped the oil and took Ellis out on the leash toward the grassy patch beyond the air compressor. He looked bewildered. I scratched among his neck folds and stroked his ears. "Hey, Flop, hey," I said. I held a pack of Shop 'n Save mini donuts and gave him one. His thick black and tan body gave itself to me and leaned into my leg, then he moved on and peed. My husband would not miss me, but he would miss this sack of hound. The payphone was right there. It was his dog.

I called my friend Clarissa instead. The only one who knew where we were.

She'd waved goodbye that morning from the wide porch of her house, having given us a Tupperware of bologna sandwiches and saltines with peanut butter. In her flannel robe, her light hair messily frothed about her face, she'd tied a sheer scarf around my neck, a gift from her daughter Tess. I'd loved the feel of the scarf, though I'd removed it and stuck it in the back pocket of my jeans. I touched it now. The phone rang.

"Hey," she said. "You okay? Are you in a ditch somewhere?"

"Remind me why we're doing this."

"I have no idea why you're doing this. I just packed you a lunch."

The phone line buzzed, a tractor trailer stuttered. I saw one of my fellow fugitives emerge from the Exxon, the one with an external lung.

"Hey?" says Clarissa. "You know why you're doing this. You know it's for Mave." Her kicked heart still opened and stayed fleshy—how? If I could love, I'd love like Clarissa, my friend since childhood.

"What if I commit murder?"

"Don't commit murder. Nan's harmless. How's Mave?"

Clarissa had a few souls to spare. She who bruised more easily than a ripe peach, who worked hard to stay upright in this world. I told her she'd forgotten the mustard.

When the time came, Mave had gone in for one round of chemo only. Her mouth parched, she puked herself dry. With that cobwebbed throat, you'd think she'd have wanted the seepage and the marsh of home, but she wanted dry mesa air, she wanted all the humidity and haze drained away. "I just want clarity," she said. "The bog's big voice is drowning me out. I want sagebrush and piñon pine and the white snow of cottonwoods along the scarce river. I have never seen the desert."

I said okay. I knew she wanted your Egypt. Your Persia. Your hieroglyphic scrawl baked by the sun. I said I would drive her west, down off the ridge of the Caudell swamp and wetlands.

"Then I want Memphis on the way," she said. Neither of us had been west of the Mississippi.

I'd prayed, May the skunk cabbage stink of her life dissipate. "Get me out of the bog, Frankie," she'd said, "and far from the damp limestone caves. I just have to get out of here." She'd shivered, her face white from the poison in her body, the metal splinters in her lungs.

When we loaded back into the Olds, Ellis licked Nan's face and investigated her pork rinds.

"Hit the road," Mave said. "Why are we still sitting here?"

Only for a second did I think I'd turn back and forget everything. Get her to a hospital, get my husband's supper on the table. I started the car. "I'm worthless now," I told her. "It's past noon, we're in the dead hours, all bankrupt."

"Don't worry." Mave rode the wind with her right arm. "If we hit tolls, we'll offer Little Gypsy Moth Hair as barter. Pay with her. That all right with you, Nan?"

"Fuck off." Big territorial crumple of pork rind bag.

You wrote me once: This is how to let the world in—say *Croatia. Argentina. Abiquiú.* Put fingertips on the globe of green and beige and deep blue and on all the scattered names. Say the names until you go there and learn what names they were before that, names pulled from the first dirt. When you're there, weep with all the people, laugh with them. Tell them everything. Love them.

I've been nowhere all my life, Ruth, except in that house across the break in the fence from hers. She and I have not wept. You wrote me once that Mavis, her full name, means song thrush, Celts pulling words from the world. From the dirt and sky. The drawing of acacia tree means sweet, you wrote. There's a bird that means soul. Let the world in, you told me—all the names across time are real, each with a heartbeat.

But sometimes I could not find the heartbeat.

Clay asked for my answer by Sunday, a Sunday back in that early spring of 1989 when Mave's drinking would get worse then better then worse again. The Good News Boys would play a set at the Chapel at Snyder's Crossing. Baptists liked announcements and liked Clay, his every contour meek. To me, they would object. Snyder's Crossing was Uncle Rex and Aunt Miranda's church, and it had been my mother and dad's and mine until I was orphaned at sixteen and quit the pew when Mave had given me the choice. Miranda, with my four cousins bunched behind her, had studied my bloodless face, put a hand to my head for fever. "What's wrong with you?" she'd said, always asking underneath, what are you, what manner of thing? The oldest of the four, my age, my pretty cousin Belinda, had slipped over and taken my hand, until Miranda had herded them off. Belinda and I had once found a baby bat snagged in a window screen in daylight, its whole body in a terrified squint, native to darkness. I'd wanted to tell her that's how I felt in the oak pew.

Friday night I'd left Mave's house for mine knowing I would refuse Clay. I'd ringed my jars of glowing beets, lined them up on the rough-lumber table, and slept. Saturday he invited me over to his mother's for a pancake breakfast.

I brought a pint of beets for Lottie. He set them on the cold woodstove. He'd made a big production of it. Cool Whip set out, too much bacon in the skillet, syrup that wasn't simply brown sugar and boiled water with imitation vanilla. He stood steadied by the good fortune of the morning, like any forty-nine-year-old man who still lived with his mother and who had never had to miss certain things—the small scent of lemon dish detergent, the assuring rustle in the other room, mended jeans. And now maybe a wife. But in me, there was bone and edge that offered no refuge—did he not know this?

You wrote me once, Ruth, that people could layer like the earth, a permafrost tundra on top and a magma heart. You wrote: That hot blood around your heart, all you feel, eventually you'll share it, it will come to surface. A thaw, or an eruption.

Clay still had all his hair. The West Virginia Division of Highways had not been bad for his back, there was muscle, but he hid a small paunch with untucked shirts. A body established, maybe, but still lean for the most part. He was a different pale than I was, pasty with a boyish face and full mouth and a scar on his chin. He'd told me his favorite season was winter, when he plowed the secondary roads before dawn. I liked that. He was careful to keep his wristwatch safe, washing dishes as he cooked, the whisk and mixing bowl and spoons.

"Your pancakes are professional," I told him. "Silver dollars."

He smiled. I was glad he said nothing. His good singing voice came out nasal when he spoke, bland boiled chicken. I sat on the kitchen chair, one of the set of four that someone had painted blue to match the bonnets of the girl reiterated in measured succession on the wallpaper trim. I asked if his mother Lottie would join us and should I set a plate, but he said she wanted to give us privacy. He shifted his weight then, facing the stove with his spatula, jeans taut against his other butt cheek just beneath his shirt tail.

Lottie came into the kitchen anyway, in slippers that suggested lightness and fleeing, already planning her retreat to the woods behind the house, to the trailer that would be new and cheap. I knew Clay had reserved the cheapest on the B&J Homes lot in Monroeville. Did Lottie see in me what Clay didn't? She habitually held the tip of her long braid when she spoke, when it was uncoiled from a bun and hung mid-belly, trailing over her shoulder. I wanted very much to see her hair completely unfurled.

Lottie handed me a recipe card for wilted lettuce made with bacon grease, as Clay brought the skillet to the table and scooped out bacon with a slotted spoon, leaving the drippings. He set the shriveled meat on paper towels doubled up on a plate. To the hot drippings, add vinegar, sugar, salt, onions, and pour it hot over a bowlful of leaf lettuce. The handwriting on the recipe card was shaky. There was a tiny rolling pin in each corner of the card. He would set aside the skillet for her, or for me.

"Thank you, Lottie," I said. "I brought you a pint of beets, there on the woodstove. You ought to sit with us."

No, no, she slipped out, having studied my face.

Clay sat down across from me. He gave the jam jar a quarter turn as if to have the label pointing a certain way, to create a triangulation with the label on the margarine tub and the label on the real-deal maple syrup. Don't, I thought, my throat got thick. I'd worn a loose white button-up blouse with thin capped sleeves because it looked feminine, my skin browning already from the garden work, my upper arms dense. I had kept slender enough though I had to resist the curve starting in my shoulders, always cautioned by Miranda's slight humpback. I was attractive enough with a thin oval face, though I wore a look of severity I couldn't help, and premature lines creased my forehead as if to stress my overthinking. Clay had competent hands. He looked briefly to the V of my blouse.

He'd clerked at Matlick Feed as a kid, stocking shelves, turning the labels out, the way he might turn my body. He would be fifty in October. My tied-back hair pulled at my temples, too tightly held in place, none of it gray yet.

"We aren't kids, Clay," I said.

"Well, no," he said. Pinched his voice.

I'd been a kid when he'd signed on to plow snow and lay blacktop for the State. He'd surely been steady and hungry-within-limits like an Eagle Scout. Would he have ever gone beyond? Would he have taken the oval rubber change purse we found in the birthday box in Sunday School at Snyder's Crossing, *Jesus Saves* on one side, the slit on the other, taken it to the woods like Dillon and Clarissa and me—three inseparable friends then—and squeezed top to bottom so the slit puckered open for the insertion of change, labial and suggestive? The indelicate Dillon who was my mirror self, who was two years younger, the boy version of me with hair just as thick-black as mine and ways just as solitary, and Clarissa like a honey-haired doll who loved us both for nothing and who melted to a blush as he stuck his tongue in the purse.

"We're not kids," Clay softly repeated, nasal and coaxing. He served me bacon. "Love can grow. After, sometimes."

In my throat, a mean clog. Usually I'd stand, stretch my body, unslump, make passage for air. But I sat, breathing poorly, I eyed the walls, I watched all the blue-bonneted girls. A wheeze threatened in Lottie's kitchen, though I had long outgrown full-blown asthmatic attacks. I stacked two pancakes on my plate and felt the weak lung and the urge to run. My feet tested the spring offered in the linoleum.

I could always run fast as a kid, especially during the years I played basketball. I went nights to the school gymnasium to run suicides in the green glow of the emergency lights—baseline, foul line, half court, again, then some pretend one-on-one to work on my layup, to work on my lung power.

Clay made conversation about the gospel band, about his bass player Stew getting a new amp—but I didn't want to hear about dark-eyed, rangy Stew—and about my cousin Ron, one of Rex and Miranda's twins, the one who stuttered, starting entry-level with the State that month, as if to say, See? We can talk like husband and wife over bacon in the kitchen.

What happened was strange, Ruth. The magma in me had bypassed the eruption and running-over, had transformed straight to ashes and a few cinders. My ashes shook down at the kitchen table. The hard No was a cinder left lodged there in the grate. I could not utter it. I should have uttered it.

Into my head pierced a sharp memory—I was a phantom point guard beating it to the baseline and dribbling like a crazy. The grade school box gym could contain me and channel me. Then, out into the night, heading home with a gym bag to Mother and Dad who were not yet specters but living people at sink and TV and supper, with a tub of Country Crock half full like Clay's.

There was a bird. I sloughed my gym bag and shoes at the hearth. I unbanded my hair and wore it like a piece of clothing, my nubby basketball under my arm. Mother's radio played, also the TV, but I heard flapping in the chimney. I put my ear to the cool stone. A bird is trapped, I said. It can't fly out. She spoke to him acidly, Why didn't you put wire mesh up there to keep them out? And he said, It'll get free, Margot, it's nothing to worry about. Tended the TV antenna with his gentle, limp hands. She pursed her face shut. Early fall, so there was no fire, only soot. The damper, when I tried it, was jammed fast, and the bird flapped like mad. It's a warbler, I said, though how would I have known that? I did not see it yellow like a Christmas ball, but I did. It flapped and stirred the summer soot into a suffocating cloud, the frail wings scraping against the chimney wall and sparking. And then, after a time, silence. I stood there. She turned off the radio and wiped her apron with a disapproving air.

See? Dad said toward the TV, his voice always sounding shoved down in a bucket. They fly back out.

My mother's face flint.

But wasn't there yet a faint glowing heartbeat? Wasn't there, Ruth, in the name *warbler* on my lips? I mouthed it, I whispered. Behind the stone and behind my eyes, it lived, barely. The silence did not mean escape. Silence meant the bird would join the others that came before it, that I'd pull the damper open one day and bird bones would hail down—how many skeletons in the chimney? A thought so horrible, my breath grew inaccessible, my throat a clogged straw. I bolted out the screen door in my sock feet, my mother righteously calling after, and ran from the bones I knew had piled there, not toward Mave's next door but toward the woods and the Train Cave. I got into the nettles, I hit a hard locust tree and drew lip blood and ran on. I could run fast on very little breath at that age, did not yet need the paper bag to hyperventilate into. I could regulate it myself. I stopped only where the moss went black at the swamp edge. I followed its creeping boundary into the cave mouth, I ducked in and stood in the dark damp expanse of limestone. There was the silent wet wall, the long hush of things so previous to me and more hidden than myself. My lip bled. I wore a Nite Glo bracelet, a jelly wire my teammate Liza had given me, and one to Clarissa too, and it made light by itself. The warbler was in complete darkness and walled—it wheezed, I wheezed—yet, as I imagined it there, I saw it shimmering with light, so it, too, must have made light by itself, in the chimney soot. A self-generated glow.

Standing motionless in the limestone, in the strange cavern so high a train could pass, my girl torso, shoulders, narrow neck could have made a chimney, and there could have been dead birds in me. I breathed. Bats rustled high, my legs stung with nettle. The bones, the odd yellow light of the jelly bracelet. Feather and remnant. I touched the damp cave wall and wrote with my finger one of the hieroglyphs you had taught me in a letter, one of the tall hieratic signs, the cursive bird looking to the right.

Clay said he'd get down on one knee if I wanted. My sprinter feet eased down onto the linoleum of Lottie's kitchen. I got as far as the nettle-feel on my calves under the jeans I wore now with the pretty white blouse. The nettle-feel was as far as I got before I stopped. In my stomach, a sharp frail thing went dull, wing into soot, but something stubbornly glowed. My throat opened, and I reached for the syrup and coated the cold pancake perfect in size and shape.

I knew love would not grow. But since I did not feel all that capable of love, I told him yes.

My own house next to Mave's, the clapboard house I'd grown up in, had a fishhook floor plan and narrow stairs that climbed to no hallway, only to a room on the right and one on the left. The front porch opened into a laundry room with an exposed water heater and furnace and deep freezer which should have been stowed elsewhere. Then the kitchen with deep sinks and the rough-lumber table Mave had built when the Formica table bowed; then steps to the small cellar and a curve to the living room with the fireplace and to my bedroom, once my parents' bedroom, tucked behind the stairs. The floors scrubbed clean, the smell of the piney oil, a hint of bleach.

I rummaged in the bureau for the deed. Mave had paid off the mortgage for me with your money after Mother and Dad died and put only my name on the paper—Frances Donne. I studied the small print to discern how I could keep it in my name. There, the paneling and drywall to which the deed referred, the light yellow of the kitchen, as though the legal claim brought things into being—the floor lamp, the framed picture of my parents and the smaller framed reproduction of a Klimt painting, a page torn from Mave's book which had been your book. There, the beets in the kitchen and the graduated cast iron stacked on the counter, one lifted out and rounded with cornbread half gone and foiled over. I would tell Clay I needed to keep the place for the bronze plant co-op meetings. Which was true.

It was noon. I stepped out on the porch for Saturday's mail, scanned Mave's house through the fence break, looking for signs of life. Two stories junked up and about to implode, always the lingering scent of grime and mold, tar paper patching the roof.

I had a letter in the box from my old friend, Liza. Between the Shop 'n Save circular and an offer from Discount Tire, her married name and *Streetsboro, Ohio*. Five pages front and back in barely legible cursive that blew forward like a sandstorm. Sorry I haven't written since last year, she started—the business had kept her busy, a husband-and-wife team mowing yards and shoveling truckloads of mulch. She gave a full page to the day she ran over a white-faced hornet nest in the ground, sucked up their rage into her mower that spit it out the clippings chute, and she was swollen for two weeks. And once she ran over a sleeping baby blacksnake and cut it in pieces. At least she still had her horses, she wrote, and a Presbyterian church she liked for the way it followed the same order each week. She'd always had horses here, two or three ponies, to pet and ride, nothing to show. She'd always liked order. Sometimes joy is a sacrifice, she wrote. My husband Gary died last week, she wrote—the line buried in the sand on page four, as though she had needed to build up courage to write it. But she still heard herself tell people she's on a husband-and-wife mowing team—isn't that strange? Out from between the fourth and fifth pages slipped a photocopied *Caudell Journal* newspaper clipping with a photo of our old basketball team. LaFaber Bronze Girls League, sponsored by the plant Clarissa and I both eventually went to work for. Liza had found the clipping in a drawer while packing to move back home to stay with her mother. She had copied it for each of us, Clarissa and me.

There I was, stringy and already fighting curvature in my shoulders. There was our Liza. Her eyes bugged, her curls gelled in a neat arrangement, her stance tidy. And there the gentle Clarissa. I would have to call her. Liza was moving back. I pictured Liza stung by hornets, stingers stuck under hems she would have carefully sewn herself, the chaos of it harder on her than the poison's pain. And now the chaos of grief. I held up the pages, translucent, to the kitchen light. All the words of the letter grit and blown.

I smelled of bacon. Was it selfish to want to take back the morning hours before I'd climbed Clay and Lottie's porch and entered that house that lay under the hill, nearer town than mine? The hours when I'd still been noncommittal up here, and proud and cold and alone, on the higher hillside that breathed—I did not like to be down under, I would not like that about Clay's house. The Bible still lay open by the foiled cornbread, which was probably about to turn and I should have put it in the fridge. An aged, burdensome heft, my mother's Bible with black faux-leather binding and silver letters at the bottom, Margot Augusta Donne. A sheafed-out tumor that wouldn't go away.

"We too must write Bibles," said Mave to me once over hotdogs. "So sayeth Emerson." Scooting away her sister's Bible, as if it were an animal skull.

And like a skull, it drew me. The Word, the world of my mother—how could it not? It was a kind of original, rough ground.

In those morning hours, I had looked for the I Am in Revelation—the one affixed to Clay's guitar case—the one who is and who was and who is to come, a girth stretched across eternity. Yet isn't the I Am a moment, a morsel of time, or maybe a pocket? I'd crossed out a few words and scribbled a few of my own in the thin rustling margin. *Blackberry thicket.* Once, I had cleared a dome for a doe in the young, soft briers. Here—gnaw on that, bed down in it, I said to the doe. Time itself was the brier room, a brief enclave in eternity that made you itch with confusion, but at least it was shelter.

Under the bacon I could almost smell my musty girl odor and taste the after-game sweat on my upper lip. A portal opened between the *Caudell Journal* girl—Number 25, a basketball held to her belly—and my thirty-five-year-old self engaged to be married and learning of Liza's fresh widowhood. The morning now felt like twenty years ago, and the coming night like another country.

There was Liza, running a Weed Eater with safety goggles on.

Dear Liza.

I would write her—I would retrieve the Discount Tire ad from the trash and write on the backside. A letter within a letter, Ruth. From the team photo on the table, our small eyes looked out from the grainy half-circle of our bodies and hair and scratchy uniforms—Liza a well-managed, capable forward, married for how many years, and Clarissa with the most delicate fringe of bangs and a curvy body that sat the bench unless we had at least a ten-point lead and it was fourth quarter, married for years now too, to Darrell who hit her—did Liza know that? When he'd first slapped Clarissa, she'd driven her Toyota to my house and stood at my front door as if a weight pulled her head down to one side, and her fair hair fell in pieces across her face, like a horse's mane. I gave her a bag of ice wrapped in a towel, I put her in Mother and Dad's old bed, and I drove my truck three miles east to the Tide family's farm. I scanned the evening horizon of alfalfa field until I saw Darrell's stout figure rendered small and harmless by distance. I took the pocked right-of-way as far as I could in the pickup then got out, grabbed the tire iron from the bed, and walked the rest of the way to find him mending fence, and he said my name as a question. I pointed the heavy tool in reply, and a hint of a smile might have curled his lip mostly hidden by moustache.

"What's this about, Frankie?"

"Don't you ever," I said. "Never again." What was I going to do? Beat him bloody? He neither denied the slap nor swore off it. I drove home knowing I could protect no one. And now, looking at our three younger faces, I felt again the keen exposure for which there is no protection—not from hornets, not from battery, not from grief.

On the back of the ad, I drew our young bodies as horses, small stick-figure ponies, each its own fateful letter, a sound uttered beside the deal for winter tread.

Everybody said I was good enough in the ninth grade to play for the boys' team. There was no high school girls' basketball in 1968, only the community league the plant sponsored. But I wasn't skilled. I was forceful, I was scrappy. I dribbled poorly, passed too hard, and shot lead balls two-handed, but I was fast and could rebound. Most games I fouled out. I had one good move, and I lived for it: I'd steal the ball and hurl myself down court for a fast break, barely managing the dribble, and my body—ever cordoned off—stopped sensing its boundaries. I felt everything at once in the tiny community building gym as I drove without grace to the basket. The building doubled for our games and—with the hoops folded up to the ceiling—baby showers and spaghetti dinners and gun shows. The smell of concessions lingered always: popcorn and hotdogs on a reel, nicotine mouths of coaches chewing Juicy Fruit. Driving to the basket, I gulped in all the adolescent salt and skunkiness, someone's perfume, the milling around of women eating cake and laughing at a shower, the caving in and down of the bleachers where hundreds sat because the scattered twenty people each had so many selves and histories, and each sound they made ricocheted against the cinderblock walls and multiplied.

That's when I could always feel Dillon.

My second self, a shadow with heat.

I could smell his burnt smell and feel the goldening of his skin from his afterschool work at LaFaber's foundry. He was too young to work legally but they gave him some hours anyway. His body lengthened in those hours of flame and then he slipped into the community building to watch us girls play. I went in for that layup able to see myself from outside, how he could see me, and if I scored I could blame that thrill for the electric shocks moving up my legs. It was not sexual in a way I could have separated out and named. At fourteen, I still felt equal parts male and female. Dillon and I swapped clothes, we fished blue gill in Heather Run with wetted oats, brown sugar, and soybean meal balled up into bait. I tented my hands over his eyes, lying in the sun. He weaved yellow yarn into my black hair.

After games, I was limp and wrung, and the close bodies of the girls were bright. I moved with Clarissa and Liza in a hot huddle, the three of us a little on fire and a little sleepy. We went to Liza's and jumped on her trampoline, though we were too old for it, then lay on the springy surface that dented under our butts and shoulder blades and tilted us toward each other. The trampoline sat near a slope that ran down to the dog pens and neat pullet cages that chirred out their constant sound, the circumference of the trampoline the edge of our young-girl heat. They teased me about him, but I'd say no, it was Clarissa he wanted, and I'd do a steamroll over both of them with hands crossed over my chest like a corpse to make them laugh. And I believed it because she was the one all the boys watched, Darrell Tide in particular, who was then a high school senior. She had real breasts and wanted to quit the team because the running and jarring hurt her; I had almost enough to cup with a very small hand.

We lay there until we grew cold, until the brightness of our bodies dimmed and we pulled back into ourselves. I wanted to stay out there longer, alone, to outspread my arms and legs with no sweater. I wanted to be cold.

It took years of shadows moving, growing dense. In my twenties something changed abruptly. Like a skin sack of wine breaking. Mother and Dad were nearly nine years dead by then, and I had also read most of your books by then, Ruth, in my house by Mave's house, she and I installed in our specific patterns of solitude. Dillon and I had both quit the Baptists, he first. He let his grandmother whom he lived with sit the pew alone. He did not tell me why. And we'd both quit school and worked at the plant. Dillon was still a boy at twenty-three and I still boyish at twenty-five.

We walked one day without talking and stood still at the fence at the far end of Uncle Rex's Guernsey pasture. I was after wild lilies to uproot and replant. I had a trowel in one hand and pulled up a loosened horde of orange lilies with the other. When I stood, I found him pressed up behind me, still silent, as was I. My jeans gapped enough in front to sag loose, I made my stomach concave, and he palmed me there then slid slowly down, crossed my chest with his other arm like a brace. I dropped the tool but not the lilies. Without noise, without meeting eyes, we threaded expertly through the barbed wire fence and headed to where Heather Run pooled into a brief pond, then walked still further. We went quickly on to the hidden source of the creek, the underground spring giving way to swamp. We stopped in a standing wrestle and crush of lilies, kissed roughly and with such latent hunger against a broad tree, fumbled then through the woods homing to the small mouth of the Train Cave. Did we not seek the swallow of it? We ducked in and felt though could not see its great inner expanse until, somewhere, it narrowed to nests and low tunnels deeper in. He wore his Army jacket, I felt him take it off and lay it on the stone and tamped dirt. There were bats, I felt their brush with my bare back, then his jacket lining against my bare back, the uneven ground beneath. In the smell of white-dark limestone and the wet of petrified drip-down stalactites, his familiar mouth took me in and uttered me. His hips and belly and all of him taut, he arched, and then a blur at our boundaries' edges, he and I wrung into the same person with four arms and four legs. We lay heaving.

And afterward, there was an awful quiet. My mirror self—a boy in that old surplus-store jacket and in undershirts that I wore that he wore, and temples that throbbed thoughts to me—afterward, wet, were we not as close as two people ever get? Yet I put my hot hand on his chest, and the breastbone that rose and fell fast was his. It was his alone. My second self obscured. This was when we split apart.

It was late on the Saturday of the pancakes and Liza's letter when I called Mave. She was bitter about the hour and groggy. Said she'd dreamed of blue horses. Said, "The nicotine patch isn't working, but it keeps things interesting." She knew Clay had staged the betrothal breakfast date but didn't ask about it. I told her about Liza. She was sorry to hear it and did remember her as the girl who came with her mother to bring weekly casseroles after my parents' death.

"The Tupperware was all labeled," she said. "Even the lids."

"That's her." I stood in my kitchen winding the stretched-out phone cord around my hand. The phone line ticked as if the connection were long distance and not across the fence.

"I was going to tell you in the morning," I said. "Are you sober?"

"That's a matter of opinion."

"Will you give me away?"

A pause. “You should have seen those horses run. There was a blue palomino, I think.”

“At the wedding, Mave.”

Ticking of the line. I heard the night sounds outside her window that were my night sounds. The summer peepers and insect trills that spill into your skull and make your mind’s action subside, let all language and thought froth down and down.

"I NEED SOME NEW CLOTHES," SAID NAN AT THE SIGNS FOR SUTTON. "You hear me, Frankie?"

I had not yet mustered the strength to address the scamp directly. I studied the skin divots under her collar bone in my mirror, the faint lip liner applied in her other life. A black bra strap peeked from her dress. She was ten years younger than I. Even with the black eye and that crazy hair, she was indisputably beautiful.

"I only had time to pack a couple things." Peevish, delicate face. I wondered what it was she was after.

Scraggly vetch purpled the highway median, and I knew my cold shoulder toward Nan was cruel and undeserved. Also, I could sense, working up in Mave then, a swarm of inner black flies—what she called the wheezing and coughing that overtook her in those days, fits at their own appointed time. "The flies bite on the inside," she'd say.

"We can stop there," said Mave, pointing to the billboard for Antiques & Primitives. "All you'll need is a loin cloth and sea shells. Frankie, note that attire in the book."

"Listen," Nan said, "this is my car and we have a long way to go, so maybe you can speak civil."

"I mean no harm, Gypsy Moth," whispered Mave with scanter air.

"Are you going to talk to me, Frankie, or just let the crazy answer?" Nan leaned forward to poke her head above the console, its cup holder full of Mave's red candy from the Exxon. "All the way to Arizona, you're not going to speak to me."

"Abiquiú's in New Mexico," said Mave.

"Wherever. It's my car."

"It's your bully husband's car," said Mave. "It's our joyride, and you were not exactly invited."

Nan muttered something. Flung herself back, and I heard Ellis the hound take offense. "Why Ab-ee-cue anyway?"

We hadn't even made it out of West Virginia. There were at least thirty road hours ahead. Mave's Pontiac had blown months before, my pickup had gone dead that morning. We'd packed the truck, intending to swing by Clarissa's to say goodbye and give her the tub of squash from Miranda. I'd turned the key in the faithful black Ford Ranger I'd bought off Rex—nothing.

Then, unbelievably, out of nowhere came Nan in Dillon's blue Oldsmobile, and why? I didn't know. Maybe because I ran the women's co-op, and she'd turned up there at our most recent gathering, early that September of 1990, looking like she held something bloody. I remembered that first encounter with her so vividly—she'd appeared at my kitchen door with that wild hair and a hand at her front, looking hugely pregnant. The other women congregated in the living room, and I met her at the door.

"Is this the get-together?" she said through the screen and opened the door boldly, forced it past where it caught on the porch floor, and stepped inside into full exposure. She was starkly pretty, though thin in the face with heavy lipstick and eye shadow, younger than I by several years, that great mound of hair, not pregnant after all but her front bulged. I saw a dark bruise at the front of her neck. She wore a green Army jacket too large for her. She held her house dress folded up in front of her, gathered at the hem to make a kind of sack, the dress a light pastel yellow. A black slip showed in front, satiny to her knees, and lovely legs below ending in black ballet shoes. Through the dress-sack, bright red streaks bled. Because of where and how she held her bulk, I was afraid she held a dead baby. I stared. She hefted, struggled toward the slab table in the kitchen. "My god," I said.

"Thought maybe I could join you all?" She made it to the table and released her load. Large topped and scrubbed beets rolled onto the surface, a dozen or more. Some fell to the floor and she laughed. "I have these to trade. You trade things at a co-op, right?" A curvy sliver of a woman with a bloodied yellow dress. "I'm Nan," she said. No care for ruining the fabric with stain.

Army jacket, loose-legged, and that hair. I had known, though she'd not said, that she was Dillon's wife.

"Looks like you got beer?" she'd said, hopeful.

But maybe, that October morning of the stalled-out truck and foiled plans, she'd driven to my house because she was hated by every woman in town since she flirted with their husbands, since she strode around in short dresses, since she'd been caught with the football coach in the high school locker room. But Dillon had beaten her before the coach fiasco; I'd seen her bruises. She found us sitting there defeated—Mave strung with tubing and me with an ice floe caught in my ribcage.

"Help me, my god, he will kill me," Nan said.

Because she was starved for something unnamed. Or, most simply, she'd driven to my house because she had nowhere else to go, and she was on this trip because she had a running vehicle.

"Tell her I'm driving," I'd said to Mave, and we'd piled in.

"Georgia O'Keeffe lived in Abiquiú," Mave said. "The painter. She wasn't from there. Sometimes you recognize yourself in a place you've never seen before. O'Keeffe said that."

I watched Nan watch the window glass and maybe all else blowing by, the exit for antiques and primitives, the skinny trees. Her eye ringed in bruise seemed to shine at the mention of O'Keeffe. I had seen Nan's drawings, the dirty ones but also the artful ones she showed no one.

Mave went pensive and deserted and professorial, as she often did, and said, "O'Keeffe woke early and immediately started painting. She went at it all day, ate a few things, little mealy squirrels on sticks, a few locusts, some honey. She slept in an old car so she could listen to the red rocks at night. She worked first thing in the morning because once you wait, the moment is gone. After dawn, half the day has passed you by, Little Gypsy Moth Head. You have to beat the morning glories that never seem real." Mave took a breath, two, three. "I think she worked sometimes without a shirt. Just brown my body and leave me in peace with ochre and blue."

Then Mave was no longer speaking. She drilled her head into her head rest, gripped her thighs, her body one long fist. She gasped and coughed hard, a full-on fit.

"It'll pass, it'll pass," I said, signaling to pull over.

She wheezed and hacked, and thick yellow spit—not black flies—flecked the dash.

I pulled off to the shoulder, skidded in the gravel, there was a tumble of hound. "Hey." I was in her face, but she clenched her eyes. "Are you taking what you're supposed to? Where's your sack?"

She got a single good breath down, calmed, coughed once more.

"I said where's your sack?"

"Give me a codeine," she said.

"Did you take the fluid pill? And the steroid?"

"I flushed everything but the codeine."

"Dammit," I said. I got out, circled to her side, and dug frantically in her brown bag in the door's lower cup holder for the pain pills. She took them with Pepsi, leaned back on the headrest, stricken head all skull, as if flesh could sometimes be an illusion. There was no way they could work that fast but she gave in at the swallow, unfisted down into the seat. I realized Nan stood beside me on the shoulder only when I felt the bird take my wrist. Her wild hair took a hit from a semi slamming past. I said nothing.

Ruth, it was clear that Mave's time was running out. And clear we were running. From what specter, I did not know then. I knew only that our lives lived in the damp black of the bog and within the tiresome outlines of ridge and alfalfa had always felt like lives haunted. And maybe Nan, too, had felt haunted as she'd sought out lovers, dodged my once-sweet Dillion's fist, and painted things with her homemade paints and her aerosol.

Mave's cells rearranged, and the pain and constriction ebbed. She was asleep before I pulled back onto the highway.

I WROTE YOU WHEN I WAS A CHILD, RUTH, BECAUSE YOU HEARD MY MIND. Since I never heard your actual speaking voice, I imagined you talking inside my head with the scratchy sound of a sad record, then I'd sit down to pad and paper thinking thoughts I would not have otherwise thought.

Once, as a kid, I used Clarissa's nail polish brush to draw my own invented hieroglyph on a clay jar. What does it say? I asked Mave—this was around the time she had come home for good. She studied it. A false star, she said. A false promise of dawn. No, a shirt on a clothesline. Or a wolf in blurred motion—see its long snout and running legs? She set it on her sill. She'd cropped off her hair. I brought the ceramic figurines from the box of Red Rose tea bags—a monkey and a sheep—and put them, and other things, in the jar for her because I understood she was lonely. At that time, I began to write you only in my head and I thought about the heartbeat of the named world, which you'd written to me about, but I no longer had your letters to reread.

❧

On Sunday evening, after Clay had announced our engagement at Snyder's Crossing, I returned to Lottie's kitchen. Shoes off, I felt Ellis's warm place on the rug by the woodstove. He'd lain there until he'd reoriented to the pool of sun by the smoky box of parsley. His stomach was a mound. He dreamed a vivid brutish dream and sounded fluffs of bark, and I bent to touch him.

Clay had cut three yellow dahlias from somewhere and stuck them in a wide-mouthed jar which gave them great leeway. As I'd walked up the driveway, I'd noted the red, white, and blue pinwheels stuck in the yard, snug to the yew bush, but it was May so they must have been left over from the last July Fourth. I could sense the inertia. They did not wheel around in the breezeless air. I knew he'd announced our engagement as he strummed the guitar and sang praise through the small amp with the backing of the gospel band, including lean and impenetrable Stew on bass, thinking who knows what about the news. My phone had rung all afternoon, but I had not picked up. It would be Miranda and the cousins—Belinda, Tuffie.

He wore a Sunday dress shirt and seemed nervous that I'd change my mind. He sat.

"I have some conditions," I said, and he said okay, what are they.

"I want to marry you on an old garden plot at Rex and Miranda's."

Relief puffed his lips. "Okay."

"They used to grow potatoes there, but it's grass now, and flat and pretty for an outdoor wedding. And I don't want to wear a white dress."

"Whatever you want."

"And I want to keep my house in my name."

The hound rotated his moon-mound belly, flapped an ear, and Clay shifted his attention there. How much warmth did he truly have for me? I saw the blush of throat before I heard the agitation in his voice. Uncustomary, didn't I think? I suspected he'd planned to sell my house to pay for his mother's trailer. I told him I'd need a place for the co-op women to meet, and he searched me, carefully, as he often did, as if to mine my cold mind. It had all been riddled with kindness and courtesy, from the first time he'd taken me to the Dairy Delite.

"Couldn't the women meet here?"

"You'll have band practice here."

"Just on Saturday nights."

"The women can get rowdy. There's a good bit of drinking you won't like. And I'd rather you and I have privacy." I stood backed up against the stove, and I knew I should sit with him, put my hands on the table where he could see them as empty and open and harmless. "I will live here with you, Clay, but I want to keep my house."

Inside my skull I pictured myself his wife. The parsley-smoked air that existed between us, two people in one room, seemed vast and obscuring. I sensed he and I would not cross certain membranes and boundary lines. Clay said okay. He stood and bent to scratch Ellis's ears with rough tenderness and the dog splayed beneath it. I slipped my shoes back on. It was a kiss goodbye he wanted. I went to him, kissed him on the cheek where the throat's flush had faintly spread.

"And I want Aunt Mave to give me away."

"Should be your Uncle Rex, since your father's passed."

"Maybe so."

He gave me the jar of dahlias. I couldn't tell whether I excited him or not, whether he might excite me. Against the house's soft rustling colors, the eggshell white of the kitchen walls lined with the redundant bonneted girl, I felt like a harsh discordant color. The screen door would shut several beats after I walked through it, with the slow measured closure of a hydraulic.

I DID NOT DRIVE HOME. I drove the two miles past my turnoff to Rex and Miranda's truck patch that sat far enough from their farmhouse for me to keep out of their sight. On the west side of the half-acre garden already vining with peas and rimmed in a perimeter of unblooming zinnias lay the old garden plot. Now fallow, this was the plot where I'd dug potatoes with my cousins—the twin boys, Ron and Benji, and Belinda and Tuffie—when Aunt Miranda still complained of a mild chronic pleurisy. Every time she lifted a child, pain—something torn loose from her lung, she said. And even when her kids were ten, twelve, fifteen, she maintained that spinal curve, as if sheltering herself. The old milkhouse, rendered obsolete long ago by the refrigerator, hunkered on the far side of the plot in a dip in the land. The stream that branched off Heather Run flowed through low slits in the walls and over the building's concrete foundation to keep things cool. A defunct structure impractical even before the dawn of the Frigidaire because it sat too far from the house. Rex had always used it for tools.

It was not lost on me that Miranda had had four kids at my age, hefting them and feeling each heft in the lung. I straightened my shoulders and walked the length of the cultivated patch toward the fallow one. A dead crow Rex had shot hung on a pole to warn the survivors away from the planted seed corn. Carnage for crows and electric fencing for deer, no strung-together foil pie pans around the border like I used to deter them. He called the pans superstitious. I squatted down at the corner where the worked-up garden met the resting plot, its scars grown over with crabgrass.

As children, we had halved the seed potatoes with paring knives, planted them in straight-enough rows. We took hoes to hill up the vines and shield the crop from sun poisoning, then we let the vines shrivel into early fall, dug the new potatoes in October. We followed behind Rex's tractor to stuff the cool Kennebecs in our sacks. I remember once, as I stood with my sack opposite Ron—the feebler of the twins, with rail-thin arms and dreamy, distracted eyes—we watched the tractor's plow force the tubers to the sun along with little balls of mice babies Rex did not mean to kill.

"L-look," stuttered Ron. "No, no, no," he whispered with no stammer, for he did not stammer when he whispered, and he knifed his bare knees into the furrow to gather each mouse into his bag, his brother Benji grubbing Kennebecs without a word, always blanching at Ron's tenderness.

Over in the wet, the seepage and the spring, all that green and softness, the bathtub cattle trough still sputtered with overflow, though thick with algae. It watered the Guernseys that stood still as a painting, watching me. Only their great stomachs moved, so slightly, with breath. One flittered an ear at a fly. I crossed in a diagonal to the edge of the clawfoot trough. I loved its cool variegated greens. I culled the algae from the other weed. I remembered the blade dragged, the earth smell, the balls of mice rolling out of the dirt, some still wriggling in the palm of my boy cousin. Some that Ron missed would be prey for hawks, or covered again to break down to whispers of bones bearing witness to the hurt we don't intend.

"What's with the fake flowers?" Mave asked.

"They're dahlias."

"They're too yellow, god." She set them on a TV tray far across her living room.

"What do you think you'll wear on my big day?" I was glad to see her dressed and cognizant and limber. I watched her move the offensive flowers further out to the hallway. She wore her steel toe boots untied. Her buttocks were square under her jeans and flat as if she'd sat on a slab of wood for too long. I wondered so often, Ruth, whether you had found her beautiful.

"This." She flayed out the front ends of her unbuttoned denim shirt, white V-neck underneath. Gravel eyes, upper lip fur, face stony and rarified. "So he said okay? Wonder if he'll ask me for your hand."

"He spoke to Rex apparently."

"Wonder what I would have said."

We settled onto the plastic pads of the kitchen chairs turned living room chairs. At one time she'd contained the spilling-out padding with strips of contact paper with signs printed all over it, for a joke: Home Sweet Home, Backdoor Friends Are Best, Laugh Often. She'd wrapped the chair backs too and the sticky paper was peeling free. The old adhesive snagged my hair when I shifted my elbows down to my knees as if sitting the bench during a game. I studied the huge dahlias from a distance. They did look fake.

She said the only one people look at is the one in white.

"I'll wear yellow, I think."

"Renegade."

One of the papered-over chairs held a stack of your books on Modernist art and a moldy Shop 'n Save circular. I told her Rex and Miranda already had peas up and seed corn in, the first errant hungry crow shot and hung as example.

"You want to watch *Ancient Worlds* at nine?"

"No, I'll go."

"Miranda called and said he announced it at church."

"Yeah. I got to go." My eyes itched.

"You don't want to know what else she said?"

I was thirsty, but we drank nothing.

"She thinks you'll be happy in time. I'm pretty sure my sister's never spent a day of her life alone." Mave scruffed her short hair. "You on the other hand. And me." She looked in the direction of my house as though she could see, through the wall, the gap in the fence I'd traversed nearly every day of my life. "Some varieties of unrest are too potent for something like marriage to resolve. There'll be wild onions in the cake. You writing?"

"I have nothing in me to write."

"Sure you do. Just inhabit your former life, all your lives, including this one here in my shitbox house, on behalf of us all."

My life, former and present and yet to come—was it not decidedly small? I left, walked into night air warm enough to dampen my T-shirt's underarms. I crossed back toward my house and surveyed my garden, a couple of weeks behind Rex's. At the periphery, the moonlight hit the pie pans strung there to say to the deer, Don't hound us, don't mess with the seedlings. I liked the way they dangled from the baler's twine and rustled. Probably were superstitious, but pie pans had been Mother's method.

I thought how Mave had raised me to be inward and pensive, but how I'd already been born heir to my mother's haggard hunger for solitude. Seven to eight a.m. daily she listened to gospel radio preaching, soaked in it, glowed in it, grew caustic with it. I could feel it when I touched her, like a static shock. She listened in the kitchen alone for a hallowed hour. I could hear the show from the front room, where I'd sit by the hot water tank and watch her private soaking and understand her life to be sealed off from me.

I never understood how some people moved through time cover to cover, as if through evenly dispersed sections in the Sears Roebuck catalog—jeans, dresses, jackets, appliances—not rushing, not deviating, with portioned-out segments for school, work, love, marriage, children, grandchildren. It always seemed to me that time spiraled, taking you first one way then another so your thirty-five-year-old self might brush past your self as a teen, then as a prepubescent pulling a red wagon.

The foil pans skirmished with the breeze, and I was almost cold. I could easily be sixteen again in winter, and there was Mave coming over to my house without a coat to tell me a truck had hit black ice and killed my mother and father instantly. My teen self stood in the doorway, turned her young body all of a piece, as a bronze statue might be turned. Mave grabbed me so that when I fell I did not fall as hard. There was a constriction in my asthmatic throat like a net I could not disentangle—though I tried to do so with my fingernails, clearing the webbing, but it was my hair and face I was scraping, like a feral cat. She tried to restrain me, but I scraped at her too. Somewhere she found a paper bag for me to breathe into, then she found leather work gloves and put them on me, then I could only bat her and myself with worn leather and I sank to her, into her solid structure and squared bones. The weight of the gloves, which had formed to my dad's large hands, finally made me go limp. My hands huge, oversized, throbbing, still.

I grew a distrust of time's gracious linear movement then. Weeks afterward, my body responded with a kind of arrest. I stopped bleeding monthly, stopped speaking, I breathed shallowly. I grew a cyst on my wrist, a hard calcium deposit with all my uncertainty and bitterness concentrated there. I did not eat, or more truly, I ate but did not remember that I had eaten.

And of course what I told no one—not Mave, not Dillon or Clarissa who tried their best to accompany me—was that I knew I had caused it. The slight but fiery filament that ran through me had pulsed with that inherited longing for aloneness, like a prayer waiting to be answered.

That night I wore the gloves to bed. Mave lay on couch cushions on my upstairs bedroom floor, sharing my grief's epicenter. She'd lost her sister, of course. So you don't scratch out your eyes, she'd said. The gloves chapped my nose and eyelids when I wiped; they dulled my contact with the wall paneling, though I still reached out as if feeling around for a trapdoor that would open into some other part of time, but I was not able to detect the slight misalignment of the boards that signaled escape.

I could not remember the funeral, but I sharply remembered Rex's fight with Mave about what to do with me. Both stood sentry on her porch, glaring and hurting. I watched, cold, through her screen door.

"Miranda's got her hands full, but there's room," he said. I thought of Belinda and Tuffie, teens then, the lingering pleurisy, and the way the twins, even as older boys, glommed onto Miranda like bottom feeders.

"Frankie can stay where she is," Mave said.

"Miranda and Margot—" Rex worked his thought slowly, like a seed from between his teeth. His shirt flecked with hay from feeding cattle, the debris of chores, his speech slow and uneasy, unfinished. There were things always felt toward Mave but not spoken. "They understood each other," he said.

"The kid can stay in her house. I'll look after her." Mave's hip to the porch post to brace herself. He nudged a broken lamp with his boot, scanned the hoarded litter. "She's already raised," Mave said. "She's sixteen. She should stay in her own house, and I'll sleep there until she can be on her own. And I'll pay it off."

"Not with that woman's money," he said sharply. There it was. There you were, Ruth. Invoked. Barred.

"Get off my goddamn porch," she said.

"You're unfit, Mave." He did not look at her but out at the black trees.

"Get off my porch."

"You're a drunk. Child welfare will come. She can stay with us till she's of age, then she can decide. She can't stay here alone."

"She's not alone." Mave kicked the busted shade of the lamp he'd been toeing around. Then her bristly lip was firm and inches from his face, his years of judgment crosshatching his skin like woven wire. "Let Frankie decide now," she said and looked at me like a wild animal in a trap.

How could I not stay with her? How could I ever betray her?

So Mave became my legal guardian and watched over me from one house over, and when Rex refused to keep the wild grape and multiflora rose brush-hogged from the break in the fence as my dad had done, Mave paid someone to do it. To clear the artery so her blood could flow to me. The deal was that I'd keep going to Snyder's Crossing with Rex and Miranda, but I quit soon enough, leaving Mave to fend off Miranda's pleas.

At first, for about a month, Mave left me only for her school bus run and slept in my parents' bed. When I could hear the bus she kept parked by her house shift into gear before dawn, I felt held by the pocket of solitude she'd somehow sewn around me. She let me stay home from school at first. In the morning, seven to eight a.m., I rose and slipped into Mother's skin, during her gospel radio hour. I would not turn on the radio, but I held her Bible with *The Living Word* on its cover. At eight, I slipped out of it, hanging up her skin as if it were an apron on a hook, and waited for Mave to cook me oats.

You can surmise, Ruth, that she was not affectionate with me. But she was watchful. She was less mother and more loyal stray dog. She sent up signs of assurance in her own way, as if in semaphore. Once, in a warm spell that winter, she pulled up in her long cavernous school bus, emptied of kids, parked, and looked over to me through the fence break and waved. This was our new world. It felt like an old world. I held the Bible shut in my lap on the front porch steps, since it was not yet eight. She went into her house, and I watched her front door flanked with porch rubble. I regretted then not going with Rex, or not asking my friend Liza if her mother would let me stay in their clean attic room. The lattice crisscrossed my porch floor with shadows like prison bars.

After a while, Mave came back outside with a wicker basket of wet laundry hefted onto her hip and walked toward her single green clothesline wire she never used, in the stilted way you walk when you carry real weight. She hung her manshirts by the tails, or by the shoulders, indiscriminate, her jeans by the waist with their pockets pulled out like tongues. The nylon line sagged between its eyehooks screwed to walnut tree and shed wall, with the weight of socks, linen towel, T-shirt. I am here, she was saying, in the best way she could.

Plenty of times she came over and held up my life like a cedar beam. Plenty of times she dragged me into her cluttered living room for PBS. But that day she had hung her laundry for a sign. And I understood.

OUR WEDDING WAS IN AUGUST OF 1989. It fell when the early corn was already in pint Ziplocs in the freezer and the late corn in tassel. I'd started the sauerkraut on its six months of fermentation in the crock in the basement of my house, now semi-barren but still in my name. The musk melons were close, the onions hung, the August prematurely cool. I made my own bouquet, wrapped a hair ribbon around the woody stems of three bluing hydrangeas.

Yellow dress, hair braided back in a way I never wore it, my body in its boyish, lean obstinacy. Since Mave would know where to find me at eleven, I left two hours early and parked my Ford Ranger in the place Rex had ribboned off for everyone, having diverted his herd. I walked past the garden now fully hedged with zinnias, magenta and orange and red, and thick with the smell of ripe tomatoes and their powerful vines, all the spines of the pole beans so loaded. No heartbeat in the electric fence disconnected from the battery. I could not help but miss the gentle Guernseys and I could tell from some distance away that the bathtub trough was spotless now, that someone, probably Aunt Miranda, had bleached it for me, and the thousand shades of green were now a singular metal white.

The milkhouse I loved sat hushed in its uselessness. I lifted the latch and descended two levels of bowed stairs to the cement slabs still cooled by the natural spring. It could still have kept jugs of milk for a day or two. Bare boards dangled from chains hooked to the ceiling beams where someone, prefiguring Miranda, had kept preserves.

Back up the stairs one level was the small workbench Rex hadn't used in years. To the underside of the upper shelf he had nailed canning jar lids and rings and screwed on jars filled with bolts, nuts, staples, seeds, the teeth of some mechanical thing, all of it now rusted out. The light from the high windows hit the jars. I realized I'd left the hydrangeas on the cab's bench seat. I fingered my braid. I would maybe stay in the milkhouse and skip the whole thing.

The workbench presented a desk, sandpaper scraps lying coarse side down, and on the smooth side, between the stamps of the brand name, I could have written a little series of letters to you—just a few lines each—but I had no pen. In the corner sat a shapely stone jar. Terracotta, a tiny cistern perhaps, shaped by a people who knew how to work the mud. It was plain, and if I'd had a brush, or nail polish, I'd have tried to paint it with birds and bats and stars and real dahlias. I no longer remembered the few hieroglyphs you'd taught me. Since I could not sit anywhere without dirtying the dress, I stood stiffly waiting.

I touched my hair again and thought briefly of my mother. Her exacting hands braiding my young-girl hair, pulling tight at my temples, her belittling gaze which, I knew, was truly a look of bafflement. After a while, up at ground level: distant sounds of vehicles parking. I pictured the bodies sitting down on folding chairs, each row set off by a single downturned gladiola, Clarissa's touch.

Clarissa in a blue dress with capped sleeves and her honey bangs curled with a curling iron by her twenty-year-old daughter Tess, and Clarissa's Darrell begrudging the interruption to the alfalfa's final cutting, possessive arm stretched atop her chair back. Miranda in sage-green cotton matching Rex's short-sleeved button-up, both sitting up front breathing a righteous air, or an air of relief at my life locking into a notch they finally understood. The twins there, still boys to me but not really boys, Ron slight with feathery hair and Benji arms crossed and face set square like Rex's. Beside them, cousin Tuffie, preferring black rayon blouse and face powdered pale, and the oldest one my age, my almost-sister, Belinda, her two toddlers left with a sitter. Belinda bursting from her silk dress's neckline, her tapered waist, her hair in a blond-brown pile of pinned ringlets that made her everywhere soft. No bridesmaids or groomsmen to flank us, only the reluctant Baptist preacher. Lottie would be a spare bundle of gray dress and crocheted shawl on Clay's arm. A gathering of bodies with hearts beating in the crabgrass, a man and wife up front almost gauzy, somehow resisting witness.

I could remember what you'd written me, Ruth, about the heartbeat of the world. You'd once gone three weeks to the Sinai Desert and had never been that alone in your life, you wrote, and something made you hear the heartbeat—what was it? Was it the ardent, clarifying work of aloneness? I heard voices up above and the tuning gospel band, Stew's bass guitar easing into sound, Stew with his chiseled, unreadable face. And underneath that, I heard the low tremor of the generator for the amp.

Mave opened the milkhouse door and called my name.

How breakable and soft the body. The inner ankle, the earlobe, the abdomen that one palms in the early morning before rising. I watched Nan's bruised arms in the mirror, ever raised in hair management attempts. Twigs anyone could snap.

We started looking for food when we crossed into Kentucky on 64. Ellis had gotten the last of the bologna sandwiches. The Indian Summer air of mid-October stayed thick, and since the Olds had no air conditioning, we ignored Nan's protests and kept the windows down. So when we pulled into the place with a nondescript Restaurant sign, Nan strewed together an impressive collection of expletives, ordered me to pop the goddamn trunk, and rooted around back there, presumably for her hairbrush. She huffed toward the brick restaurant and left the trunk open.

"Why did you dump your pills?" I asked Mave. Nan addressed her calamity's reflection in the building's window, starting at the frightful tips.

"Let's just leave her here," said Mave, "let her hitchhike."

"We could," I said. Nan held her lipstick tube in her teeth.

"It's like being naked in a burlap sack."

"What is?"

"Living inside time." Mave patted the paper bag in the door. "I didn't dump the good ones."

"If anything makes you feel out of it, it's the codeine."

"Keeps me lucid."

"Keeps you numb. You took too many."

"There's less chafing."

"Let me see your eyes."

"End of discussion. Back to Little Gypsy Moth—since you won't desert her, you might try talking to her. The silent treatment puts all the pressure on me, and my pipes are bad." She watched Nan flit into the restaurant.

"What do you think she wants?" I said.

"I doubt she knows."

"You feel sorry for her?"

"Me? Hell no. The only one I feel sorry for is the ransomed dog. Come on, boy—" She got out, air tank in hand, opened the door to the backseat and hooked his leash and Ellis fumbled forward. "—he's got no idea where he even is. Look, Dog." Mave pointed up to the sign she led him towards. "Don't you love that? Just call the thing the thing—Restaurant." She floated on the pills and he hobbled to keep up.

Why not Florida, Nan had whined, to the beaches? Why the desert?

Because it has rained here for forty days and forty nights, said Mave—

No it hasn't, said Nan—

Something is rotting, Mave went on. It's my feet, I think.

But it's true we were drowning. The swamp would have to rupture and drain; there would have to be something else, something new and strange, even for Nan. The red rocks—wouldn't they have the secret? Some message etched a billion years ago into their sandstone ledges?

Again the conviction to call Clay, and, again, I dodged it. I grabbed my wallet and circled back to shut the trunk. But first I surveyed Nan's rubble, her black overnight bag unzipped to its skimpy contents and various cosmetics spilled from the bag. I fought the urge to rummage. Some brown powder dotted the trunk bed from a compact; I dusted it off and felt a bulge, something solid and bulky beneath the thin carpet pad. Under the carpet corner, a handgun. Mave's Browning pistol.

Unbelievable—when had she stuck it there? I looked over to where she'd disappeared with Ellis. I'd seen the gun before, loose in her hands, or sitting off to the side, her gaze blackened, the gun like a hairy spider about to jump. I covered the pistol and gathered Nan's tubes and mini jars into her bag and shut the trunk.

Inside, it was dim, everything orange plastic and brown. Old-fashioned bar stools lined a counter where a few truckers had installed themselves, one waitress in white tending them. Sun-bleached photographs of wildlife hung above the diners' heads on the wall where the sun hit in full force. A buck with a washed-out rack, a wolf pair running, a bear in a grove somewhere far from I-64. I saw that Nan had claimed a booth in the back and had also attracted the attention and talk of a man middle-aged. So be it.

I headed to the bathroom. Two stalls, both empty. I sat to pee in the cleanest stall. On the door, drawn in lipstick at eye level: a huge calla lily with stamen sticking out enlarged, an obvious cock. I recognized the signature curves in Nan's lines. The crude provocation but also the quick artfulness, no question. I smeared it with toilet paper, riled more by the gun in the trunk than by Nan's lewd graffiti.

At the booth, Mave sat on the outer edge of her side, elbows on the table, not moving. Nan was slunk up to the wall under an aged photo of seals sunning. I sat beside her. I planned to take up the topic of the gun another time. I couldn't tell whether Mave knew I knew, whether she cared one way or the other, her nonchalance aggravating.

"Our mascot says to order him a T-bone," Mave said.

Nan was already nursing a Miller Lite. "Compliments of Patrick." She wiggled her fingers at the dumpy man now watching her from a stool at the counter. Her lips calla lily shade.

"Little Tramp," Mave said, "do you love anyone?"

"Patrick."

"Right." Mave's alien tubing looked too normal to me. "Under the voluminous webbing of your hair, what do you think about?"

Sip of Miller Lite and quiet. A woman with two toddlers struggled into the place and made a brief racket.

"Fish and chips please," I said to the grim waitress. Nan ordered a burger and Mave two T-Bones, one wrapped to go. I mentioned the bag of kibble on the floor of the backseat, but the order for Ellis stood.

"Perhaps you don't love anyone," said Mave. "Perhaps you think of nothing, like a chimp they would teach the signs for milk and hungry." Her face grimaced at a secret pain then went slack, its edges softened by sickness and painkillers. I wished I still smoked. I guessed this was supposed to be her suicide mission, and I had not agreed to that. I sipped on the huge Pepsi cup of water and watched her put both hands palm up on the table in some kind of surrender or game. I was angry. Nan tucked a piece of hair and eyed the seals in their heap by the sea, and her smallness and softness agitated me further.

Then, out of nowhere, in this nowhere diner stale with beef and starch odor underscored by the bleach I could always detect, in the booth of weary brown padding, Mave spoke of you plainly for the first time in all those years, to this backwater girl we didn't even know.

She said, "Nannette, I'm going to tell you about someone named Ruth. This is going to be a truth-telling trip. Ellis and I decided that out back where we raised our legs to piss."

Nan's black eye pulsed.

"Save your air, Mave," I said.

"Who's Ruth?" Nan said.

"Somebody I love." Mave like a rock face, like a too-big boy. Like somebody dying.

"Love as in *love* love? You love women? I had you figured for that."

"What's funny about you, Gypsy, is that each time you open your pouty little mouth, I grow more curious about you, who you are, why you're with a brute husband, why you think you're nothing."

"I don't think that," said Nan.

"Truth-telling, remember," said Mave. "I'll tell you what Ruth is like. She is not like me, that's for sure. She has a way, she's warm, she treats people like they're small animals. Or big ones. Really, to her, we're all chimps she'd teach to sign milk." There in the booth, talking of you as present, as nearby. The waitress set a steak with fries before Mave, then our orders. Smell of grease. A greasy to-go bag for the hound. Toward the steak, Mave leaned down, studied its gristle and juice. She said, "Ruth has no family. She wears a loose braid." I did not know these things.

So this is how I came to see you, really, intact for the first time—you of whom I'd not seen one photo, whose story I'd only glimpsed in Mave's rare drunken anecdotes, whose face was no face to me, and whose body had always been the ashes of letters. I saw you alone and braided and animated and tending scared animals. I wanted Mave to stop.

"You took too many pills," I said, even-keeled, trying to deflect. Nan picked up her beer as if I were trying to take it. How could Mave say things about you to Nan that she had never said to me?

"Ruth chooses the underdog," said Mave. "Perhaps because of her own ailment, a leg fractured and poorly pinned and screwed back together. She's acquainted with pain. The fury toward one's limitations. You wouldn't know it to look at me, Nannette, but I have a graduate degree. I'm her diamond in the rough, so to speak. Picture me, this product of alfalfa and ridge and mountain bog, poor as dirt when I go up north, and I sit in on her lecture. She speaks into the room like she's reading cue cards written by a poet. She's old Boston money—huge inheritance—but lives like a pauper, except she's vain about her hair, like you, Nannette, like you." Mave's eyes all fog, her words a slur. "She has gray silk hair in that long-ass braid. And some pricey pieces in her apartment, she can't help herself with those few things. And east wall, south wall of a house—where the light hits matters, Ruth says—she faces the Janus head bookend north and south. Thirteen years my senior, and my professor, but a body lean like a jaguar. She does like cashmere."

Nan sat greedy and rapt and I was erupting, the battered cod in front of me stirring up nausea.

Mave's voice grew more slurred and scattershot and her eyes bugged out, still clouded with drug. She said, "I met her and knew her already—like learning a language and the spelled word surprises you with familiarity. She's a linguist. You may not know what that is, Little Gypsy, that's okay. Frankie can explain it to you. Only men in her field, but Ruth is the one who went to the Sinai Desert alone and listened to everything for the first time. Language does more than signify, you need to know that. It originates. It makes a little bread." Mave took a bite of steak and chewed. "She studies hieroglyphs. Words that have gills and scales and skin and fur. It's so simple, even you will be able to understand it, Nannette."

She studied Nan's slunk body unmoving, seemed to decode her. Then she studied me but still spoke to Nan. I was beginning to think that Nan was a conduit.

"Ruth wants to make the world right. When the Black students picket the Quonset Hut, she carries a sign, even with her limp. When the pregnant girl gets kicked out of the dorm, Ruth makes up a cot. When I go to her with all the iterations of myself, in a bundle of scraps, and all the possible ways to live, innumerable—" Mave stopped in the middle of the thought. We were quiet. The waitress filled my big water cup and left the scribbled bill.

"So where is Ruth now?" Nan asked.

"She tatted lace once," Mave muttered. "Can you imagine that? She always wanted to fix cars, too, but only because she likes to say *spark plug*. She loves to say *piston*."

I'd had enough of your unveiling. I felt all the private, secret years exposed in the shoddy light of the booth. Mave took long draws of rough breath and she was finished.

Nan waited. Her bruised young face expectant. "Where is she now?" she asked again. She looked at Mave, at me. Everyone in our dim booth so breakable and somehow out of place.

I said to Nan with a plainness I hated, "Ruth is dead." My first words spoken to her since we'd left. And now I write the preposterous words here, on a dollar-store notepad, in this letter unending. I write to you, the dead, about the dead. To stay alive.

Another Miller Lite appeared, the waitress's white uniform dissolving to ghost. Attentive Patrick at the bar nodded his head and waved. Nan slid the bottle over to me, and I took it.

All these notes froth up and spill slowly from the rim.

So I started learning real facts about you at a diner just over the Kentucky line, and you who were always otherworldly to me took on a mundane bodily form and almost a face. I write to you now, though you've been dead years, because I need to keep my hands doing something and because, for that brief time in my childhood, I had written you almost daily and in secret, and you had seen some kind of promise in me. Also because you were the one Mave loved, and I did not know, I never really knew, what she harbored toward me, only that I was her counterpart in the universe. But love? In O'Keeffe's *Ram's Head, Blue Morning Glory*—a print I still keep folded up somewhere—was I not the blue morning glory and she the one with intact horns?

What can I say of you, Ruth, most intimate stranger? What more do I know of you besides a gift of lilac soap delivered by Mave and the flutter of words—and, after a greasy Kentucky supper and beer, those revelations yielded up to Nan, the loose gray braid that might have resembled my mother-in-law Lottie's? When I still had your three years of letters, maybe I could have formed you from them, with a fully rendered face, as if you were a paper doll.

Your letters to me that blew up my head.

Always with Mave's name and Massachusetts return address so Mother didn't know they were from you.

I first wrote only to Mave, and she shared my letters with you. I was eleven when she left for Northampton at age thirty-nine or forty, beginning at Smith College on scholarship so late in life, after years as an autodidact, then on to her master's at Amherst. I didn't know all the details of her circumstances then. And I didn't know about you at all. I remember the occasion of my first letter to Mave clearly. A Sears Roebuck catalog appeared, thick and promising, in the mailbox, too large to allow the metal door to shut all the way. I saw it from the house, like a tongue sticking out. Then I saw a boy I didn't know, dressed in a collared shirt and nice pants, steal the catalog and run. He ran out of my sight, toward the back of the house. I went down to the cellar to look for him out the high-up smoky window that faced the back, and there he was among the thick wires of black-eyed Susans, hidden from the road but not from me. I pressed to the window, standing atop a crate. He propped open the catalog in the big flowers, unbuckled his belt, and pulled fast in his underwear, struggling mightily against the underwear band, until his body shook stiff and still. My one hand warmed the cellar window glass. My other trailed along me, along the thigh in my jeans, along my blouse and neck and ear. He wiped his hand in the grass, the tree leaves red rust. Fall was beginning around this boy. He disappeared, and soon after, I heard the knock at the front door. I listened to muffled voices from the cellar and reached the kitchen as the boy handed a pamphlet to my mother. I understood he was a Jehovah's Witness boy witnessing.

A foreign pole of ache formed in me, throat to pelvis. Through the front window, the catalog tongue stuck out again from the mailbox. I did not fetch it. In my mind I flipped through the sneakers and tents and Maytags to the negligee, the beige and white silks, the brown eyes and long hair he must have turned to. I did not exactly want the boy to touch me, but I suddenly wanted him to be me and me him—I wanted us to switch places. Our private moments had come in contact to make an exquisite loneliness. I felt within me plenty of boy and plenty of girl, and I then wondered if that was what Mave felt since my mother had told me, confusingly, when I'd asked why Mave was not married, that she loved like men love.

Mave lived at an address I knew only from a paper in a kitchen drawer. I could still see her in boots upon porch steps, and I missed her very much. I had so often climbed the stepstool she'd put by her sink just for me, and I had accepted wet mugs and plates into a dishtowel from her strong hands, sometimes extra aware of my own hands moving and holding as if they were someone else's.

So I wrote a letter to Mave. I asked if she was both man and woman and told her about the boy and the things I felt and how I did not think Mother would understand. Then, when I finished all that, I continued onto another page writing about everything and feeling freedom in it. A long letter about basketball games, Dillon, Clarissa and Liza, the sad colors of fall that came so quickly and how the winter would soon look like slate. And she wrote back to me, a brief letter, in her all-caps print and incomplete sentences that made me fill in the gaps myself, writing the same way she spoke. *Inside, maybe we are multiple*—I remember she wrote that. After three exchanges, she enclosed a letter from you.

Your letters came on soft blue paper, written with care in blue ink, not quick and choppy like Mave's handwriting. You did not write to me as a stranger addressing a child, asking what grade I was in and did I play any instruments and what was my favorite season. You wrote about books and sometimes music, always news of the world though never news of yourself, not what happened during the day or how old you were, or why you were writing me. Instead, you wrote about the painter Jacob Lawrence—his newest Dream painting of a Black woman sitting in a room dreaming, in one window a wedding and, in the other, someone holding a vase of flowers, always a vase of flowers, you said—and you wrote about the Civil Rights struggle, which was not much spoken of in Caudell. You suggested I study the words *tribe*, *nation*, *race*, words to be peeled open: where were the words born and how did we come to wield them like weapons, one nation of people over another? *Nation* in the Latin and the Old French peeled back to expose *birth*, to be born, to be uttered into the world, a spectrum of Black, White, Male, Female, each of us simply uttered like a particle of human light.

I found you peculiar. My hands shook when I read your letters.

Often you wrote of the desert, how in the Sinai you heard the original language inside of language. How in Persia there could be no larger sense of night, of scope. Mostly you wrote about words themselves, and about my own letters to Mave, which you had been reading all along. Words without limits, blurred at the edges like bog land; words as rooms one walks into, words holding million-year-old species like amber—see the trilobite and the ancient fern, the spinal column of something extinct still preserved in a word's withered curve.

Then, when I wrote back, though I didn't understand who you were, I wrote Dear Mave and Ruth, as if to the same person. The blue letters answered me, enclosed in Mave's at first, and eventually only the blue letters in envelopes with Mave's name, so Mother never knew about this woman who wrote to me something like (I don't have it now to read exactly)—*What is beautiful is you don't write words to be remembered. You are a tiny leaf miner carving tracks in tunnels of chlorophyll on ephemeral leaves, writing out only its desire for food, like someone making tracks in snow to disappear. Because of that, the letters bring me joy here in Northampton.*

You called it a second waking. We wake to words in our mouth—think of that word Mouth, lips wide and back for the O, then rounded, narrowed for the U, the diphthong. We speak what we hear, we name what is named for us: this is your mouth, these your toes, your sheaf of paper and flower seed packs, and they pet our heads and say Good as if we're puppies pissing in the right spot. Good, you can survive. What is this? They check us, pointing: Dog. Chair. Dress. From speaking to writing, when we start to write, it's in shadow of the spoken, an echo or repetition, the voice saying, Repeat after me with lines and shapes, and the hand in its proud flourish matches the names with the correct marks, dots, and sticks.

But some have a second waking, you said. It comes when a word does not chase after a thing, but engenders it. You write the word Light and there is light, a dim glow maybe, almost secret, but there. You write the word Bird and a new species of warbler sings. You write the story of the Tree and the tree thus grows. It all felt like myths or poems to me—bits and pieces of Egyptology and hieroglyph, these first words that wrote the real trees, the flooded river banks, the freedom of all people and nations among stars rising, and all people's beauty, a person's beauty as something to name and to call forth. A vase of two cut lilacs with ants furious and alive in them. Have you ever seen them so furious? you asked.

I understood to some degree what you meant about that electric current in words. I understood that when I sat down to write *Dear Mave and Ruth*—and eventually, during the three years, simply *Dear Ruth*—the air shifted, and I had a feeling of starting over from the beginning. Of being changed into myself. You sent me the collected letters of van Gogh, in which I mainly looked at the plates of paintings. I told no one, not even Clarissa, about the strange letters on blue paper, but I showed Dillon the van Gogh paintings, and he loved them.

Then you died, without my ever having met you.

Mave came home, with the money and books you left her, and moved back into her falling-down house where she and Mother and Miranda had all grown up. She carried all those hundreds of books in pillowcase sacks, one by one from the car, like heavy litters of kittens to be drowned. She had no bookshelves so she used bricks and plywood and two-by-fours. Shelves leaning and bowing, a sorry shrine. I was fourteen. I had sent a few letters that you had not answered and these Mave brought to me tied together in a bundle and unopened, and Mother saw and questioned until Mave confessed I'd been corresponding with you. Mother demanded those unopened letters and all the others I had from you, so I gave her the box of blue letters and she burned them in the fireplace—why didn't I save some of them? Why didn't I fight her? Maybe because Mave didn't fight. She simply squatted in her boots and watched the fire and drank whiskey from a jar and accepted the reproach. Mave passed her hand through her coarse cut hair, so short. I wanted to touch it and was surprised that I did so. With my hand on her head, we mourned you.

"Why did you come back," I whispered, "and not stay in the house on Aldrich Street? Wasn't it a beautiful house? And so full of her?" I had no pictures of your house, but still I saw the oak bookshelves, the tall windows with green drapes, the hung hieroglyphs on parchment and reed. It was as if Mave's face were a scrim lit from behind by your beautiful life.

Mave didn't answer. After a while, toward the flaky ash in the grate, she said, "You keep writing. Write a book. She believed you could."

I remember in one letter, Ruth, you told me to cut flowers daily. You said, They don't have to be yours. Ownership is illusion. Make a vase by hand, change them out when they wilt the least bit, the prolific peonies, the daisies, but they don't even have to be blooming. They can be stems. They can be twigs. They don't even have to be real. They can be scribbled down.

When Mave came home widowed, it was late winter, too early for anything to bloom, but buds were out. On her dining room table, I cleared the already-collecting debris of bread crusts and loose mail and candy wrappers and set out a jar of green wood branches I'd twisted off a tree. They stuck out, helpless, in all directions. Some days after that I brought a clutch of fragrant waking-up alfalfa grass. Later on, a wild lily or a primrose I'd steal from Miranda. Later on, dandelions half gone to seed.

Dear Ruth.

I HAD A DREAM, THE NIGHT AFTER MY FIRST SEX WITH DILLON ON THE WET FLOOR OF THE TRAIN CAVE. Since I was twenty-five with his twenty-three-year-old body now folded into mine but already wresting itself free, I felt uncontainable by my childhood room. I lay on the kitchen floor alone, still dressed in filthy jeans smelling of sulfur and duckweed. From my vantage point, lying on my back, the hanging tea towel billowed from another world. I felt my shoulder blades resist the linoleum and I studied my hands in the dark, lit by my animal light and etched by the Clorox and Murphy Oil that always leached through my surgical gloves at LaFaber. Then I slept.

I dreamed Miranda took me to a revival meeting at Snyder's Crossing. The evangelist like a tree trunk, his Bible held intact with black electrical tape. He opened to the story of the demon-possessed man who lived naked in the tombs and caves. I was younger in the dream, in a sheer blouse, with no bra, with two rose-eyes seeking Dillon among the congregants, but he wasn't there. Only a blur of faithful faces. The preacher took up most of the space, as if hogging a camera frame, and read me the story. Jesus sailed to the country of the Gadarenes, across from Galilee, and the naked crazy man housed nightly in cold stone ran to him and said with the voice of the spirits, What do we have to do with you, do not torment us. The revival preacher grew loud—It was Legion speaking, he said, it was a host of demons that seized up the man, made him cut his arms and break his chains and stay outside in sun and rain. Legion begged Jesus, Don't send us into darkness, send us instead into that herd of swine. So Jesus cast them into the two thousand swine nearby and they whinnied, terrified, and flung themselves one by one off the cliff into the sea and drowned.

The preacher steamed and swaggered. He said the possessed man came into his right mind, his eyes became a new blue, and Jesus boarded the boat and left. What did it feel like for the man now free? the preacher asked me directly. My girl self said I didn't know, then the evangelist shape-shifted into the man shed of demons. He had scarred arms, years of ratty hair full of dead things, blinking his eyes at all the colors now too bright. He was a lonely loon watching Jesus become a dot on the far water, and he said to me, I do not want a real bed. I do not want what I am supposed to want.

And the swine? Squealing, barreling their thick wire-hide bodies off the cliff—what did it feel like when the demons slipped into their fatty tissue and bones? Like a tongue, slithery, sensual? Like a tongue. The radiant lonely man loomed in hazy dream-light, in his neat house with a roof and ordered days. The swine with haggard flat faces were gone in a wild morbid parade.

I strayed into the man's former caves that were tall enough for a train, the tombs fogged in moonlight. I chose the tombs, in the dream. I chose the terrified swine. I woke up soaked on the kitchen floor, groping in the dark for the tea towel.

❧

EVEN AFTER CLAY AND I HAD BEEN MARRIED A MONTH, the house still felt like Lottie's. She cooked, I scrounged up a side as if bringing a dish to a potluck. Clay had positioned the cinderblocks at the four corners of the trailer lot behind the house but had gotten no further.

I woke early at the start of the second month and sat on the back steps in two flannel shirts, smoking furtively in the September chill—I rarely smoked around Clay. It's not that he forbade it in or near the house, but it filmed my skin with a grime noticeable to me next to his clarified flesh. He seemed to me wholly rinsed in body and mind.

"Frankie," he said once, on a walk toward town while I smoked, "do you like the house? Would you like a porcelain sink to replace Mom's stainless steel?" And though I reeked always of astringent cleaners, it was his phrases, not mine, that were ruddy and scrubbed kind. I did not answer the first; to the second, I said the steel was fine and there was no use wasting a fine sink. We turned around at Matlick Feed and the motel that sat derelict. "We could paint the stairwell," he said.

"But it's fine," I told him, "really," tossed my cigarette to the feed store pavement, maybe trying to reduce the differences between us.

On the back steps, I studied the blocks that propped up nothing. I liked the semi-darkness of morning in which no one shuffled around—Clay had left already at five thirty, in State Road clothes that smelled of fuel and sun, and Lottie still slept in her recliner, which she migrated to in the middle of each night. Her head lay back against the spray of lace doily, and she held her long braid across her front by habit. Sometimes I now wonder whether you slept this way, Ruth—and how long your braid. Ellis formed a heap on the kitchen floor. When I started the truck, the hound appeared in alert silhouette at the window behind the couch, backlit by the lamp I'd left on.

I drove to my sparse house to harvest the butternut squash. Backed the Ford Ranger up to the garden with buckets loaded in the bed. The foil pans along the perimeter had worked up an artful patina in the weather, rustling in the scant breeze like a string of spirit charms. A dozen butternuts were ready on the vine—two for Mave, two for Clarissa, two for Lottie's kitchen, and a half dozen for the LaFaber co-op trade. My house stood by, a dark gray witness. The taste of the coffee in the thermos I'd brought was different, the proportions for Lottie's pot never quite right.

I drove back and chose the two most shapely squashes. In the kitchen, Ellis ambled over and flopped his ears back and forth in a fury as if to shake loose a bad thought. "Hey, Hound," I said, "hey, Flop," sensing the warmth of the house and stripping off the flannels down to my long-underwear layer. I held out a squash to him, and he put a thick paw on it. I scratched his ear and spoke the doggerel that came from the easy soft place, unpinched, and I labored with a dull peeler on the two squashes in the sink. Ellis yawned and watched and smelled—I imagined that, in one sniff, he could smell everything on my body I had tried to wash off, nicotine grime, urine not wiped clean from the hair, my sweat, the sandy soil. I scooped out the seeds for a baking sheet, oiled them, sorted out the viscous strings, and he sniffed all that too, then pressed into my dropped hand chalked with resin.

I'd trained myself on the whereabouts of spoons and knives. I chopped the squash in coarse pieces and set them to cook down later in a little water, found the brown sugar neatly labeled in Tupperware by the same hand that had written the wilted lettuce recipe card. I salted the seeds that would roast bronze in the oven, then slid to the floor by the hound's head, which he put in my lap.

That first month, Clay and I had lain down each night on sheets that somehow still smelled of their plastic packaging. We had skipped the honeymoon, felt too old. His every movement was slight and gentle. Mostly I thought about how I'd fouled out each game as a girl, elbowing, egregiously forceful. Mostly I slept on my back, feeling that I should not sleep in my usual fetal clutch, as if that posture were selfish. He'd reached for me, tentatively, only a handful of times.

It seems important now, Ruth, to say more about Dillon, to try to understand what became of us. He'd just barely missed Vietnam, too young, but all he had ever really wanted was to fly fighter jets for the US Air Force. He didn't have the eyes and wouldn't wear glasses since he thought he could get back to twenty-twenty. All I wanted was to breathe inside his body, like a baby newt, breathing him through my skin. We were restless and rough; he matched me in roughness.

He was wearied by the years of foundry work at LaFaber, firing the bronze trophies, grave markers, nameplates. I was wearied by nothing, body on edge. I sensed continually the nightshades past prime, their juice seeking us like something homing in, and him pulsing like a varied thrush, with a black ring bib around his gold-orange neck I could bite, a nectarine, both of our bodies flinty and thin and drinking in the other. But at the core, he preserved a loneliness, like something kept out of reach on a shelf. He always wore his uncle's Army jacket; he always squinted and looked past me, to see things in the distance, to read billboards, make out the model of a far-off car to convince himself of his improving sight. I took him to Rex's barn crammed with square bales, with nothing to see in the dusky air but me, my body, hair, mouth. I hardly slept during those months; I rarely spoke to Mave or Clarissa. My bond with Dillon was not a generous kind. I could have choked on my greed for him.

That summer the gypsy moth got bad in the trees around Caudell. You could see the webbing everywhere, around the thousand-egg masses that had wintered over to hatch out when the oaks and sweetgum would go into bud. We could stand in the heart of the summer hardwoods at the perimeter of the swamp and hear the sound of worms chewing and frass dropping like a light rain, the moth slowly stripping the trees from the crown. Dillon got part-time work, after foundry hours, setting pheromone traps and loading the canisters of Bt onto the planes. Near the end of the summer, he took me up on the ridge to watch the plane drop, the spray drifting down like fallout and paralyzing the larvae so they'd stop feeding and starve. We lay on our stomachs, propped on our forearms. Turning from the dissipating cloud, we rolled to our backs. My hair fell into my mouth, he pulled it out and played with it, facing me.

"Pretty cruel to the moth if you think about it," he said. Cheeks and forehead tanned dark with a crescent of pale beneath his eyes, humidity curling the black hair at his temple which I touched.

"I can read your thoughts," I said, circling my fingertip there.

"That right? Well, what am I thinking, Frankie?"

"Things that would make some women blush," I said.

He smiled but pulled his head back slightly, looked again to the distant fog of poison in the treetops. "Might be my chance," he said. "To fly." He squinted after a rising bird, a turkey vulture. "My buddy told me the Forest Service has a school in Virginia to train pilots for the pesticide planes."

I watched the vulture dive and duck out of sight. "You should do it," I said, though my breathing thinned.

"I mean, it would be a lot of travel, on assignment and everything. A lot through the South, I think."

I watched him seek the buzzard, or maybe the plane and its pilot.

"But it would just be seasonal," he said. "I'd always come back."

But he didn't go at all, not at first—it was August, September, and he stayed and brooded. Slowly, Dillon talked less and less, then quit altogether, a kind of fade-out. In time, he seemed unable to speak, his mouth plastered shut. His body itched somewhere deep.

One night we walked, and a ranging dog padded alongside us, hopeful and mangy, and Dillon kicked it hard in the ribs. I saw, as through gauze, my old revival dream, of the possessed crazy man by the sea, and I thought of the other gospel story about a boy possessed by a mute spirit. The dog slunk off to the woods and Dillon buried his fists in his pockets, squinting ahead, his face in profile, and I saw the gospel's mute boy, like someone seized up before a sneeze. Unvoiced words transmuted to a black blood I could see gathering in the boy's ears, his cheek quivering from the clench of jawbone, as though there were some secret he could not loose but badly wanted to.

In the story, the demon threw the boy onto hot coals, into water, into dirt. A person's head, discomfited by its own ideas and sealed-in secrets, will knock out its own lights on the concrete floor, will crack its skull—or someone else's—for release. Dillon scared me because he was so soon stoppered, he cricked his neck, got red-faced. He punched walls.

Clarissa had long been dating Darrell Tide by that time and they were planning to marry, and Darrell was stoppered the same and I did not warn her. Maybe because I did not want to believe in our dangers. The two men seemed forged in the same furnace of disillusionment, since Darrell had always been expected to take over his father's farm and had no out.

In the gospel, Christ cast out the mute spirit and the boy foamed at the mouth, convulsed, and nearly died. Then color returned to his rigid lips, and I pictured the kid opening his mouth and speaking, stunned by the ring of his own voice. But the near-death and the quickening did not come for Dillon.

He disappeared in late fall. To flight school, I found out later. I put my face and most of my body into Heather Run, supposing I would stay there among the bluegill and pondweed and drown. I surfaced wheezing and of course showed up on Mave's porch a stricken fish, my wet jeans cement. She cleared a dismantled radio and orphaned shingles and plastic flatware so I could sit on a porch chair. She did not hold me. She went inside and brought out a notebook, said, "Write something down. Anything." She said, "Cultivate the ground, Frankie," then receded into her half-gone bottle.

Who was she to tell me to write to stay alive? To maintain some kind of faith in the inner life that words can stoke and preserve? She who had no working pens in the house, only a blanching television, only a drink and a temple made of your books and bowed plywood.

THE ROASTED BUTTERNUT SEEDS LAY BRITTLE AND GOLDEN, cooling on the baking sheet on the stovetop. Early afternoon kitchen so warm and humid, and somehow it had become slightly more my own, mine and Ellis's. Ellis darted to the door like a pup at the crush of gravel as Clay pulled up the drive. He got out whistling a simple tune, then a truck pulled in behind him, beautiful and red with intricate flames detailed up its hood. Stew's truck. I felt the sweat-damp of my thermal shirt in the cave of my underarms, at the base of my neck. I rarely saw Stew anymore. I went to Mave's during their Saturday band practices.

The two men were framed by the storm door window as they walked up. They removed their ball caps with deference. Stew's hair black as mine, his chiseled handsome face always and ever opaque. I trained my eyes on Clay's snug work jeans tailored by time and squats and kneeling to pavement on the job so the denim was thinned white at the knees. The sweet humid air softened their faces as they entered, Clay still encountering me in his own kitchen with some surprise, or embarrassment, and uncertainty. Stew nodded and kept his lanky form near the door like a stray unused to interiors. I wanted to smoke with him out front. He wouldn't have minded, he minded nothing; the world came at him and he took it all easily. He'd taken, without a fuss, a wife named Jennie, the raising of three kids, his dad's body shop where he banged out dents and sanded rust.

I knew Jennie disliked me because I'd lingered at the body shop when I'd taken in my truck with rust on the fenders a few years before. Stew seemed to take long with the job. I would watch him work before going in to LaFaber to clean in the afternoon. We smoked, I liked his permanently greased hands, his angular face and his calm, his leanness. He rarely spoke but when he did it was about the Fords and Chevys and Pontiacs strewn in the yard outside, the parts ordered, the way one of the Ellafritzes had dented up the hood. And he always looked out and up, squinting, so he reminded me of Dillon in that way, but not wound so tight. It was as if he squinted at his feeling out there in the distance, silently watching it approach, knowing it would beget another and another and he wanted to know the genealogy of the feelings before he let himself feel them. He took in my company in this unique ease. He, at times, studied my body when he thought I wasn't looking; he'd touch my shoulder, my arm, as I handed him a glass of water. But nothing ever happened. He had seen the feeling coming and chose to head it off. One day I got there and the fenders were done, painted with new black. As if to say, that was it.

"There's supposed to be an early frost," Clay said, "so we should take advantage. I was thinking we could go for that load of wood." Voice hopeful and high and gentle.

"Those downed trees on Rex's?" I asked.

"Yeah, I was thinking that. Rex is okay with it."

My own house had baseboard heat, but his and Lottie's had a wood-and-coal boiler and the woodstove in the kitchen. I said I'd be glad to, and I meant it. There was the smell of the seeds and the heated-up and browned promise of work for my hands, one of which, right then, brushed some debris from the shoulder of Clay's work jacket. In my periphery, Stew shifted his weight.

"You mind if we use your truck?" Clay asked me. "I usually borrow."

I turned off the burner, left the cooked-down squash lidded on the stove. I lay a towel over the roasted seeds after offering a handful to Stew while Clay sought out Lottie's small, feathery self in the front room. Stew chewed the seeds slowly, in meditation of the trucks or something out beyond the screen door. I admired his profile, features both smooth and angular at once, an artful face and neck thinner than most men's. I asked how he was.

"Business is a little slow," he said, fed himself a few more salted seeds. "Been working on your cousin's Jeep, that CJ-7 he's fixing up. Ron."

"Miranda says the Jeep's been good for him. And the flagger job with the State. His stammer's not as extreme."

"Nothing wrong with a stammer. It's hard to talk." Stew turned from the door to study the wallpaper trim of bonneted girls and flushed slightly with relief when Clay returned. There was some reconfiguring of vehicles because the driveway was narrow, single-file—Clay pulled his Bronco off to the side in the grass, and Stew gingerly backed out to the road and let me pull out so he could park in my place, then he disembarked and waited by his cab, as if on guard.

A new bite in the air, so I pulled back on my two flannel shirts. Stew needed a coat, wore only a white undershirt. His truck was spotless and waxed. The racing stripes up the side weren't new, but the flames were, up the hood—they shot out of the radiator, orange and yellow with blue highlights, licking at the windshield with mean tips. We of course could have loaded the wood into his truck, but it was off limits. Couldn't risk a scratch. Clay retrieved the chainsaw from the shed, and my body surged with its own ungivingness. I stood there and smoked alone, looking at my pickup that had taken a beating but had no rust. The surge traveled up my inner pole to my sternum, to my throat, and I felt a little peeled when Clay turned up beside me with the saw in hand and a fistful of work gloves.

"You want a pair? These are Mom's old ones." Leather palm blackened by use.

"No," I said, but I took them to hold and gave him the keys. I climbed to the middle of the bench seat and straddled the floor gear shift, feeling for Stew sideways, invisibly, as if in the dark. Clay's hand fell on my knee after he shifted. I held Lottie's gloves in my right hand and settled my other atop his. I wanted the splinter, I wanted the hotspot preceding the full blister at the base of my ring finger wearing its new thin band.

I knew and understood myself in work; I could still smell the pungent squash vine from the morning hour. I was eager to handle bark and brush and, in that eagerness, the air grew familiar and good in the cab. We didn't need to agree on rolling down the windows, despite the chill, we let the September wind wrap us, and the core pole in me that carried the surge up and down—to chest and neck—heated like a coil, like the engine as Clay shifted into fourth headed east on Hollow Road toward the edge of Rex and Miranda's farm, where the good locust trees had fallen in a storm, the hard wood that burned almost as hot as coal, Clay said. Heat gathered in Clay's hand upon my leg. Stew watched the world pass.

I felt stripped down to that radiating coil once we pulled in the tram road cockeyed and parked and spilled out to start the work. I left the gloves I had refused balled up on the vinyl seat, tied back my thick hair, shed the flannels, pushed up the sleeves of the long underwear shirt to carry the firewood bare-armed. I worked with speed and hum, each bending of my body alert to the scent of the saw's two-cycle oil, the burn in the sawdust, the men's awareness of me. Stew acquiesced to smoke silently with me as Clay cut, and when the saw shut off we all picked up and stacked the full cord in the bed. If the pieces were small, I took them in twos, and the knocking together of the locust sounded musical, like thick wind chimes, a deep tone in all that dense grain. My biceps tensed—I knew they watched—my forearms went taut, dust caught in the arm hair, and the surge centered and swelled in my abdomen, pelvis, upper thighs, a capacity opened up. My groin heated as I squatted in the duff for another piece.

We worked until the evening dew started to fall and we could feel it on our faces. I tasted cigarettes and the salted roasted seed bits working free from in between my teeth. When it was time, I said I'd drive. Clay took middle and I drove too fast, given the weight in the pickup's bed, but Clay said nothing. At the house, I lumbered the truck a little off the road since Stew's red pickup barred the way to the woodshed. He offered to move it and then help unload and stack.

"I'm tired," I said. "Clay and I can manage it tomorrow." No one got out, and there was the lingering question of supper and whether we should ask Stew to stay and not leave in his blazing beautiful truck, and I knew Lottie would have soupy meat ready for which my cooked-down squash would be a side, and she was surely adding a plate for him right at that moment, right before spooning a bit of broth over the dog's dry food, which would melt Ellis to ecstasy. I blamed the sudden ringing in my head on the residual song of wood striking wood and I felt them looking leftward at my face's profile in the cab, in the dying evening sun and the grim porch light. It was up to me, it was my call. My mouth felt wet and forceful.

"Good night, Stew," I said, "we thank you." And that was it.

Stew backed out his red truck with care, switched on his headlights, and took off. Clay and I walked toward the porch and I grabbed his wrist. "Not that way," I said, "this way," and tugged him toward the side door that led more directly to the dark stairwell, bypassed the kitchen golden with light and pot roast and starch and carrots. He stayed silent, simply followed, a mild large body, but I still turned and said, "Clay, shh," finger to my lips. The wooden stairs barely groaned.

You might consider my force a subsided sea, Ruth, and my beckoning cruel, given my singularity and my obstinate apartness. Given that I did not love him and he knew it. But it seems important to me now to speak to this, too, this day with him that was not nothing. I untied my black hair so it hung like drapery and I did not bother to pull the comforter down to the stiff sheets. I lay back. He said something about a shower, he smelled of One Shot chainsaw oil, I said no, it was okay. He said, "Now? I mean—" and I palmed the skin of his back beneath his shirt and felt it contract at my touch then sigh down like a released breath, or pant, his skin panting, his strong living back. He said again he should clean up first, but I helped him find my ragged shirt hem, my stomach, my bra wet with sweat. I pictured the woods and the stand of alder and locust flaring, I let myself picture Stew, even Dillon, for only a moment, all eyes squinting to see me. Clay hesitated and hovered. My inner surge soaked a cavern in me that wanted rough entrance, that wanted everything. Always everything, I could hear myself almost hollering for it. I said, "Just undo my belt."

The white of Nan's eye within the purple bruise, that center of midnight poppy, began to hurt me every time I looked at her. Her body took on meaning. Part of that meaning was her witness to what my Dillon had become; the dark clouds I'd seen gathering before he left me behind unleashed their full fury of storm upon this, her body. Her twenty-some years of life seemed to swell.

Now, with your presence in the air of the car, Ruth, the girl went thoughtful, mulling things over. She regarded Mave with sorrow and intrigue, and with me she was careful but somehow pleading when she'd catch my gaze in the mirror, since I'd shown her that my body, too, had some give to it, and a tenuous bridge had appeared between us. I knew she was in the blue Olds with us for reasons beyond her fear of a beating. Mave feigned obliviousness to the small shift in our triangulation of feeling. She studied the atlas.

What is the body, black and blue and straining to breathe? Angular, furred, beautiful. What did your face look like, this face she found beautiful?

I remembered Mave telling me, "There is no soul, but you can have one if you want one. It's a free country." We'd looked at the skinless man in the science textbook I kept after dropping out of school—digestive system, respiratory and circulatory systems.

"The body diagrammed like a cross-section of an engine," she'd said. "Breathe."

I'd breathed.

"That corporeality, the sensate—it yields up everything in bottomless creative action. Breathe and feel it." She'd left my kitchen table brusquely then, out the scraping screen door, to pass through the break in the fence and retrieve your books. Merleau-Ponty, Husserl who said the earth is our *original ark* and our senses everything. I watched her return, her godless, stony face godly to me, and my breath, where I'd sat at the rough-lumber table, extending to fingertip and toe and almost visible.

In the car, about the atlas, Mave said, "You know this was printed in 1984. These roads might not exist. The one we're on could be erased."

"Then we'll drive off into the Kentucky horse fields," I said.

"In six years anything can happen. I-64 probably got rerouted, like a river." Mave flipped to New Mexico and lifted her glasses to read the tiny names of desert towns and landmarks and reservoirs. I'd studied that page.

"I want to see one of the Great Lakes," Nan said into the car's new and generous wind. "What do you say? I hear they're so big, they're like the ocean. Let's hit one on the way. We'll all need to buy bikinis." She was now banking on an increase of friendliness.

"Thank you for your contribution, Nannette." Mave took out a pen and circled something in New Mexico.

"How about it, Frankie?" said Nan. "Go for a swim? I bet you tan good."

"Geography's not Little Gypsy's strong suit," Mave said.

"Oh, fuck off." Nan laughed and Mave turned and smiled with an ease that pricked my jealousy though there was a bit of fresh hurt in Nan's laugh. Then, "Could I at least get some clothes? I left with nothing. And smell like wet dog." I heard a reshuffling, Ellis's heft being shoved off, a flopping of ears and a huff.

Mave told me she was circling all the monument names where white people tried to make it up to the Indians, we should see those. "Important for your book," she said.

"Okay, Nan." I watched her confused face in the mirror, considered her body in its apricot dress, a collection of veins and organs and bones not skinned visible like the science textbook man, all bodies really only glimpsed. "We're coming up on Elizabethtown," I said. "We pick up the interchange for I-65 there. Should be a mall or something."

"If I-65 hasn't been rerouted," said Mave.

I PULLED INTO A SMALL PLAZA. Dismal-looking, but there was a Family Dollar next to Double Dragon Chinese takeout. "This okay?" I asked.

Nan didn't answer but lit out toward the automatic doors.

"I'll get some eggrolls for me and the wet dog." Mave doodled now in the thin margins of New Mexico. "Make it quick."

"You want anything?"

"Polka dot bikini."

I followed Nan. The late afternoon sky fell on the bald plaza, on the shopping carts gone wayward in the parking lot. The sales in Family Dollar were announced in marker on neon-pink poster board. Toddler clothing 20% off, it said. Hot dogs and buns for your Labor Day cookout, a month-old sign. My body felt emptied from the drive, weak against the store's air-conditioned gust, as if I lacked substance, as if this trip were without a purpose and it were true all the roads might disappear. My throat closed a little as I watched Nan hold up a dress to appraise. Maybe the trip was indeed aimless, or maybe I was afraid of its unspoken aim. The unspoken gun.

The normalcy of Mave's cancer ebbed away into the camouflage-print onesies and left behind the disease's acute strangeness—sudden sting. Nan waved at me, as if we were friends. I felt as though I'd walked through a spider web and caught a struggling fly, and she couldn't see that it buzzed loud and hopeless against my brain.

I pulled out one of the onesies that said *Born a Rebel.* Another one, plain white, said *Cuddlebug.* Another, splattered with colorful decals of food stain: *Good Thing I'm Cute.* I wandered toward the little girl aisle, the lace-trim toddler dresses perhaps still 20% off, the purple rompers. Unwise, given my floaty body and unmoored head, given the indelible mental imprint of the little girl I have not yet mentioned to you, Ruth, because I mention her to no one. I got out of the aisle before I would have to ask the bored clerk for a paper bag to breathe in.

"You like the stripeys?" Nan asked like a child from outside the fitting room. In her twenties, still nubile, in a dress from the Junior section.

"Sure," I said. It hugged her and hit her mid-thigh. My jeans sagged on my nearly middle-aged hips, I fingered my leather belt. Sexy as a feed sack. "Just hurry up." Maternal and warm as a thing of bronze. "Hurry," I said again, and Nan registered a wound. Offense throbbed in the black eye.

Over by the cheap jewelry was a mirror at face height. I loosened my ponytail and let my black hair soften down onto my shoulders and back. Only a few grays and still thick. I wished for a brush. When had my skin settled into lines?

The clerk was a teen with big black-framed glasses and a full figure. She cut eyes at Nan while she rang up the dresses, underwear, some T-shirts, a black bikini. Nan threw in a bag of barbecue pork rinds last minute.

"Thirty-six seventy-five," the girl said, defeated, pushed up her glasses.

Nan looked in her red wallet, looked at me. "Frankie, seems like I'm out of cash."

"What do you mean you're out of cash?"

"I guess I spent my last on lunch."

"You guess."

"I'll pay you back."

"When?"

"Soon. I promise." Imp. Trickster. Little crushable pretty hand.

We just stood there. The clerk bagged up the slinky stuff.

"Wait," I told her.

"I will," Nan insisted. She could rot in that apricot dress. She could starve. Throw her to the hyenas, Mave would say. But Nan knew I'd buy. She knew we were already bound in ways we couldn't yet understand.

I snatched the pork rinds from the plastic bag. "I'm not paying for these."

THE I-65 INTERCHANGE WAS HAIRY, CONGESTED. We didn't talk. I narrowly dodged some shredded tire. As soon as we were sailing on, I tried to keep focused on the road, hands at ten and two, extra mindful of the bikers on old Harleys, the speed limit, the brake lights of others slowing me down. I wanted it quiet but, inevitably:

"So what did we decide on the Great Lakes? I think we could use a dip."

"Nah," said Mave. "I'll spit in the desert dirt and make some mud and you can roll around in it."

"You said this was a truth-telling trip, Crazy, so why do you want to see the desert? O'Keeffe lived there, okay, so what? If you ask me, her big flower paintings are the best. All that color. I want life to get big and colorful, not shrivel up, and we're going a long way to a dried-up nowhere."

"You might tell the truth about how much cash you've got on you." I avoided her midnight poppy in the rearview.

"I said I'd pay you back, Frankie. I needed that stuff. I left everything in that house in the goddamn swamp."

"Caudell is rightly a boreal bog," said Mave.

I read the license plates. Old Bush-Quayle stickers.

"The ancient glaciers left their mark," Mave went on. "You could feel them sludging back toward us at home, couldn't you? The glacial shadow creeping up on the sedges and the black spruce. It was best to blow town. We were to the point that the shallow pools would never dry up, like a weepy cut in dog days."

"The hell you talking about?" Nan's voice scratchy.

"I don't think anybody noticed the wreckage coming but us, Nannette."

I read on a Ford Escort *My Other Car Is a Piece of Shit Too.*

Why the desert, Ruth? For Mave, it was of course because you loved the Sinai. And the open plains would give us space, let one word find form and purchase and time, let it spread out its ample limbs. No longer stifled by the losses junking up our lives like the TVs and rotted things subsuming Mave's porch. The trip was not supposed to end everything, but begin it instead.

I focused, the road beckoning. I focused hard to guide the heavy blue car. We'd come from the swamps, we were bog people. Thick, we wanted to slim down, empty out, bottom out, crush into campfire smoke. There was a long history of this, of course. I'd read in your desert-fathers wisdom books that the stick-people leaned into the wind, the fourth-century hermits who'd fled the city for the Persian desert, as you did as a younger woman, before you crushed your leg, before you met Mave, and you must have never fully left there. Your books, your hieroglyphs, your photos of the three-toned dunes, the sand I imagined always in your long gray hair.

"You might watch out for that, Frankie," said Mave.

"For what?" But I hit it. I ran right over the large deer carcass before I could swerve, a huge rolling thump. "Shit." The car fishtailed and I struggled to regain control. I pulled off to the shoulder without signaling, my hands shook. "Shit, sorry, I didn't see that. How did I not see that?"

Mave got out to inspect the tires. So did Nan and I. Rust flaked under the black stripe up the side of the car, like a bed's dust ruffle. But the tires looked okay. We forgot Ellis and he plodded off to poop in the grass, and I saw it was a little runny. "Sorry," I said again. "I need to focus."

Portable tank in hand, Mave walked back several feet toward the mangled heap of deer. Nan followed. I hooked Ellis's leash, and he was shaking like me. I told him I'm sorry, I'll focus, I'll be careful. It's okay, Flop, we're okay.

Cars zipped past, all with sense enough to change to the left lane. The two women, one aged and sick, one hungry and small, gazed steadily at the head of the deer pointing toward them. I installed the hound back into the Olds and joined them to study the doe's head with most of its skull showing. Its eyes no longer there. Its body a pile of bloody ribbons. It was impossible to tell what part of the damage we had done. Nobody said anything else. Eventually we piled back in and I slowly edged us back onto the highway.

What I focused on then was the skull. Because, for me, that was why the desert, Ruth. The best paintings are the skulls. The faces of the other two fugitives watched the early evening interstate—median and tree line, respectively. I had this feeling we should have strapped the doe's horrible body onto the roof and carried it on.

This trip was for Mave, but I wanted to see Abiquiú too, where Georgia O'Keeffe had once had a roofless room to let light in so she could paint the longhorn skulls, souvenirs of death. And Mave had looked pale as death as we'd watched an O'Keeffe special on PBS, and I'd found a book of prints afterward on her shelves of your hundreds of books and flipped to *Cow's Skull: Red, White, and Blue.* The skull more like a tattered shirt than solid bone. My fingertips made their way down to where there would have been jowl-heat, where its nostrils would have heaved wet, now turned ratty bone. Womb-shaped head, I thought, complete with horns, shredded womb. I assumed that was what I looked like inside. That hostile and ungiving.

On the next page, *Cow's Skull with Calico Roses.* Big white plastic flowers on the has-been head. One rose at the wide brow, one stubbing out the frayed snout below. The roses were fake, the ones that had modeled for her still life, like the ones decorating the Snyder's Crossing Cemetery on Memorial Day or the ones beside porch steps in Caudell, speared into the ground with the Fourth of July pinwheels moving slack year-round. O'Keeffe saw drought take the animals down, skeletons everywhere. Graves on top of the blasted earth and nothing to exhume. Death bald-faced.

"Let's go there," Mave had said, thinking, I knew, about your vaster desert sojourns. This would be as close as she would ever get.

And I said okay because she and I both needed to go but felt ourselves aimless. I said okay because it seemed to me the desert is where you go when you've got nowhere else to go. Skin to leather by the sun, stick to witch for water, mind to clarify, more silence than not. We would have space to figure it all out. But it was not supposed to be the end.

I studied Mave's profile in glimpses, then back to the road. Her body—what did it mean? How could it ever not be beside mine?

She was thinking of you, you like the deepest itch, perhaps telling you the plan, what she would do under the desert night sky outside some motel when Nan and I would go out for Chinese at a Double Dragon.

Since I did not smoke in Lottie's house, I smoked in my own. The morning of the September LaFaber co-op meeting, I sat at the empty rough-lumber table to smoke and think. I had invited Liza, widowed and now moved in with her mother. The scrubbed half-dozen butternuts waited in a five-gallon bucket on the floor. It's possible, I think, to be held by a house. The cheap paneling, the brick-patterned linoleum, the hushed repository of the upstairs bedrooms.

Outside, at Mave's, a high-pitched idling pealed out. A belt of some sort went bad and snapped, then a potent explosion of car engine followed by her froth of swearing. I looked out the kitchen window to find her ancient brown Pontiac belching smoke in the middle of her driveway. She had spilled a feed sack of black walnuts gathered from her tree into the driveway ruts for the car to run over and crush, to expedite the shelling process. She did this every fall, crushed the black walnuts sheathed in their bruised green hulls and pungent, but she never finished the tedious project. Mave pounded the hood, crumpled the empty feed sack, marched up the driveway to her school bus parked on a tilt and kicked the tires.

I stepped out to the porch to witness Mave's fit through our path that needed clearing. She batted smoke from her face and disappeared into the house and came back with a can of primer and a brush. She painted *Farm Use* across the passenger door and fender. Drunk early. I tried not to laugh, yelling, "Let me call Rex."

She ranted on, now about both the shitbox car and Rex.

If she could crush the walnuts she could shell a jarful to have something to trade with the other co-op women. Last meeting, she'd brought key chains from the service station and a grommeted banner with pilgrims on it to hang at Thanksgiving, and the women had been reluctant to trade a pound of newly dug red potatoes for a trinket. Mave got the hood up, and I lost her head and denim garb to the smoke.

I didn't call Rex; I'd forgotten the phone was disconnected. I went down to the cellar, left the light off so there was only the moted sun coming through the thin windows at the house's foundation, windows through which one could watch the world in secret. I still had three-quarters of a self stowed in this house, and three-quarters of my preserves. The cellar was walled in but not finished—the door without a knob or latch I kept shut with a brick at its base, only one side of shelving installed. The potato bin in the corner had never been enclosed, and its mustiness gritted the cellar air. I listened in the dark for Ellis padding after me with claws ticking on the floor, needing to be trimmed, but he was at the other home, the other life. It felt good to naturally miss his barrel body and his eyes like woman's eyes.

I pulled the light bulb's cord to survey the jars of unbright peaches, beans, Romas. They had taken in the summer sun and settled it down to a muted mature color for winter's duration. I chose a quart of half-runner beans for the co-op crate, a quart of peaches, some pickles, one pint of beets I could part with, and two pints of kraut, Liza's favorite. I hoped Liza would come—on the phone she had said she would bring some of her mother's raw honeycomb, voice hoarse and quiet and black. She had been back for a few months, but I'd hardly seen her, she always made excuses. I propped the full crate onto my hipbone and left the cellar dark, nudged the brick jam back into place with my foot.

I thought about Liza's industrious hands; it was she and her mother who had taught me to can with a boil-bath canner. Miranda had helped, too, on scattered brief afternoons when the twin boys peeled from her. Until I could grow my own garden, Rex and Miranda kept me in food. They feared I'd starve with Mave, who survived on oatmeal, Campbell's soups, sardines, oyster crackers, and Jameson. They watched our two houses—mine and hers—as though watching the onset of catastrophe. I did not tell anyone that I often dreamed I fed Mave my curled-caterpillar body and sometimes it looked like a dream-snake eating its tail and sometimes like hands holding. But Mave took care of me, in her way. She paid the bills, paid off my house with your inherited Northampton money.

And she guarded my mind. She kept it stoked, banked like a fire. A month after my parents died, she sent me back to school, but I cared for nothing except the new biology teacher, Doreen Betts. Ms. Betts, with her large horse teeth and wild eyes, came into class and unfolded a napkin of vitamins, like precious metals she'd mined—holding them out in two palms like that—all colors and sizes and shapes. No one knew what they were. This was 1970. Vitamins are the future, she said. She'd worked in embryonic research in Oklahoma, she said, and it had led her to capsules and candy-coated pills. She didn't teach from a book; she stood squat and solid in front of the class, eyes searing and bright, and told us about her experiments, about the hearts of unborn babies ticking like tiny bombs. She was fired within a few weeks, which set Mave livid, and Mr. Dolan took over biology but was more versed in geology so we moved to intact stone with no ticking heart about to blow my world apart.

"I quit," I told Mave.

"Good call," Mave said. "I'll teach you my goddamn self." She ignored Miranda's fits and the phone ringing off the hook.

I had only two years left, and maybe it was a shame to quit because they started a girls' team for the school the next year. Mave put up a basketball hoop for me, over a dirt patch lousy for dribbling. Dillon stayed in for two more years. He came over some evenings and fed me balls for jump shots; he'd let his hair grow to his chin and watched me through a dark shag, a silent body leaning into my own silence. I got the job as janitor at LaFaber, only half time, working from one p.m. until supper. I liked the scrubbing, I liked what happened to my hands at the mercy of the chemicals, I liked that I had the early hours to read whatever Mave dropped off in the morning dark before her school bus run. Fiction and poetry, biographies, semiotics books and Egyptology books from those chaotic shelves, the library all yours, with R.S. initialed inside the covers, with your annotations written in the hand I knew from the blue-paper letters. How thickly you were with us, though Mave hardly ever spoke your name. Often I read nothing but your annotations, which built small, crude rooms in the margins. In a translation of the Pyramid Texts, next to the line *You are born for Osiris,* you'd scribbled a list in pencil: *sugar, rubbed sage, masking tape, baguette, clothespins.* A shopping list, I guessed. Further down: *no, no, no*, your disagreement with the translation. And then a sketch of a boy with big hair and an elegant nose, perhaps Osiris himself. Beneath the sketch, these lines:

I kissed him on the forehead once, for falling from a limb.
I washed him and set him in new towels and talcum, lavender scent, even though he is a grown man.
Because he is a grown man.

In a book on meteors, I found inked in the margin: *Some bodies are see-through, are honeycomb. And I erupt.* I understood almost nothing except that there are layers and inner rooms in books; there are so many thickets.

None of my learning was straightforward. I knew little about what Mave had studied in graduate school, but it seemed to me her accumulated knowledge was a stack of papers and someone had opened a window—perhaps at your death—and the loose pages scattered in the wind. Every so often, she snatched a page midair and read it aloud to me. That's what her homeschooling felt like. When I learned the word *entropy*, I realized that's what was happening, the books entropic, my mind getting sucked out of windows and into others, everything being blown apart like I'd wanted when listening to Ms. Betts detail her godless experiments. I was grieving and isolated, but I was writing in a notebook and, in the midst of chaos, feeling myself form.

Mave's direct tutorials were enigmatic.

"Sadness or anger," she said once. "Which is the wiser sister?"

Or, pulling a pressed brittle leaf from a book: "Look at this leaf. Don't screw up your face to study, open your pores. Eat it. Tell me what it is. That's how you read. Understand?"

Once, she drove up in her emptied bus, I made us pancakes with Bisquick and she found peanut butter for them. It was winter, I was layered in sweaters over long johns.

"Needs syrup," Mave said. She squinted at something indecipherable in the paneling and pursed her mouth. "There's a whole wilderness in a thing called a mother," she said. "What does that word mean, inside out? There's a wilderness in it." She let that sit, took a bite. She told me about the Ellafritzes, though I already knew about them. The Ellafritzes fostered only for the money and sometimes adopted. Mave had checked her route around six that morning, to see if she would need chains to the make the hill. Off Randolph Road, she saw a tiny light in the bus stop—could have been a lighter, that small. Six a.m., single digits out.

"I came upon two of my bus kids, a girl and her little brother wrapped in blankets, two hours early for the bus, holding a flashlight. They were Sandy Ellafritz's two natural kids, not the fosters. She was high on whatever, probably forgot what time it was. Doped with Bernard on the floor. So here were the kids"—Mave gestured her hands in a V toward her plate of dry nutty pancakes—"wrapped in wool blankets and sitting there in the bus stop shelter like puppies ripped off the teat. Left to fend. They don't fight the encroachment of the cold, Frankie. Instead, they fight the fireweed in their hearts, the brutal monkey vines that have claimed their mother and the word they name her with. Understand? I pried them out of the shelter and carried them around on the bus blasting the heat. The inside of a person—the inside of a word." Mave studied the fridge, scanned my face for comprehension. What did my face show?

"A word is a living thing," she said. Her whiskery lip so near me, leaning her face across the table, her head like a boulder set down. Then she stood, and I knew she was off to get drunk before noon, then sober by the afternoon bus run.

I said, "I know a word is a living thing." But she didn't seem to hear me. Out the front door. Alone, I went to my mother's bedside table, to her Bible. *The Living Word* it said on the cover. *The Living Translation* it said inside. I opened it to the beginning and pictured Mother following along with the gospel radio reading. I felt her voice like a grater, shaving me down in slivers. I thought about the Chapel at Snyder's Crossing and the pretty oak pews and my cousins still stocking them, Belinda missing me sitting beside her, me wearing a dress that would have been her castoff, too big in the chest. I turned up the heat and read cross-legged on Mother and Dad's bed all the way up to the story of the maidservant Hagar in Genesis 16, then stopped. Something about Hagar's story was personal—did you know this story, Ruth? She was a woman used up, made pregnant as a surrogate and then punished for it. I saw her wild hair swirl, I saw the bony donkey she rode out on and her dress straining at her belly. The ancient story hung in my parents' bedroom like swamp air, despite the winter. The story had layers of green and moss and sedges, so many greens. I thought of your Osiris sketch in the margin of the Pyramid Texts, and I sketched Hagar's unruly hair in the bottom corner of the page.

Hagar said she saw God and God saw her, at a spring in the desert that she named the Well of the Living One Who Sees Me. The wind whipped up her hair; I drew the crazy strands. I could smell the red smoke and feel the rock. I saw her son, poor Ishmael, held by the web of veins inside her globe of belly. Her voice rang in my ear and my voice rang back into it, as if into a rock canyon. I scribbled in the margins the things left out, what God saw in Hagar's tangled hair and the doves that came to her and brought twigs to make a tea, how one lay down and died for her. She roasted it on a spit. She lived. She said, *Here I am below this sky.* She said—like you, Ruth—*I erupt.* I knew her and I thought, Here I am too, erupting. Her words were still being written somehow. I sat on the musty quilt and understood that words were being written inside my own rock canyon and cave and black wilderness, my own teenaged skull. I heard the pen scratching.

The next morning Mave brought over a book about boreal bogs of North America. I'd slept in my clothes, not something she'd scold me for. I accepted the book, put it on the stack, and finished Genesis when she left. After her bus run, she found me belly down on the brick-patterned linoleum with a pen and the Living Word. She sat heavily at the table.

"I like parts of it," she said. "The poetry. I like a good beheading. And there's the seven-headed beast."

"I know you don't believe in God," I said.

"No, I don't. But you do. Margot shamed you with her gospel hour and Sunday school, but it's more than that, you think?"

"I don't know," I said.

"Well. You should read what you need to. You should be stubborn." Something stuck in her teeth and she tongued it. "As long as you read Cicero too," she said. "And finish Virginia Woolf."

I mixed up the Bisquick and milk in the warm kitchen, poured us both coffee. She started in about boreal bogs.

IN THE EVENING, the gray of the half-empty kitchen steamed as though alive. Voices rose as the co-op assembled. My first co-op meeting as a married woman, that fall of 1989.

"I didn't quite finish," Hope said, "so I brought the stock pot." Hope was one of the two women who worked in LaFaber's foundry. Her voice like a mist, her body the width of my stove she commandeered. From behind I saw the length of ribbon added to each of her apron strings so they could meet in a knot. She planted her feet wide and explained the vegetable bouillon she'd brewed herself for the co-op trade—carrots, celery, onions, the cabbage in the crawl space, any old vegetable lying around, chop it all, cover with water and cook, then press it through a colander, boil again—garlic powder and cumin, poultry seasoning and so forth. Cook it down, pour it in little Gerber jars and freeze. When you want a little bouillon, she said, you just take a knife and cut out a chunk. I still had some of Hope's homemade ketchup from the last co-op night.

"I cooked this down for sixteen hours but it wants to go a little longer." She left to get the empty baby food jars from the car, I rolled up my sleeve to stir, peered into the dense broth. I heard others pull up, slam car doors, embrace. My cousins Belinda and Tuffie entered the kitchen and set down quart jars and beer and a crate, all of it from Miranda, except the Budweiser. "Is that this year's?" Hope asked someone on the porch.

"Living in the flesh," Tuffie said to Belinda in my bare living room, plucking a can from the six-pack she'd slunk in with, "like it's a bad thing—right, Frankie?" Her cocky voice thinner in the room with no rugs. The sound ricocheted. Though grown, they both still lived at home, Belinda with two toddlers and unmarried at the moment. Belinda was a replica of Aunt Miranda—all soft curves, a slouch in the spine, generous bust she hid but didn't, voice like a purring hen about to lay. But she wore Miranda's righteousness more easily as she answered Tuffie with something I couldn't hear. The bouillon steam coated my face and worked into my hair at the scalp.

Rayletta, as large as Hope, unloaded seven quarts of sausage onto the counter, '89 marked on the lid, so, yes, this year's. She was the other woman in the foundry and the only Black woman at LaFaber in our mostly White town. "There's the new bride," she said and hugged me sideways so I could still stir, tucked up her yellow headscarf that had come loose, gold sheer against her dark skin. "I sneaked you a hambone," she said and set the throwaway pillowcase with its bulge on top of the fridge.

Rayletta had been the first to respond to my sign on the break room wall: LaFaber Women's Cooperative, bring your wares. It was an idea from Mave's book—your book—on social movements in South America, and she'd flagged the chapter and, in a rare lucid and sober moment, had come to my porch all parental to say I was too solitary. I was twenty-six then; this was right after Dillon had left abruptly for pilot training. My body was young but turning to slate, and Mave, of all people, said I needed some fellowship. Perhaps she could see I was becoming her. Ray hadn't known me, she'd looked me up with my industrial mop bucket in the elevator and said she'd be there. Told me she was from Cincinnati and had stepped down off the bus here by mistake but stayed and married a shy hog farmer.

The foreman's wife Delores brought a basket of biscuits covered by a tea towel, set them beside Miranda's pink apples, two jars of pickled eggs, and frosty Ziploc pints of frozen sweet corn, my own preserves, and the two quilted potholders Lottie had contributed though she'd stayed home. Delores was the secretary in the plant office, wore a pantsuit out of tune with my house and this crowd. She produced a rectangle of butter from her efficient dairy close to Monroeville, a boutique dairy she called it. She asked Hope if her grapes had yielded, said she'd put an ad in the Penny Saver for a bushel of grapes, as her vines hadn't produced.

"Bud will produce," Tuffie told Delores, and Delores took a can and laughed. Tuffie's black eyeliner dramatic, black hair like mine but thinner, with a single lock bleached and dyed psychedelic blue. She was in her late twenties and still at the Citgo, had never worked at the plant, but she and Belinda always came anyway when the co-op met every few months. Ray's golden headscarf like a moon rising beside them, Ray took a sip.

No Liza yet. No Mave.

Out the screen door, one more single headlight, and that would be Clarissa, her driver-side light out. Hope took over at the stove, I pushed open the door that faithfully scuffed the porch boards. I walked through the scrim where the kitchen air met the cool of September. My old friend, my long friend who loved me, though I was a woman of flint. I could dimly see her hair falling in pretty pieces about her face, pestering her eyes. I waved. She hoisted a cardboard box from the backseat of her and Darrell's sorry car and bumped the door shut with her hip. The white ankle socks with loafers caught the porch light and made her look younger than we both were. Her curvy body always tentative, wary, her voice weighted by deference but face full and open.

"You made something new?" I asked.

"It's nothing." She hid a smile. I told her I put two butternuts back for her so she could trade for something else.

Inside, most of the goods heaped up on the living room floor on an outspread sheet: black-eyed Susans dug up to replant and rubber-banded in wet paper towels—I hadn't seen those come in—my scrubbed squashes, the dwindling beer, the quarts of ground sausage like brain matter, a carton of Belinda's Virginia Slims. Belinda was explaining the contribution.

"You are not."

"Again? Damn, you're a baby-making machine."

"Aren't the first ones fifteen months apart too? They have ways to prevent it, you know."

Belinda reddened, said Jack was straightening up. They were getting married for sure. Her third child, and he would be her third husband. Still, Belinda, under her blond bangs curled with an iron and aerosol sprayed, beamed innocence at us. Ray gave her a sausage jar and opened the carton to pull out a pack.

They made way for Clarissa. She set down her box and took a padded stool, humbling her hands in her lap. Delores reached into the box and picked up one of the necklaces of waxed thread strung with a small slab of painted gourd, a tiny scene. Everyone ringed around. At LaFaber, Clarissa designed the bronze memorial plates: for headstones, for pews refinished In Loving Memory of. The necklace went from hand to hand and reached me. A tuft of lilies sprouting a tiny cabin with porch and chimney, big enough for a bean beetle. She'd used fingernail polish for color, she said, old eyeliner pencil for the sketch, some lacquer.

Mini bouquets on some of the others, a nativity scene for Christmas, an abstracted head of a girl with two braids and you could tell it was her daughter Tess. A doe and fawn, an eagle, a stand of two-centimeter pines. All scenes small as a thumbprint on dried-out and chipped birdhouse gourd.

"Just an idea I had," Clarissa said. Delores brought biscuits around with butter, and Clarissa said she had enough necklaces for everybody. Goods collected at her feet in thanks. "Darrell thinks they're too country-looking," she said. Tuffie slid on the eagle necklace and petted it there above her flat chest, her rim of lilac bra showing.

"Darrell's a dumbass," Tuffie said. She set both jars of Miranda's pickled eggs beside Clarissa's loafers.

Clarissa frowned but didn't defend her husband. We all knew she locked herself in the bathroom to draw and paint. Always his sorrowful head would hang after a slap, the handprint not yet faded from her face, though she promised me those days were over now. She pulled at her sweater, done with the attention.

"Rayletta," I said, "remember that time you brought a baby pig to the co-op in a cat carrier?" And we went down that road and conversation picked up again and Hope returned to the kitchen, called out for a ladle and funnel for the ready bouillon. I went in search of what was left in the drawers and said I'd look for a ginger ale for Belinda.

I wished Mave had come. From the stove, looking through the kitchen's archway into the poorly lit living room, I saw the huddle of faces all skeletal then fleshy, depending on the orientation of each face to lamplight. Hope carried half a dozen filled Gerber jars into the living room to deal them out and give instructions on freezing, and Tuffie replaced her at the stove.

"How's the sex going?" she asked me. "You getting anywhere?" Raised her eyebrows.

I laughed, ladled more pungent liquid into a tiny jar. She said to do it once a month somewhere other than bed. "When Lottie's napping." She winked, screwed on the Gerber lids, wiped the dribbled bouillon. Then I could see the specter of Clay's head, like a little boy's that I guided between my legs, like a sipping calf at a bathtub trough, like a bird mouth. Trembling. And close on the heels of that image, the unbidden force of the long-absent Dillon quivering into my skull, our bodies itching on Rex's alfalfa square bales as we rolled off the ragged quilt heedless and hot. And where was he now, and in whose arms?

Behind us, the screen door scritched the porch. Tuffie and I turned. Liza stood holding a plastic shopping bag, wet hair brushed back and clipped, willow-weed thin in a blue coat fully buttoned.

"Liza, you made it," I said, glad for her quick, clearing wipe of my mind. I remembered her as military and certain, but here before me she stood washed out with grief.

She held up the bag. "I brought something I made."

I took it and thanked her and said come on in. We entered the living room's rising warmth and humid air. I wiped my upper lip. The bag was almost weightless. No raw honeycomb from her mother, something thin and folded instead. Liza put her hands in her coat pockets.

The room of voices gentled. Delores gave the broken easy chair to Liza and buttered her a biscuit. I pulled out the cloth from the bag and unfolded a white cotton nightgown, eyelet trim, two darts at the bust along the sides, one embroidered purple aster at the chest. It would hit mid-thigh. It was girlish. Belinda complimented Liza, Hope made a joke about it maybe fitting her left leg, Tuffie touched its hem. I turned out the gathered seam at the front, all the seams so neat and perfect, not the nests of thread ends that plagued my few sewing projects, and I remembered Home Ec with young industrious Liza and how we'd laughed at my inner seams looking like ratted hair and how I'd stood watching her work, the rhythm of the Singer machine calm, like someone brushing fur. In the chasm between eighth grade and the co-op night smelling of simmered bouillon fell Liza's widow heart and empty bed, and I could feel the women shutter it out.

Nobody wanted the nightgown, I could tell.

The pretty thing hung like an apparition from its ribbon straps hooked on my forefingers, purple aster like a wound. "I would love this," I finally said. I gave her a squash for it, I gave her all the kraut, her favorite, and I gave her the pint of beets. Delores said the nightgown was perfect for a newlywed.

An hour later, Mave made it over. She was lit. It was about eleven and everyone had gone but Rayletta, who gave me one more from her pack of Virginia Slims. She stowed the rest in her purse with the black-eyed Susans, their roots double-bagged and getting thirsty.

Mave stayed out on the porch, holding a lidded pint jar and a fifth almost empty.

"Mave, where you been?" said Ray.

Mave was still on the nicotine patch that blued her dreams. She bore a look of deep offense and ached toward our smoke through the screen mesh. She said, "I couldn't get the Pontiac going." The car had sulked in the driveway instead of rolling over the walnuts in the ruts. I pushed open the door and she hobbled in, steel toed boots untied. She sat on the bench beside Ray and set the jar on the table, the bottom barely covered by a few shelled-out nuts—she said she had pried them loose with a ball-peen hammer. Just a handful and an IOU. Rayletta accepted the jar and wrapped Mave's hand around the last quart of canned sausage as if it were an even trade. I stuck one of Lottie's potholders in Mave's shirt pocket.

"Couldn't start the Pontiac," she said. Whiskey wafting from mouth and skin, but the black walnut meat was still the stronger, more bitter smell.

I SLEPT THERE, AT MY OWN HOUSE, ALONE. I let the muggy air and the sound of their voices sift over me. I wonder now, Ruth, what you would have made of this congregation, the things made, cooked down, bundled up. It was all uttering, wasn't it? Uttering like prayer, a way to connect to the life inside our lives as our outer lives unfolded in ways we had not expected. Sleeping in my childhood bed, I corralled my thoughts away from memory, from Dillon, and toward the next unfoldment, what I might next say to Clay at supper—maybe a request for a new porcelain sink after all, maybe for a trip together, maybe my hand would be at rest upon his shoulder as we spoke.

I headed back to Clay and Lottie's in the morning, almost forgetting the hambone in the pillowcase on top of the fridge. Pulling into the driveway, I saw Ellis from a ways off. He was the one for whom I intended the bone, though I knew I should make a soup with it. The hound was excited, jerky, scampering and dancing like a younger dog, not his usual languid, thick self that was supposed to draw toward me in welcome. I couldn't tell what he was doing, circling the yew bush. He didn't notice me and I didn't see Lottie's face appear at the door's window, so I parked and switched off the ignition and sat in the cold truck cab with the goods stacked up beside me. Mini jars of bouillon, the sausage, what was left of Delores's block of butter that I needed to get to the kitchen, the doe and fawn gourd necklace painted tenderly in the insufficient light of Clarissa's bathroom. I pulled the pillowcase holding the plastic-bagged hambone into my lap. Nowhere to go but here, I said inside my head, to this other house and this unfolding day. My hangover was subtle, my jaw sore from something. Despite my mental gestures of the night before, I felt a stab of fierceness for myself, as if the life inside my life were a thing I might hoard. Beside the necklace sat the cotton nightgown that would fall to mid-thigh, though I would likely never wear it.

Ellis paused by the yew, stalked, prepared his haunches. I saw him dive in with an instinct prior to his domesticated days. I was out of the truck with the pillowcase in hand, and I ran sluggishly to find too late that he'd chomped a small bird from the low nest in the bush. No, I said, no, drop it—he watered his eyes at me, caught and longing, but he unclenched and let the broken thing drop.

We both looked at it. Its head nearly severed from its tiny body. It twitched and would not live. I knelt on the ground and took the dog's brown face in my hand. I shoved him a little, his woman-eyes stupid and hurt. I felt my own stupidity or helplessness or hoarding as I postponed entering the house. He nuzzled the pillowcase, and I didn't want to give him the hambone from Ray, but I gave it and it felt good to do so. I put my hand out and his wet nose came out of the snuffled sack of bone, the salty marrow of some other beast, and his grateful tongue hit warm and sandy on my palm. I bent into it, on my knees, in our small huddle of want and greed and harm. "Hey, Flop," I said. "You cruel thing, come here." Another tiny bird, bereft in the thick center of the bush, chirped open-mouthed and upward.

Ruth, I remembered, as I knelt there in the grass in front of that strange home, one of the birds, the carrion birds, a hieroglyph you'd sketched in a letter. The gray kite that scavenges. Its shrill sound the sounded-out letter attached to its drawing. The bird is its sound—the living sound that means mourning and sadness, but even so, the living sound.

Mave said she needed to get horizontal. She shifted in the vinyl seat, pulled her wallet from her back pocket as if it were agitating her, and held it. I'd looked in the wallet once—a photo of Miranda and my mother Margot as girls with carefully arranged hair. A pressed flower gone brown between two pieces of clear contact paper cut in a square. "All my plumbing is rusting up," she said, hovered her hand over her chest and scanned, down and up. "Yeah, all of it."

"You do need to lie down," I said. It was dusk. The blue signs cropped up and brightened in the headlights. I looked for offerings of lodging with food nearby. Fast food at the next exit and a Motel 6.

"I want to know why I can't drive my own car," Nan said from the back.

"We're going to take this exit," I said.

"It's my car. We could at least take turns."

"We're going to find a place to sleep."

"Frankie," she blared.

"Nan. Why are you bringing this up now? We said I was driving if we let you come along, and you said okay."

"I changed my mind. This dog fucking drools."

"Be useful, Nannette," said Mave, "throw yourself out the window." Voice airy and light and inwardly focused, like a voice trying to remember something.

"She doesn't mean that," I said. I told Nan that this was as much her car as the bag of new clothes were her clothes.

"What's that supposed to mean?" She stuck her head between our seats.

"It means Frankie drives," said Mave, easing her posture as we got within a mile of a bed. I studied her past Nan's head for the illness and drugs filching the light from her skin. It had been a couple of hours since she'd taken something. She was fading out. Nan jutted in further.

"Give me shotgun tomorrow, Crazy." The back of her hair was exploding, flattened in a wide spot.

"Tomorrow you get the trunk," Mave said.

"Fuck off," said Nan, as if they were now a comic routine.

I exited, heading for the huge red six on a pole sprouting from a Denny's lot. Mave waved her hands in front of her. "Let there be hash browns, let there be cable TV. And I saw that it was good."

"I'll go in," I said.

"I'll go in," Nan mocked from her angry slump.

"You're welcome to pay for the room."

Mave got out and stretched, scratched her butt. Shook her oxygen tank, like a can of shaving cream. She said, "We'll wake to the Warm Morning stove, bank the fire in its belly, dress languidly. Nan last so we can linger on her little body. Then a Western omelet, hot coffee, and hash browns," one hand spreading up and out like a slow firework. She kept talking, walked toward the streetlamp in the evening gray. We watched her, Nan and I.

"How can you tell when she's talking out of her head, and when she's just talking?" she asked.

"Sometimes I can't."

Mave leaned her back against the lamppost, closed her eyes.

"Nan," I said, turning to the backseat, "why did you drive to my house? And why are you here with us in this motel parking lot?" No response. "What is it you want?"

A murmur, delicate face in profile, pointing toward Mave.

"What did you say?"

"I said I just wanted more." She faced me but eyed Ellis and stroked his head. "I want the more that you two have. Like a bigger life or something."

"There's nothing big about my life."

She didn't say anything else, so I said, "Probably no pets. Keep him down on the floor, okay?"

"Yeah. Ask if there's a pool."

Smoking or non, I told the clerk smoking. This was White House, Tennessee. She studied Mave under the lamppost through the window and I saw the woman's kind yellowed eyes go tragic on the oxygen tubing. People always studied Mave to ascertain—man or woman, crazy or drunk. She spied Nan, too, in the lot's light. The TV bolted to the wall blinked out the weather, colored globs all over the US map, rain on its way. I grabbed the *Tennessean* for whenever the other two watched TV. We would need dinner.

"Anyplace to eat besides Denny's?" I asked.

"Not especially." She wanted to ask how long does the old woman have or something more trivial: are you headed to the Grand Ole Opry, where's home, who slugged that pretty girl in the car? "You're in 110, around back," she said. "Here's two keys."

I thanked her and asked for extra towels, and she ducked out to a back room. In a full-length mirror in the lobby, between piled chairs, I caught my own yellowed eyes. I thought of the antique mirror Clay would walk past, heading upstairs to bed wondering where on earth I was, how the glass would yield to him his gentle oblong face washed softly by the hall light and, beyond him, the cavernous house with the blue kitchen chairs where we had sat and he'd offered me pancakes and offered me everything only a year and a half ago, and what kind of steward of his offering had I been? I'd not even been able to carry his child.

The motel felt moldy like a holding tank, but I already sensed the desert coming, where eyes could unyellow. Where there would be no comfort, no routines, no supports, no gentleness to confuse you. Nan was mistaken. There was no enviable largeness to my life, only an internal useless clutter of confusion, crowded like the landfill of Mave's porch. Mave had said, as we'd packed, that we would take dirt baths out there, she would wash her remaining hair with sand. She'd said, "Your mop will take longer."

I glimpse you sometimes, Ruth, in the Sinai, in knee-high boots, treading. Upon the barren scrub, could you not see yourself in the light, in the red dust, finally with absolute clarity?

I thought meanly toward Clay—There is lasagna in the freezer. Sing your pious songs, Clay, you are the kindest man really, but you knew, didn't you? That our matrimony would settle over us like soot in a summer chimney where birds get stuck and pulse and quicken and then give in? Sing the refrains that sit like stacked bowls in the cupboard of your mind. The clerk appeared with a clutch of thin towels and I jolted, as if she had caught me in a low-down, untoward act. I returned to the car.

"You see a pool?" asked Nan.

I looked up and said it would rain soon.

We got Denny's club sandwiches to go. Room 110 was poorly lit, everything beige except for the matching beach paintings. I breathed in the lingering tar smell emanating from the walls.

"It stinks in here." Nan dropped her overnight bag, crinkling the Family Dollar bag inside.

"I used to smoke," I said. "I prefer smoking to non."

"Maybe there are more people on this trip besides you."

There was a table with two chairs and Mave sat, unwrapped the Denny's foil, and Ellis snapped to attention at her elbow, waiting. He got the pickle and cheese. I said I forgot something and walked into the drizzle. I popped the trunk to feel for the pistol bulge. Still there. I would hide the keys. Nan slipped out of the room barefoot and walked to the vending machine a few doors down. She wore Dillon's Army jacket that must have been in her bag. Fritos, Twizzlers.

"Where'd you get quarters?"

"Found them. Twizzlers are for you."

The little bit of rain slimed the road dust in my arm hair. In the room, Nan sloughed the jacket to the floor, bolted to the bathroom with her bag, and started the shower with the door open. Mave watched the open door as she lay down.

I sat and scanned the *Tennessean.* Top headline read "Two Dead Babies Found, Omaha, Nebraska." The first paragraph said their skeletons were discovered in a septic tank outside the city. Near a Catholic home for girls. I quit reading and took up the notepad with the big red six on it, the Bic pen.

"Work on your book," Mave said.

"Yeah."

"Eat something."

"Not hungry."

"You cannot write of hunger unless you are hungry."

"I think I should call Clay."

"And say what?"

"That Ellis is with me."

"You can take dictation for the book if you like, you can quote me. This codeine should kick in soon, and I'm liable to speak French. Should be profound."

"Are you feeling pain?"

"I feel like a tiny man stole into my body through my butthole and is sucking away my air and he's taken an electric sander to my left lung. Also—if you'd like an inventory of the details—I'm in a shitbox motel with you and Gypsy Moth making our way at crawling speed to a desert I may never see. I have only one more of these portable tanks. And you forgot to say no mayo on my club." Her arms spread out like Jesus. "I'm fine. Write something from your dream head."

"It's empty. Sorry about the mayo."

"Then use something else."

"I've got nothing, Mave."

"Then make it up whole cloth. Shit, you know you don't know what to say until you start. Use the goddamn brain I helped shape."

"Helped warp," I said. I held the notepad. "I'll just call Clarissa again."

"Write about the day. Write down her pathetic but sincere offering of Twizzlers."

"I don't have time."

"I'm the one with no time." Voice sharp. "You're lousy with time, you're rolling in it, you're like Ellis in carnage. You have the stench of time scumming up your fur."

I almost mentioned the gun but didn't. I rubbed my dirty arms. The Army jacket lay heaped like old skin. Nan sang in the shower.

"You okay?" Clarissa asked over a fuzzy connection. "Where are you?"

The payphone in the lobby was within earshot of the clerk, who feigned busyness.

"Has Clay called?" I asked.

"Twice. What do you want me to say when he does?"

"What did you say?"

"That I don't know where you are."

"Miranda?"

"I told her Mave's with you, that she had an appointment."

"What about Dillon?"

"Dillon wouldn't call me, Frankie."

I felt quiet and thick. I felt him all at once, unbidden—he was dark and young and compact, his limbs were my limbs, he tied things in my long draping hair and I left them there for days, didn't comb out the knots. I heard Tess in the background.

"Tess says to get her a turquoise ring." More muffled talk. "And to live it up, you owe it to Mave." Clarissa laughed. "Frankie? You there?"

"This is stupid. I don't know that she'll even make it." In my throat, the admission gathered itself and lodged. "I know she won't." A petty cry, too, for Mave's thin suicidal breaths and for everything else buzzing—for Nan's body unto his mouth in their home I'd never seen, and Nan's pathetic but genuine clamber for some kind of life, and Clay's kind hands handling me and that time he said he hoped it would be a girl that looked like me.

"She'll make it as far as she needs to. Listen, just sleep awhile—have you stopped for the night? Just sleep."

Back in the room, I found Nan's dirty doodles on the notepad, vulvas in lip liner. I lifted the top page and underneath, on the next sheet, a sketch of a woman with arms reaching out, a feathery movement, her hair in mid-swing. Sketched fast but with skill. It looked familiar; it reminded me of something Clarissa might draw. Nan's disastrous hair was flattened wet and harmless, and she donned the striped blue and pink dress, the price tag hanging off it. She held the newspaper, irked, pacing the wall by the heater not on, back and forth, antsy, under the paintings of palm trees and ocean and conch shells. Any calm Clarissa had willed into me dissipated to restlessness. Mave lay horizontal and quiet, holding a pillow over her eyes.

Nan started chattering about the horrible headline story I'd already had my fill of, how the tiny skeletons had been there for years, how the nuns probably made the teenage girls get rid of their babies, they're like that, nuns. Maybe the girls hadn't even known what happened to their newborns—whoosh, taken away—and they probably didn't get drugs for the birth even, nuns don't give drugs to wayward girls.

"Cool it, Nan," I said. "Mave's trying to sleep." I found my toiletry Ziploc. I wanted a shower, but she kept on.

"I will not cool it, I know what I'm talking about. I know some things you don't, despite what you and Crazy think about me being second-rate." Young face going stricken and a body in a dress I'd bought her.

"I'm showering, Nan. Watch TV or something."

"I heard your husband's band play once," she said.

I dodged it, knowing my nerves were frayed. "I'm going to shower, just cool it."

She blocked the bathroom door, agitated and fretful. "Look at me. I said I heard Clay's band, they were pretty good. He looked pretty good to me. I'd sleep with him. You wouldn't care, would you? If I fucked him?"

The slap was hard and loud. Her head swiveled back to the right. Stayed there. Mave creaked the bed. Nan slowly raised her face, her eyes welling up.

"Finally got that out of your system," she said.

All heat in my face, I needed air. "Nan, I'm sorry. I didn't mean to do that."

"Yes, you did. You expect the same thing from me as everybody else. You think the same as everybody, that there's nothing to me. But I told you, I want more."

My hand was hot, her left cheek red in the bad light. Her eyes darted to Mave, who I knew was watching.

Nan said, "Dillon found me when I was selling these dumb leather bracelets at a road stand in Georgia. I embossed them and painted them, they were pretty and worthless. You know how intense he is, those eyes that see everything and make you feel like you've got layers, and his silence that seems shy and sweet at first. He's a slow smolder, but I knew early on he was dangerous and he'd trap me. He got me pregnant, but I didn't tell him. I didn't want it. I didn't want to be bound." Nan in the new striped dress on a truth-telling streak. "Ask me how many I threw away."

"How many what?" I said.

"Ask me how many babies."

"How many?"

"Three. His was the third." She smoothed her dress with the *Tennessean* rolled up. "I'm not proud of it, but I thought I could be an artist or something. More than a body for men and babies. They didn't give me enough drugs for that last one. And the nuns and priests protested outside the clinic. They had all these blown-up pictures of unborn alien babies. They said horrible things about me, but they didn't know me."

I felt my jealous coil heat for a moment, my throat constrict at the mention of a child by Dillon and the choice to throw away a thing I could not stop from slipping through my fingers. Mave stayed quiet.

Nan said, "I was in bed for a few days after that one, told Dillon it was flu, but, when I could, when he left for a half-day flight spraying for moth, I got some paint and I found their church and I painted huge cocks on the walls. A bunch of beautiful colors."

Mave started laughing softly, and Nan smiled at her own transgression.

I said to her, "I lost one once. Last spring."

She didn't say anything, but nodded. Dead babies hung in the nicotine air, and she moved away from the bathroom door, all renegade and sore, slapped. So beautiful in her wild look. She said, "I should have kept going, painting all the walls everywhere, really painting. But how? I ended up bound to Dillon in the end, baby or no baby."

I felt the Ziploc still in my left hand. "I'm sorry I hit you," I said.

"It's all right." She bit her lip.

"No, it's not. I'm sorry." I entered the bathroom and shut myself in softly and got the shower as hot as I could upon my back, my closed eyes, my neck, my belly.

I LAY BESIDE MAVE, NAN IN HER OWN DOUBLE.

"I have to say, I miss the hibiscus," Mave said. "The flora of the homeland."

"There are hibiscus here," I said. "We're only a few hundred miles from home."

"I miss the walnut trees."

"We're in the same temperate zone."

"I miss the sphagnum moss. That we've surely left behind. We've left the swamp farts. All the putrid skunk cabbage pussing out marsh milk."

"Okay, yes. We're out of the swamp."

"But the changes are imperceptible. I want it to look different, Frankie. Blasted, like another planet."

"Should have gone to Miami then," said Nan. "Told you. Climb a fucking palm tree."

Mave laughed and so did Nan. I twisted loose my thick rope of wet hair and strung it out on the pillow above my head. I laughed and it felt good to laugh after tonight's heat, after telling our horrible truths. Mave said we'll swing by the bus station and send Little Gypsy packing, we'll drug you, she said, and you'll wake up in your sunny Florida. Nan kept laughing, loose and easy, lightened. I breathed in the tar, stretched up my arms, hands meeting in the woods of my wet hair. You know—I could almost see us young and unfettered and untrapped and full of promise. I could glimpse a shape under the baby blanket wadded in a wagon. Pulling the Radio Flyer behind my girl self, and there was that shape of a thing I could almost see, something almost born, before cousin Belinda got in, whining for her turn to ride. It was a body haulable, transportable. And small.

I'm up at three a.m. writing you.

One time Mave said, "The spring snow is so marvelous. My mind is white and bald as that. Or maybe it's white as garden lime and burnt." She stood in her filthy bathrobe facing the window as I scrubbed her floor, though she hadn't asked me to. I cleaned the grime to reveal tongue fitted to groove. I used a Brillo pad and cleaned a square of floor to blondness. And what was my mind like?

In the spring of our first year married, Clay's band got invited to play the Good Friday fish fry under the pavilion at Snyder's Crossing. I could easily conjure the smell of trout and crappie and catfish in tinfoil and the cheap punch in Styrofoam cups, the crackle of the tinny amp and Clay's new song. He said he would need to hold extra practices in the house. We sat at supper, the two of us, with asparagus I'd cut from Lottie's overgrown bed and lamb from Rex.

"You'll come out and hear us," he said in a vague tone somewhere between question and statement.

"At the Crossing?" I speared asparagus at the tough stalk and bit. I hadn't been to the church in almost two decades, even to see the bathroom that Belinda's contractor husband—her second one—had installed. I said, "Last time I was there, the outhouse still stood, with that prim lattice around it, like something of another century." He turned his face toward the dark rectangle of screen door and the spring night beyond it. "Clay, I get to hear you every practice. Private concert."

"I don't ask for anything much," he said, and the supper glow—plate, milk, tender meat, the things that compose the comfort of supper that man and wife share routinely—warmed his oval face that turned now from the door to me. His ease so evident whenever we courted normal routine. "The other wives come out to hear us."

"I'm not the other wives."

"Frankie."

"Clay."

He lost his ease in a soft snort. As offering, I said I'd prepare snacks for practices.

He said, "And I need you to tend to Mom," salvaging at least a feeling of the glow, a hint of it.

"Of course," I said. Lottie's body had started to fail.

I did as he'd asked, and I attended each practice.

Stew always arrived to practice last and plugged in his bass with no preamble. I watched him like a cat from the kitchen for the first few measures, then looked in on Lottie asleep and retreated to the back steps to wait for him to smoke with me. Sometimes he did. Sometimes I set a kitchen chair beside Clay strumming and singing—he sang well—and I held a plate of sweet breads.

I remembered once showing up at the fish fry, about fifteen years old, in Belinda's indigo taffeta pageant dress. I arrived before my mother and dad, and the Easter snow lingered like icing in eddies of shade. I had no sweater, only a sheer organdy overlay down to the capped sleeves that were pure flutter. Belinda had won Miss

Fireworks in the July Fourth pageant, and she of course had boobs, so I balled up socks to pad my training bra. There stood everyone, wearing jeans and flannels, as I knew they would. They ate the battered fish and set their punch and paper plates on the big white oak tree stump, and here I came in my cousin's borrowed eveningwear.

Dillon was there, part of a half circle of boys much older. He watched me with some amusement and allowed me, as always, my privacy. There were no amps then, only an acoustic. The guitar started and Aunt Miranda's waify voice began the Good Friday hymn—*Were you there when they crucified my Lord?* I knew the refrain and waited for it—*Sometimes it causes me to tremble, tremble, tremble.* I shook. The hymn so old and heavy, and how gloriously sad, the Lord's body coming down into the good, dark Friday night.

I knew the older boys, finished eating, would take off for the Matlick Feed parking lot in their fathers' trucks, and the girls would clump up at the Dairy Delite for shakes and would watch the boys from across the street, one or two bold enough to cross over and slip into a truck cab and let things be unbuttoned. I cried listening to Miranda, her voice stronger than her stooped body. I felt my own body skinned, so keen to the cold air. The earth itself seemed like God's huge body, crocuses coming up all over God's chest and face and into the thick hair of rye pasture, creating new wounds each time. My yearning was real but scattershot. The smell of Belinda's lilac body spritz I'd stolen mixed with the Wesson-oiled air, and my stomach churned. *Were you there when they crucified my Lord?* Miranda finished, all somber and bent.

"Frankie, you want your trout on paper or fine china?" asked one of the boys, and people laughed.

I boiled, gangly in the big dress. My nausea swelled. I looked at the big fryers and the closed cooler holding hostage the fish yet to fry, the channel catfish and crappie—I pictured their living selves and tiny O mouths—the flashes of their faces burbled in me and sent me toward the outhouse behind the chapel, head down, watching the dress's ruffle darken with wet grass. I rounded the white-painted lattice that hid the outhouse door, uprighted the door latch, stepped into the darkness, and vomited.

Pee and vomit go far down in an outhouse, Ruth. You hear the earth swallow it and can imagine the limestone underworld, the stalactites in the throat that catch the excrement. I wiped the mucus strings with toilet paper, shut the lid, and sat. I no longer smelled the fish, only fake lilac and the fake berry of the air freshener. I hooked the door's hook into its eye. I could see, in the dusky light coming through the high air vent, the friendly small spiders stirring in the pyramid stack of toilet paper rolls. Someone had stowed, in the corner, a blue cross eraser with *He Lives* at the center, where the haggard body would have hung.

Dillon knocked on the door and said my name, but I didn't answer and he left me alone. I was cold and wanted his Army jacket to wear. The dress gapped forward, and through the gauzy deep-blue organdy I could see my small breasts and my hard chest bone, and I thought about how one is supposed to receive the Lord who lives into the heart, right in that space, with the balled knee socks. My desire was crocus blue, a vague intensity, as before, but I became aware inside the outhouse that whatever I was yearning for was something I could not have. I longed to have a Belinda-like body and the normal sweetness of the Dairy Delite girls. But more so, oddly, I had a great want for the clean smell of grass after the Easter snow, which falls so lightly you can mistake it for heavy dew, and this was of course right outside the door, beyond the outhouse lattice, and still I knew I somehow could not have it.

I smoothed the taffeta, my ordinary adolescent cravings swelled and sobered by Good Friday. I had this idea that everyone in the churchyard was opening up into larger selves as they flipped fish and poured punch by the big stump—as natural as breathing, this largeness—but I couldn't find a way to meet them in it. Why not?

In the middle of everything, my longing reared its head just like a spear of crocus, up through ice and snow, and I mashed it back down. To save it. Or to deny it.

One Saturday night, Stew didn't show for practice. The other men tilted their trucks off the road, half in the yard like always, and Billy lugged in his rhythm guitar as though it were heavy, Danny the new high hat for the drum set. But no bass guitar. No Stew.

I'd baked the pumpkin bread Stew liked. I wore a fitted eyelet dress with tiny circles of skin visible. Clay dug into his new song about the suffering of God. It's true he did not ask much of me. And he was, really, gentle as a leaf. Danny and Billy set up, and in the kitchen I crossed my legs and studied the circles of skin beneath the white material, the embroidery rounding up the circles' tiny rims. Clay thought his guitar riff was new. I considered taking a slice of the warm bread to Lottie as I ought but I sat waiting for Stew, picturing his squared jaw, the lines etched around his eyes.

Framed in the living room archway, Clay scribbled on his pad with his boy-tongue in his teeth. His butt at the edge of the easy chair, he shuffled his Bible concordance and paraphrased out loud, maybe to Danny affixing the wide cymbal, Hebrews 2:9: "We see Jesus, made a little lower than the angels for the suffering of death, crowned with glory and honor, that he, by the grace of God, might taste death for everyone." Glad for some easy rhymes and leaning into *taste* and *crowned*. Out on the town, but he for you crowned. Taste death, waste breath.

I pictured myself led down a path in darkness. I would see nothing, not my feet not my hand, only taste the darkness. Taste being the most intimate thing, more intimate than understanding.

Billy and Danny thickened the living room, started tooling around with rhythm, with tuning, with simple chords. When present, Stew was lean like a piece of leather, like a body wrung to dryness, and his clothes folded smoke into themselves. Clay had never lost his baby face. I surveyed the kitchen, the sauce pans hanging on hooks, the fragrant nutmeg almost a visible specter over the cooling pumpkin bread, the ever-present blue chairs, one of which held me, and I placed my hands there—right there—upon my lower belly and fought some nausea. What would death taste like?

The phone rang. I rose from the blue chair, muting my childish desire to cry or to vomit.

"Frankie, it's Jennie." Stew's wife. She asked for Clay but I said, "Where is he?" more adamantly than I should have.

She was quiet. Then, hoarsely, "Sitting in his truck."

"What?"

"Give me to Clay."

"Is it running?"

"Not anymore it isn't. It's his third DUI." She said they towed him from the ditch to the front yard, booted the truck, and took his license and let him sleep it off. "He hasn't dismounted," Jennie said, "just sits in there. He's so stupid, he's locked himself in, he won't come eat."

"How long?"

"Could they come over?" She was pissed and justified—I could see her full body bracing for some kind of retribution, as one braces for bad weather; I could hear the hurt dragged behind her voice, the way Clay dragged his dissatisfaction now, his song's limitation and haltedness, as he came into the kitchen—I held out the receiver, "It's Jennie"—and I watched him try to leave his feelings wadded in the corner in Ellis's empty bed.

We all knew Stew loved nothing more than that red truck. The feel of the cab, the six horses he had painted on the underside of the cab roof running in full slant. Clay and the others left in a righteous line of vehicles. They would try to pull him out, but he'd take his flask from the glove box, anchored. He would sit there into the night, a backslider backlit into silhouette by the shed's dusk-to-dawn, sitting behind the wheel, looking upward, as if in prayer to the horses kicking up the dust.

I had sat in Stew's cab once, secretly, during band practice when they'd crowded in the basement. The Good News Boys were rehearsing for the next morning's concert at Monroeville's Heartland nursing home, where the old people would tap along out of sync. The tire tread looked good and uncaked; the truck was beautiful as ever, with its flames up the hood. I climbed in and stretched out on my back across the bench seat, pulling the door shut.

It was magnificent. Why paint a cab roof, why paint up there unless you're going to lie down and look up forever? A stampede, musky, the manes and tails blowing back, almost glowing in the dark. I thought how Stew must drive faster knowing half a dozen horses were in full gallop above him. I lifted up my blouse and put my hands on my belly; it subtly filled my hands but was taut. Looking down, the horses saw my black hair fan out as if in water as a body sinks, my face half whitened by the porch light.

The drums carried, and I listened for the final trailing off of sound, when Clay would climb the stairs and seek out sweet tea and walk into the kitchen, saying my name, but I did not detect the silence when it came. I felt the bob of the pickup bed under something heavy, likely an amp, and I heard Danny's voice and Billy's more faintly, then Stew's, close to the cab window. I didn't sit up. I pulled my shirt down, the glow-in-the-dark horse manes like wicked little lashings—what would I say? But Clay hollered something that took Stew back inside, something he'd forgotten to pack up, or a final detail of the show for the old ones who would touch their own filmy sweet skin through the plodding choruses, and who would fall back to watch some fleeting self painted on the inside of their skulls, always there, running forward at a slant. When Stew opened the cab door, I was already gone, having spilled out, making sure I missed the other two. I'd sneaked to the back porch where there was no light on to show me to Clay or anyone.

Now, with the men gone, Clay's new song drifted around the silent house and into my head, and I thought about the taste of death and how it must mean more than simply dying. It was more intimate. It was like replacing the thing you love—your very life—with the palpable absence of it. I conjured Stew in the cab with the engine cut.

The nausea persisted, but I finally sliced a piece of pumpkin bread for Lottie, slathered it with apple butter. I took it to her hospital bed that had a rail—like a child's crib—where she slept with the tip of her braid in her hands, haloed by the wide white doily upon her pillow. I set the plate on the TV tray and watched her milky eyelids. The industrial bed was discordant with her rust-gold room with the cherry dresser and nightstand. When she'd fallen on the stairs and broken her hip, we had made the quiet, damning modifications to the house: bed, shower chair, color-coded arsenal of medications to thin the blood, to ease the blood's pressure, to thicken the blood in turn. Without discussion, my caregiving days opened out in front of me like a road draped with heavy branches. I quit my janitor job at LaFaber, I packed my coveralls with name patch in a trunk in the attic and watched my future self waver in the light, holographic. I saw my long black hair fade to white and shimmer.

The day I quit, I got drunk quietly on the back steps, the two-by-fours with gaps between to mind, facing the trailer ruins barely visible. Iridescent orange ribbon marked spindly trees to be cut that would not be cut, though the cinderblock corners that Clay had set in our first month of matrimony remained cemented there. Lottie would stay with us, and I'd keep my view of the woods from the kitchen window. I studied the ruins of a thing never built.

My heart was no caregiver's heart. I remembered a section from the Book of Leviticus, read during my homeschooling years barely supervised by Mave, instructions for how to ready the she-goat. A sacrifice to atone for such things as black thoughts, charred self-pity, narrowness. The exacting sacrifices of the old temple were in place for when your heart didn't meet the standards of contrition. I remembered scribbling in the margin—words like hands shaping mud, the shifting, sliding muck of extant text. I wrote the tending and the dishing out of sweet pellets and making of straw beds in the barn, all the stroking of the short hair on the head between the dull eyes that ever sought high ground or food or mischief. How the she-goat would butt up against me and leave a bruise. Was she really demanded of the faithful? Or was it the faithless she died for? I drew the marsh reed in flower, remembering from one of your letters that the reed meant an address, meant O, as in O Lord, forgive me.

O—and there was the shabby snow of fur falling, shaved from the neck before sacrifice. O Ruth, didn't I hear a bleating?

In my eyelet dress now, in the house emptied of The Good News Boys, I left Lottie's bedside for the bathroom where I leaned upon the sink and cooled. In place of her old porcelain and pearl, softness and peach highlights in the towel sets, there was now steel and plastic, all things firm. But I was glad for the new bar bolted in by the toilet as I braced myself to heave.

I knew when I'd conceived.

A few weeks before, in the waiting room of the Monroeville clinic where we took Lottie for her appointments, Paul Rose had been there, a retired Army colonel, with his son, and they were talking about practicing boxing in the front yard, and two women I didn't know were talking about paint for their walls. One woman held up pink paint samples.

"You want Hibiscus?"

"No, I want Dreamland," the other said, "just because of the name."

The colonel made a comment to Clay about his capable son and Clay stuttered, which he never did. The men felt like a dense web, with the whole room turning Dreamland pink; I could see Clay shrink and I could see his seed in him, translucent and useless and humbled. I thought about how I guided his head for him in love-making, and how I pictured Dillon all the while with his dark wet hair and felt more relief than a trembling, and, if that fantasy did not work, I pictured Stew. Sex with Clay was all mechanics and gentle-ness, but that night I urged him to go at me hard, I coaxed him to it, I moaned something genuine and pictured no man but him, and the coming was bright—his, not mine, but I did not care, I knew he was getting his hurt out, his flaccid living. That's when it had taken.

Some of the pumpkin bread was nibbled away, but Lottie dozed again with braid in hand like a branch clutched by a dove. How ill-equipped I was at the sickbed. From skeleton out to aura, I felt thinned and vague. What I most feared was the bitter milk I'd deliver, like a Guernsey's laced with ingested wild onions.

Lottie roused, sat up, and spit out a morsel of bread.

"Lottie," I said, "I thought you were sleeping. Why didn't you swallow?" Strings of apple butter spit striped her nightgown.

"Good bread," Lottie said, lying back down. I wondered whether she could sense my pregnancy as I dabbed her gown with a washcloth and put my hand to her damp forehead. "Good wife," she said.

She soon slept again. The downstairs was still empty except for Ellis sprawled in his kitchen bed. I put on my work boots to walk. Stew's place was a couple of miles away, so by the time I'd get there, the men would be gone. I would see him silhouetted by the shed light and leaning his head back under his horses, Jennie inside bulling in the cabinets. I should have changed from the eyelet dress.

It was dark. I felt, on my arms, the wet April air, the ever-present damp of this climate I had never not known. I could hear the seepage in the ditch. In the opposite direction lay Rex and Miranda's, where spring water cooled those milkhouse stones, always the wetness, like a blacker color to things. No fade-out whitewash, no sun bleach. Even then I thought about how the desert must be bright and blackless and clear.

A mile and a half down the road, about a hundred yards off, sat the Ellafritz house, and Stew's lay beyond. Under the front porch light were two of the adopted Ellafritz girls, one standing and one sitting in a kitchen chair. The seated one lazily noted me with her gaze but said nothing. They were no more than fifteen but had a baby each, and some flesh spilling over their jean-cutoff waists, stretching their floral tank tops. They were doing each other's makeup on the porch, taking turns, it seemed, in the chair. I watched from the road as one worked on the other, cigarette dangling off her lip, and I wanted a smoke. The seated one's eyes closed and her lids went sheen with violet. A coffee can of soot for mascara, applied by Q-tip. I got close enough to climb their six steps, though they pretended I wasn't there. An infant cried in the house but "Just a little longer" said the standing girl, her movements deft. She needed to get the coral perfect along the high ridge of cheekbone, brushing the cake of it in the compact and slanting the upward application, until her breasts hurt enough, like homing devices, longing for the tiny wailing mouth and squinted face. She went inside, leaving the other on the chair to light up.

Belinda had told me the girls nursed each other's sometimes. Neither of the girls was pretty. They weren't going anywhere tonight; they looked unshowered. Grandeur only from the neck up. We were both in our own skulls, the girl and I, but she turned and looked me up and down. I felt she could see my belly hard. She could see the child starting there now, just a hive of cells. She picked up a shard of mirror, tilted up her chin.

"What do you think?" she said. The foundation was caked on, but her lined eyes and her lashes sooted with homemade mascara did jump out.

"Looks pretty," I said.

The other returned with an infant at her breast. She started in with lip liner with her free hand.

I walked on, and the way their screen door sounded behind me, as one of them went inside, invoked my mother through the long hallway of time, the way she had stood on the porch once. She'd boiled water for ear corn and, afterward, walked outside to throw the silk-littered water off the side of the porch and not in the sink, and stood listening to the supper-hour night. I remembered her looking kind in that moment, though she was not kind, an image in the porch light to wake in the mind of her daughter years later. And now this one inside me would recall me in some way. I put my hand on my middle, over the eyelet, over the pair of eyes forming in the dark.

By the time I got to Stew's, the dusk-to-dawn on the shed was the only light. The house was dark, Clay and Danny and Billy were gone, Jennie likely asleep. I saw the beautiful red truck, the prize, its tire booted. Whenever Stew would speak, the words were like sparse growing things. Once, when buffing the rust from my pickup in his body shop, he'd simply said, "Come," showing me the work he'd almost finished, kneeling to study the fender as I studied his temple and ear.

I walked up to the truck in my white dress and put my open hand to the driver-side window. I waited for him to sit up full of horse taste, my palm like a light. I drew closer and tented my eyes to look in the window and saw the cab was empty.

❧

I WALKED THE NEXT HALF MILE TO MY HOUSE. I still kept a few changes of clothes in the closet. I changed into a blue blouse I'd once loved and jeans and hung up the belted eyelet dress. Outside Mave's, I saw the basketball long left in the peony bushes beside the house, lead-like. I wiped off the grime of old leaves, shot it toward the hoop Mave had put up for me on a two-by-eight. Air ball. Only the hoop was left, the net had disintegrated. I took a few more shots with the dead ball and, with each, I felt the darts in the sides of the blouse restrict, then I let the ball roll on.

"Hey, come in here," Mave called out the window. "I've got the bog people on." She wore bathrobe and boots, gray hair frizzed. "The ancient Danes."

I refused a beer but sat with her in the PBS glow.

"I wore this blue blouse one time," I said, "and Clay said I looked nice. Then I hid it in my house and didn't want to ever wear it again."

"Then why are you wearing it again?"

"I don't know."

On screen, the bog bodies of Denmark writhed without moving. A man from the fourth century BC looked like he'd simply gone to sleep except he'd taken an ax down the nose bone, *bludgeoned* was the word used, probably a human sacrifice thrown to the bog, which sucked the body down and sealed out all the air so centuries later he'd come up looking made of bronze. As if out the throughside of the LaFaber foundry. He still had lips, the voiceover said, and kidneys and spleen, his hair.

"There must be something else out there," I said.

"Other than the old sacrifice?"

"Other than this."

"Thinking in broad strokes, you have it pretty good. You have not been bludgeoned to death." Mave held out her hand to chop, demonstrated the blow to her face in slow motion. "You're not big-league in the tragedy department."

The voice said archaeologists could test the hair and know what he'd eaten, could study his stomach and tell us his last meal. Both skull and brain were intact. The peat moss, the cool bog acid, like vinegar, dissolved most of the bones but not the skin.

"You're shitting me," Mave said to the TV. "Skin pickled like eggs."

I said, "Every day Clay hands me his lunchbox to wash and a thermos with coffee stains. My breathing is erratic. I feel the air sealing off."

"How's Lottie?"

"The same."

"Maybe you're lucky with no air. Your hair will be preserved just the way you fix it."

"Bury me in this blouse after you bludgeon me."

"But once the body hits the air—look at that shit. They brought him up into the Denmark air and the change was violent and fast, he oxidized. They had to get him into that capsule before he dissolved like salt."

In my head, Clay turned to me his boyish face the color of an antacid tablet, of cat tongues, and said, when he entered the kitchen, You look nice. The blouse cool on both arms, against all my skin except where the bra was.

"Maybe what you need is to oxidize," she said.

They went on with Grauballe Man and Elling Woman of the Iron Age, then the Bronze Age Cashel Man of the Irish peat bogs, the oldest fleshed body crouching in the peat longer than anyone.

"I bet we have our own around here," Mave said, "pickled in the Caudell bog. We should start foraging for them in the skunk cabbage."

"I'm pregnant," I said.

She looked at me. Didn't say anything with her mouth, only her eyes. She looked back at the TV.

I didn't picture myself bludgeoned. I pictured my black hair growing long and wrapping around me like a coat so all you could see was my head, my face, but the rest was shrouded and cut off, my limbs tangled. With my arms restrained, I wouldn't be able to hurt anyone.

THE PAPERY MOTEL BED SHEETS CRUSHED UP TO MY CHIN, I lay imagining the aerial view of the New Mexico desert, radioactive and bombed out, the mesas blue at sunrise, haggard white by noon. The New Agers would have their open-air market, trading in spiritual goods—come get your new life in the wide rocky spaces, get a Navajo turquoise ring for twenty bucks, and I'd get one for Clarissa's Tess. Get a buffalo scrotum purse for twenty-five. A purer soul for thirty. But, aside from the racket, there would be the true wilderness of conversion. Be changed, it says. It says: I will not restore you to the same. It says: There is no tourist trinket for what I will do, for what it means to become nothing. I thought of that, Ruth; I thought of the relief.

I turned to see the vague outline of Nan lying on her stomach, ear down on her pillow, face toward the pastel palm trees on the wall, arms wide out in free fall like a child's. The hair, tamed wet last night, had sprung back into its wild nest. Ellis had chosen her in the night, a pile tucked to her side. The thick drapes kept me in question about the time, but their rim of bright sun said we were up late.

Mave was gone.

I sat up and checked under the mattress for the keys. Still there. I went to the drapes to check the car anyway, looked for a popped trunk, but it was shut. At the foot of the bed, Mave's suitcase. My gym shorts and tank top clung. I'd let in enough light through the window to wake Nan, who groaned and shoved the mound of dog.

Out the window, I watched Mave exit the lobby door with two cups. She wore her favorite red flannel shirt. She managed the oxygen in her armpit, like a rolled *Tennessean*.

"Am I in Florida yet?" asked Nan, mooning from a spillover of the night's goodwill.

Mave crossed the lot to our room, her stiff walk, her unshielded squinting eyes. She saw me spying so I opened the door.

"Could have left a note," I said. Daylight pounded in.

"It's Sunday. Had to make the call early to catch Miranda." She gave me a coffee.

"Where's mine?" said Nan, sitting up in her silky and pink, strap off the shoulder. The dejected Ellis snuffled for an ear scratch.

"You called Miranda?" I said. The coffee tasted day-old, I gave it to Nan. "What did you tell her?"

"I caught her before church, but she'd already been out to the primrose."

"What did you say to her?" I felt the headache all at once, long after it had settled. Like somebody throwing elbows in my mind.

Mave sipped, winced. "The primrose, I mean, imagine. Little gaudy things. Some people pry the day open, that's Miranda. But with a fingernail file, not a crowbar. Hers is a gentle force, prying with equal measure at all edges, and then she eases the lid off."

"Enough circumlocution," I said.

"Hey, watch the language for Gypsy—keep the syllables down."

"Fuck off," said Nan. She rolled out of bed languidly and slipped into the bathroom.

Mave's face softened and suspended itself elsewhere, and my eyes absorbed the encroaching ache in my head. I breathed in the last of the tar and nicotine from the linens, the walls, the carpets. I asked her if she'd taken her pills. I asked about the primrose.

"Her women's group will pray for me in Sunday school as they always do," Mave said, "as they have since the beginning of time for the cancer people and the lost. They lower their lashes and picture us like shelter puppies in a pen, in amongst our turds."

Nan flushed and emerged and brushed her teeth on one stork leg flipping through the motel welcome book, deliberate to be part of the conversation.

"It's okay," Mave said. "Miranda goes out to the primrose already dressed for Sunday, salting the slugs, taking a cutting for the noon table and usually one for me. I can see her stoop down every day I am alive. She hitches her skirt, her nylons are runner-free as they slide into her muddy garden shoes. Her hands are flecked with wet parsley and they smell of whatever they have kneaded and seasoned. There's a pot roast in a crock pot for the twins and Belinda and Tuffie and Belinda's brood and Rex's square head. There's a loud croak in my heart for Miranda and her concave body. Someone who mothers. I know nothing about that, Frankie. The lived-in world was always real to my sister. I fit into her hunched curve at one time. I see now she chose to let it all be wrung from her. I think it was a free choice. I may have been wrong to try to dissuade her."

Mave watched Nan head back to the bathroom sink to spit, grabbing clothes on the way.

"I told her she has lived a real life." Mave sipped the bad coffee and winced again. "I wanted to tell her that before I die."

"I know what you're planning to do," I said. "And I won't let you. We're going to see the desert and O'Keeffe's roofless room, and we'll get some souvenirs, then we'll go home and you'll do treatment again." My eyes watered out the ache.

"Some turquoise," she said. Mave so tired and pasty, breathing there, her lungs mostly on the outside, wearing that shirt I'd seen every other day of my life though it looked clean this time, sleeves rolled to the elbow. She sat.

Out of the bathroom, Nan said, "I want to see the Grand Ole Opry," dressed now. "The motel book says we're only a half hour from Nashville."

"Me too, Nannette," said Mave. "Let's get on the road."

We piled our meager luggage in the trunk atop the hard lump of mute gun. Nan seemed to have come to terms with her backseat status and was the first to climb in, rubbing sleep crusts from Ellis's eyes. It was such a tender gesture, gentle with the pad of her forefinger, somehow keeping the red-painted nail from interfering, he held still for it, and afterward licked her wrist, bedded his head into the lap of dollar-store striped dress. In those four seconds, like a barely redirected spring, my thought shifted to touch. I pulled into the same Denny's for breakfast sandwiches to go, then we left White House, Tennessee, behind.

Mave stayed quiet, removed the cotton balls from above her ears, detached the tank's network of tubes to rub where the plastic hose weighed on the cartilage. I thought of Clay's touch, as if I'd walked into low-hanging crabapple branches, then backed away. He would pull down my T-shirt nightdress with decorum after, cover me up, his eyes set close together but a face not unhandsome, only uncertain.

Then I was out there, a sack of organs in the world, sense organs, set of orifices—all of myself hungering now—barreling southbound in that beat-up blue Oldsmobile Royale on Interstate 65 with two other disparate bodies, one with a lovely face unpurpling, the other with a face drying out as if already accustomed to sand and scrub. In the desert perhaps our dead babies would come back, to haunt us more substantially. We should have named them.

One of hers had been Dillon's. He'd worn a leather bracelet as a boy, I remembered, imprinted with the name Augustus, for his grandfather he said, and someone had stamped it by hand with metal letters and a mallet, and then he had met Nan when she'd been hawking leather bracelets. One of the children would have been named that, Augustus, Gus, Auggie—Come eat, Gus, come comb your hair.

Mave's cotton balls were yellowed. She held them out to Nan between our seats. "Here, have my ear protectors." I saw Nan wrinkle her face in the rearview and laugh.

"Who do you love?" asked Mave. "You never did answer me, Gypsy." She replaced the cotton, hooked the tubing over her ears, into her nostrils. "Come on, this car is sacrosanct. This metal box is a place to let it fly."

Maybe, Ruth, we were looking for a land that suggested the heart opens out, under the bare chalk-tick of a white sickle morning moon and unto flat craggy ground. Because it's thirst that's expansive. It's thirst that lets everything touch you at once, even parts of you never touched before.

Nan said, "You wanna know? I love sex in general." Mave raised her eyebrows and nodded. "And funnel cake," Nan said. She laughed, and Mave beckoned with her hand to say that's fine, keep going, what else.

"Okay. I also love to paint. But not just the dirty pictures in aerosol. I do scenes. I actually make the paints myself sometimes, from stuff around the house. Like berries or mustard."

Once, I had seen Nan's work, wall-size, still wet. I had not yet asked her about it. No sound inside her pause but the engine and the rhythmic seams in the pavement. Then: "Sometimes when I paint," she said, "I forget where my body ends. Like I don't have edges. Do you know what I mean, Crazy? I bet you do. I bet you know things like that."

"People will miscalculate you, Nannette," said Mave. "People always miscalculate. You bear some resemblance to O'Keeffe, you know, in calculations. Her lover made a mint photographing her nude—did you know? Everyone fascinated by her sex, by the generous give they could feel in her fleshy canyons in black and white. He groomed her like a horse. Like her dark rippling hide belonged only to him within the frame. I don't give a shit really—give me her own stuff, her reds and rocks, her many skies. What she made with her hands. Give me her color, all untuned. And the bones and buttes. Nobody could give out her body except her."

I stayed quiet. They did not ask me what or whom I loved and I was not sure how I would have answered since I was not sure I was capable of love. I was sure only of thirst. I was sure that I always reached for the notepad and for the pens that engrave more than write, their cheap ink drying up. Maybe I was sure then, behind the wheel of the blue Olds, that I would eventually write all this to you who would never read it and, in that act, is there possibly some form of love?

Nan said, "I do like to draw sexy pictures too." Big smile and a purse of lips.

"I know you do, Little Gypsy," said Mave. She consulted the atlas for which exit to take off I-65 for the Opry, but the signs on the roadside took over the job.

"It won't be open," I said. "It's Sunday morning."

"I just want to feel Saturday night's leftovers." Mave rolled her window down all the way and the wind roared. "Catch a few of Patsy's refrains."

The lot was huge and built for buses, and the building imposing. This wasn't the old downtown Ryman Auditorium I knew from posters. We could see the unlit horrible chandeliers through the full front windows, the unlit sign. Gaudy in the daylight, but I could imagine the excitement that took over at night, how things would be transformed. I stayed in the car, they got out, and Ellis took his opportunity to sniff and piss on a paper cup. Nan and Mave stood side by side, with this new flow between them, and I felt my separateness in relief.

"We better move on," I said from the car. I was crisp.

"It looks like a casino," said Nan.

"But you can hear some clips, can't you? Sing it, Patsy. Hank Senior, Ernest Tubb. There's the Texan drawl."

Nan nodded. "Sure can, Crazy."

We tried to find Nashville's Broadway where the honkytonks were, and the places to buy boots, though we knew they'd be closed too. The streets almost vacant, the shutters locked down over windows from which, on other days, crooning would pour out to the street. I wished for more for Mave, real music, some life in the city. Someone walked his dog and Ellis put paws to the car window and whined. I took rights and lefts following the will of the one-ways.

"Better look for interstate signs," I finally said. "Time to get moving."

Mave's window was still down, and I heard singing then. It was a hymn, gospel. The next right I took put us in front of a Holiday Inn with a lot so I parked and said, "Turn to the Nashville insert in the atlas." But Mave's nose went out the window. The singing swelled, coming from the hotel. Or from just outside it. The hymn I'd heard faintly now grew louder and soon bowled into the car, many voices like one big voice with spokes or avenues—*Let the redeemed, let the redeemed, let the redeemed of the Lord say so.* The three of us gazed at the hotel pool with its low white fence perimeter, at the crowd singing and becoming one body of sound. Maybe thirty people, many dark-skinned people, several white faces, many were children, some of the women wore white dresses, gloves, some wore jeans. A small boy stood separate in a white undershirt and white flood pants, his thin dark brown legs and arms jittery, as if he had to pee. A tall man in a white button-up shirt stood in the pool, the shallow end, and the pool water deepened the gray of his trousers. He raised a large inviting hand to the boy in the white tee at the edge of the pool, and the boy settled and looked up and took the man's hand.

The voices softened though still sang. The poolside hotel bar was closed and a row of young boys and one girl climbed up on the bar, jockeying to see. Two other kids stood beside the boy holding the man's hand, and a woman in a formal blue dress printed with white lilies gave a towel to each kid, and each held the towel like a ring bearer his pillow, with both arms out, as if the Holiday Inn towels were sacred.

The man spoke but I couldn't hear him. I turned off the idling engine; still he was too gentle to hear. He spoke to the boy whose hand he held, and the kid nodded, then opened his mouth to speak when the lily-dress woman, I assumed his mother, touched his shoulder as if to say, Don't just nod now, speak it out loud. The kaleidoscope of faces was still but in motion at the same time, eyes on the boy. I noticed his chest was so tiny, his hand like a brown moth in the man's huge darker hand, and the boy put his other hand on the railing and started down the underwater steps that were there to ease in his body. His eyes widened and teeth clenched, so cold, but he moved steadily down into the pool toward the man, close enough for embrace, face to torso.

"Father, Son, Holy Spirit," whispered Nan from the back seat.

The man palmed the boy's back and leaned him down into the blue water, as if giving him a swimming lesson, teaching him the back float, except the boy held his nose and disappeared for two seconds, except there was a mist of voices that began to intensify again, blooming out into the chlorinated air. When the boy burst up, the woman in lilies wept. He smiled and wiped his eyes and jumped a little, put his arms out to his sides, ready to play Marco Polo or dive for coins with his friends whom he looked at now, their arms bearing towels. He climbed the steps, almost princely, and the two were shy for this split second after the rite. He was cold—he took one of the cheap little hotel towels that hardly wrap once around a body, but it was big enough for his small self. He dried his face, his eyes, his neck. His two friends remained tentative. He was different now.

The mother grabbed him in a quick hug that broke the spell, and he squirmed to get out of it. He broke free, flung the towel around his back and held the corners under his chin, took off running, the towel his Superman cape, and the other two followed, running, since he was again the boy they knew, and no one scolded. The kids on the bar hopped down and gave chase, the singing pronged out, the tall man still in the pool upraised his arms in a formal benediction while the soul saved and sanctified took the corner and kept flying, toward us, cracking up. The girl in the bunch waved at us as they raced by and then turned to head back to the congregation now talking and visiting. Someone brought towels to the preacher rising from the pool. I watched his large hands take a towel, shake another hand, rub his own head of close-cropped black hair, reach into his pocket to pull out something he'd forgotten to remove, now wet through, and he laughed.

We stayed quiet, we three fugitives. The pool water tremored. Mave soon flipped through the atlas to find our coordinates in the city, suggested a direction, and I started the car.

"I loved that," said Nan softly.

Mave said we'd see signs for 40 West once we crossed the Cumberland River. I just drove. My arms felt wobbly, as if energy had surged through them and then nothing.

"I loved it," Nan said again.

I kept picturing the gentle touch, man's hand on boy's slim back, his barely back, just a slip of person. I watched Mave's hands acutely, bitten nails and bony fingers, watched her trace the turnoffs on the page over the tiny string of blue that meant *river.* How rarely we touched, she and I.

"Take Jefferson," Mave said quietly. None of us wanted to speak loudly or stir the air very much. Mave said then, "Give him a page in your book, that kid. Give him a whole chapter." She watched the storefronts pass, the signs and awnings. "Write a chapter on a boy dunked in a hotel pool and wrapped in skinny towels."

"You don't believe in the Father, Son, Holy Ghost," I said.

"I believe in that boy's cape."

"I don't know," said Nan, "I just loved it. I'd like to paint a boy getting baptized then flying."

The traffic had picked up. I swelled with a sense of things blurring by too fast out the windows. I switched the blinker on, but I wanted stillness somehow. Maybe it was the boy running and the look of Mave watching. I wanted to freeze it. Indeed, paint it. I wanted more time. I thought about her earlier farewell call to Miranda, and I thought about the gun, and I wanted Mave to live. Maybe she would live. I turned us onto a bridge and the sign for 40 instructed me into the right lane. There was a shoulder, narrow but big enough for the car, I put the hazards on and pulled off.

"What's wrong?" asked Nan.

"Not here," said Mave, "next turn."

I still saw the tremor in the pool. My arms were weak. I gripped the steering wheel then popped the trunk and got out. I shoved aside the suitcases, lifted the thick carpet cover, and unwedged the Browning pistol. Mave opened her door, but not in time. I threw the gun overhand into the river below. Tiny splash. I got back in the car.

In the rearview, I saw Nan about to speak but she didn't. Cars zipped past, honked, complained. Mave's door was still open and I asked her to please shut it.

She put both palms on the atlas and smoothed it out and did not look at me, she set her jaw. She took a breath that was not deep, and I panicked with a second of doubt, but I summoned the magic of that kid in his cape, dripping wet. I wanted her to live, Ruth, don't you see? We would finish this joyride then go home, get treatment, and she would live. And I believed it as I signaled and pulled us back into the flow of traffic and onto I-40.

My cousin Belinda had always had an inkling. She got pinned like a bug early. A beautiful body pinned to the mat and felt up by boys at the fringe of supervision. And pinned by Miranda stooped and hopeful to have a second-self with pageant potential, not too smart, thank god, nothing of Mave's ruinous genes. "Not the brightest," our mothers said at the kitchen table, whether or not Belinda was within earshot holding her rouged doll by the hair. They petted Belinda's head; my mother did so greedily, wishing me more like my cousin, softer, more in line. Miranda certainly saw me as heir to the ruin and ill-colored and strange, and then after Mother and Dad died, a feral animal raised by an unnatural drunkard. From the start, I was left to develop my mind in peace and wear boy clothes without hassle. Belinda wore everything fitted to her early-forming breasts and slim waist, a body like carved ivory.

But she had an inkling of what lay beyond the frame, like someone studying a photo's narrative beyond its border: there is more than the posed figure, there is more than this. By rights, she felt sorry for my dearth of everything—Pity you never had boyfriends, god your chewed nails, here's a dress I don't wear anymore, here's a spare husband, a baby you can hold and coo at.

When we played as small girls, she made shadow puppets of her life to come. She played house, able with a broom, played beauty shop or soap opera. I played tractor trailer and pulled my wagon. Once, as I tied a bandana around my neck and got ready for a cross-country, she said, "It's God you haul in there."

"It is?" I said.

We looked at the empty Radio Flyer wagon I had not yet stocked with cargo and I supposed it was true. There was God's poor body, there were the sores between the God-toes, there God's sleeping head.

"Now me," she said and crawled in atop God, folding up her skirts and holding onto the edges, knees up so I saw her pretty blue panties. "Haul me to the Train Cave." And I took off down the gravel drive.

"Slow it down!" she yelled.

I ran faster, flinging rocks. The wind whipped.

"Slow it down, there's potholes!" Her voice rattled. I took her off-road, into the rye grass along the fencerow, down the right-of-way that crossed the Heather Run culvert.

I stopped, panting, the old T-shirt of Mave's hanging mid-thigh, my boy boots a good fit. I bent down and squinted into sweet Belinda's face, her hair blown back as if aerosol sprayed. She had an inkling, I knew, about everything; she had a vast heart with new living birds in it, vaster than mine would ever be, and eyes that could see even though she'd turn to look the other way, always and ever, my cousin, like a sister, same age as me. Our futures would bear out as they willed, without asking us.

"You smell like a cow barn," she said.

I pulled her pretty hair. I took off toward the cave before she could hold on, but she held on, wailing.

❧

In mid-May, I was five weeks pregnant, and Miranda and the Snyder's Crossing women held Belinda's combined bridal and baby shower in the community center. This was the spring of 1990. Belinda was waddling into her eighth month. They'd hinged the basketball backboards up to the ceiling and set out tiny white cakes sprinkled with edible snow glitter, marshmallow snowmen for favors, mints and salty peanuts. All decorations had been held over from the shower planned for December, when Jack had gotten cold feet. Then he'd come back poking around and the wedding was on again.

Belinda sat in the metal chair up front by the table of presents, boobs and belly straining her dress, giddy like someone who wasn't on her third marriage and third child. Our pale Tuffie took the seat beside her to feed her gifts. At twenty-eight, Tuffie had a plank for a chest and was snide and protective and stricken.

I sat at Miranda's table feeling like my soul had grown a goiter. The smells from the LaFaber League concessions booth lingered—popcorn, hotdogs, fritters. On the far side of the court, my adolescent self went for a layup, pounded the ball in a graceless dribble. And did that phantom girl not always summon the ghostly Dillon, watching her every move? And what would Dillon think of Clay's child growing in me like a tiny bat hung upside down?

"Oh my gosh, oh my gosh," said Belinda. An ornament with B & J in puff paint, *First Christmas*; a black nightgown miscalculating her bust; a pretty wooden rattle.

Jack's was a family of churchgoers. The women in his family were all there, and Stew's wife Jennie, my old friend Liza thinning down and closing up, dangerously, and Liza's careful mother, and Clarissa and her daughter Tess, on break from art school, who was starting to wear her hair piled up on her head in ropes. Mave was reluctantly present and accounted for. Rayletta and Hope were on shift, but Hope had made a clothespin bag of calico, in the shape of a baby's dress hanging on a clothes hanger, and had sent it with me on behalf of the co-op.

I watched Miranda across the table from me. I resembled her despite her fair coloring and hair. In profile, her shoulders were mine and I stretched mine back. Her nose was mine, her gesture too: left arm crossing the stomach and propping the elbow of the right as her right hand cupped her cheek, held her own face, as if, when it came to tenderness, she had to see to it herself.

My own palm to cheek, I watched Belinda strip plain brown paper from a box and lift out something sizeable. She looked at it for a few quiet seconds then held it out for us to see. A two-foot house-like shape, edged in metal, a mosaic of tiles all over the front. There were four small wooden doors, or shutters, asymmetrical. Tuffie reached over and pulled open a door gingerly to reveal a piece of patterned cloth behind. She pressed the door shut and opened another, different cloth. It brought to mind an old Advent calendar, it abstractly evoked a doll house.

"It's mixed media," Tess said. "For the baby's room." It was a disturbance of style among the muted pastels of burp cloths and Christmas ornaments. I could tell Belinda was moved and confused, I could sense her secret self, her knowingness, her inkling, lodged inside. Then she turned babyish, in-turned her feet, pressed together her knees.

"Thank you, Tess," she said. Tuffie took the art piece and peeked into the other two doors privately.

Clarissa glowed, Tess just finishing her second year of art school in Cleveland, Tess whom she had gotten away from the violent moods of Darrell Tide. Tess wore a long scoop-neck sweater and camouflage leggings, her hair in that messy pile, boots that looked like Mave's steel toes but blacker. She sat close to her mother, like a sister.

I felt my face, thumb at my jaw. Belinda *oohed* over tulip placemats, but her heart had shot out a sliver of its raw self, had come up for air before sinking back down.

That morning a bird had kamikazed Lottie's picture window and I'd found it nearly dead in the leaves. I'd ringed it slowly with my whole hand, slid its feathers and wings down, put it in a box with no holes punched in it. The comfort of the dark, or the terror, had roused it back to life. I'd lifted the lid and it had fled. Now my hand was on my flesh and fur, my red hue, warm. Who is it we touch, Ruth, when we touch our own skin? Is it not, often enough, someone other than we expected? We miss her, the expected one, by a split second—she has just slipped out the storm door, and we seek her, up at the skin surface, not understanding.

"Classic, Mave," said Belinda flatly. She'd unwrapped some kind of metal dragon incense burner, held it as if it were a dead kitten. Mave stood against the wall with her hands shoved in her pockets, loving the gag. A gift to her from one of her school bus kids who was into fantasy and picked on, and she'd rewrapped it. Miranda puffed her downturned lips.

My abdomen was hard and watertight. Only Clay and Mave and Clarissa knew I was pregnant, and probably Tess. Clay wanted a little girl and wanted to tell everyone, but I'd said not yet. And I would not sit in that seat near the foul line on the gym floor. No baby shower for me. I'd refused the bridal shower too—instead, Mave had come over with a set of nesting dolls made in Ukraine, each one with perfect circles on the cheeks. We'd both cracked up.

I tried to unwrap the sticky paper from a glittered stale cake, then abandoned the effort. The pink mints looked like tiny hard pillows for a tiny hard woman to lay her head on. After the gifts, women milled about and got ready for the games—they would guess Jack's favorite color and shirt size, the baby's name, the mother's measurements.

"You got an eye for decorating," Jennie said to Miranda. One of Jack's sisters fawned over the gift table, but kept at some distance as though the art piece might bite. I stood to go and said goodbye to Clarissa.

"But you'll miss the fun," she said, and Tess handed me a favor from the table, the stale marshmallow snowman, laughing and widening her eyes. I said I had to relieve Clay, he was watching Lottie. Mave would stay to heckle; she waved me on. I crossed the gym floor's faded out-of-bounds line, removed the snowman's licorice-smelling hat, and put him in my hot bitter mouth.

It's true I meant to head home to help Clay after Belinda's shower. He'd been sitting with Lottie, and he was due at Danny's for practice. They practiced there now, because of her, so I hardly ever saw Stew after he sobered up and rejoined. But instead I drove to my own house sitting spectral on the hillside. Tess was on my mind now, and I wanted to find the book of van Gogh's letters you gave me, with his plates of paintings, thinking I'd give them to her. They were somewhere in the closet of my old room, with the LaFaber League participation trophies of gold plastic and the bedspread I'd lain under as an orphaned teen. I was tired; I thought I would lie down a while in my room.

Screen door scuff on the porch, a sound I always heard before I heard it, such dust on everything, an extra layer of dark. I stood still. Inside me, a hot cinder. I made it as far as the kitchen table, then sat, my legs light and boneless, my palms to my belly, its tight hot skin pulsing through the dress, then pain, god, like a wrenching. I gripped the table, reached down and pulled back blood. My throat closed to a wheeze, I fumbled for the paper bags still kept in a drawer, I breathed into one, sucking and puffing out the bag. I made it to the bathroom, another deep cramp and I dropped the bag and held onto the towel in its ring so to not fall, and with the other hand I held a cake of lavender soap, some version of it sitting forever on the white saucer by the sink year to year to year. I held it, smelled it, knew I needed to get to the phone, vaguely remembering I'd disconnected the phone, then so dizzy I let go and felt my body sway as if it were someone else's, toward the edge of the tub.

A dream—still sharp to me now—held me in strict channel, vivid like a memory because it was a memory as fully as it was a dream: I am on my house's porch in the full frothed air of a summer noon. My mother alive but like a colorless lithograph. Mave there too, but it's in that season when she is back and forth from Northampton and starting to pull away. All hands occupied with work, and on the overturned washtub sits a jar of water with a molded peony stem, ugly, like a furred typhoid tongue, so big that I know I am small. The dense air wads into curled blooms fallen from the Rose of Sharon, the white infolding the dark pink stain. At the edges, the forsythia, long done.

On either side of the washtub peony, Mother and Mave string half-runner beans for the canner. A colander and a soup pot full of picked beans sit on TV trays. Newspaper stretches lazily across each lap to catch the throwaway caps and strings. A bowl between them to catch each bean strung and snapped. Where I sit on the porch floor with my own smaller bowls, I am eye level with their laps, with the newspapers that crease down in between their knees. The pages—the funnies or world news—flap down off their thighs like the V-birds I know how to draw in a landscape. You make little Vs in front of the round sun for effect, some just above the trees, some small which means far off, some big and wide to be up close. There's a broken wingtip when the lead breaks from pressing too hard. The V-birds ring your head like buzzards in a bad picture, but might be eagles in another, herons mallards swans, little wrens or swallows. Usually they are swallows, flying around Uncle Rex's cattle barn I know how to draw well, with a hayloft and a small loft window.

"Sit up straight, Frankie," says Mother, "you look like Miranda." Her voice scrapes. I unstoop myself, I take a drink of the iced tea made with Red Rose tea bags, it's still warm from the boiled water mixed with cold, it's too sweet. They drink hot coffee, and my mother says to Mave, "It's so sad, and the little thing is an orphan."

The hundred Red Rose tea bags hide tiny ceramic monkeys I love, pink-colored zebras, blue elephant figurines for the windowsill. One comes free with each box, and as a child I assume the tea leaves have grown them, as if from figurine-seed. I often draw the small hard animals, a monkey face looking up at the V-birds, and I draw my mother's face, which is a face afraid and somehow emptied. I love what I don't draw: her back, sitting at the edge of a bath she fills for herself. Coil of her hair knotted perfectly upon her head. The discolored white nightgown against which her morning body strains when I come downstairs and ask her questions she doesn't answer, as if they confuse her. I do draw the blue elephant figurine, her favorite, on the sill.

She talks about a Lithuanian boy from gospel radio and her voice, for him, is tender as lamb's ear.

"I said sit up straight." A different voice for me.

"Margot," says Mave, who winks at me. Mave is slow and clumsy at the bean work, she is here visiting, having come from the someplace else. The someplace else is in her voice and will never leave it now. She wears a big belt buckle with a blue stone in the middle and a shirt somehow soaked in men's aftershave, her face and whole being strong and thick. She slits the tip of the bean easily enough, but struggles to catch the string and pull it the full length of the bean before it breaks. My mother, though, is expert, exact. I watch her thin, thin wrists at the end of her arms that come out of the capped sleeves of her top, and I want her to look at me.

"It's the saddest thing" goes her sweet voice above my head, meaning it's the most beautiful thing and not the saddest. "Cancer of the brain," she says.

I am eye level with the V-bird newsprint that catches strings the way a beautician's floor catches ringlets, and the V-birds tremble a little as my mother and Mave ease out their legs, as they maybe get closer to having to pee, which I suddenly need to do now, but I want to hear what my mother is saying about the boy with no family and the orphanage with no doctor. The Lithuanian boy who has cancer, he has made it across the airwaves onto money-raising gospel radio that she tunes into from seven to eight a.m. daily. He has no running water there, or decent bedding. "His village ruined by famine," she says gently, "and they say the other children bring him their bread and sing him songs." Her voice is a tendril, a petal, somehow rehearsed. Mave says nothing but watches me.

I've got to pee, as well as the other thing now, and my bean bowl lies still so my mother can tell. She says, "Go on, you're squirming"—in the harrowing voice—but I want to hear the talk about the boy. I can't hold it anymore. She says, "You come back quick to finish your beans," in the tone of someone talking about a picture that's indecent, that should never have been drawn.

I set aside my beans and rise and huff past Mave, who touches my arm and says, "There's special soap for you," in a supple voice even though Mave is neither supple nor soft. "It's lavender from Ruth." Ruth. The first time I hear the name. As I go inside, I hear Mother's voice turn angry toward Mave; something has upset her, but I don't stay to listen.

I find the soap wrapped in crinkled paper and sitting on the sink next to the bits of yellow Dial my mother saves to slivers on the saucer. I unwrap and hold the purple square of it after I finish and flush. I love this sweet-smelling thing that's come into my world from someone named Ruth or someplace named Ruth—this is before the blue letters. I love it all the more so because of the boy in Lithuania, his small body a secret nursed inside my mother's voice. He has never smelled something like this—and does his head hurt, and what in fact does he smell in his rough bed? Orphans in short, raggedy pants keep wary of him and give him their supper because of his throbbing head, his worried skull.

I switch off the bathroom light and close my eyes a minute. I am filled by the thing in my hands. I see myself in the bathroom dark and the Lithuanian boy in his bunk in a stone room. And I grow big, huge, with wanting. I want my mother, I want to live beyond her bony instructions, I want her voice to croon that I am beautiful, I want her to understand me like Mave does, I want the place Mave lives in and has come back from and will go back to in her man boots, her world as big and true as the name Ruth. I want the loveliest life. A span of pain, as if my skin were stretching, comes all over me—I balloon out and crowd the boy up against the hard wall till he cries, till he can't breathe. Then I stop.

I wrap the lavender soap back in its paper and tuck it into my pocket. In the kitchen, the light is dusty on the pitcher of sweet tea. Mother pulled out the tea bags, wrung them, left them beside the pitcher on the counter. Red Rose bags browning there and drying out. All at once I bust them up with my lavender hands, crumble them onto my bare feet and the floor, I sprinkle tea crumbs on my head, tea leaves that grow the rose kangaroo, the tiny blue elephant—they can grow a tiny me too, tiny and pretty and simple and loved forever, a greenblue Frankie, wondrously small, a tiny hard figurine. No, still too large. I want to be the farthest bird, drawn there, barely a tick of pencil before the evening sun.

In a jar, drowsy heads of blue iris, but not on a summer porch. On the linoleum square pattern of my bathroom floor, blue iris against red in awful amounts. I woke to bathwater running. I tried to move.

"Easy," said Clarissa. "I think you hit your head on the tub. We'll get you to the doctor, but let's clean you up."

My inner acres of muscles hummed hot and cold. My palm to belly, I felt the cool tight drum, still cramping mildly. My mouth filmy, I coughed. The blood on the floor was thick and black. She unbuttoned my dress and unsleeved each heavy doll arm.

"It's okay," she said. "I need to get you up and in the tub." She propped me and heaved gently, I winced.

"My god," I said. "Clarissa."

"It's okay." She cried with no sound. She peeled off my soaked underwear, eased me down in the water with my bra on, then unhooked it. I looked like someone maimed. She soaked a rag in the bathwater, brought it soothing to my neck, my back. I shut my eyes.

She said, "I was bringing irises for Mave, I saw your truck."

Their terrible bright heads there in the jar on the floor. I was still bleeding. She washed my breasts and my face.

"It's okay," she said. Then: "You know, the painting prints Tess gives me never show women as they are." She shook her head slightly. "Naked women in baths who are never hairy. Ever notice that? Like pearls. They should paint us how we are." Hair around my nipples, down my belly to my matted nest obscured by red bathwater. I sobbed, dry and hard. "It's okay," she kept saying, stains down her white blouse.

"I didn't know I wanted a baby," I said, "but I did want it. I wanted her, but she didn't know."

"She knew."

"I'm cold."

Clarissa worked the rag from water to skin but soon the water was not water, so she pulled the plug and stood me up, wrapped me in old towels, the few left in the closet, my groin and thighs a low-frequency throb. She said she'd lay some garbage bags and blankets on the car seat and come right back, we'd go to the hospital.

I stood in the tub and watched the irises. I knew the baby would have been a girl on a bike finding her way, knowing me, understanding me, and studying the heavy heads of two irises, like two blue planets—one of blue glacial ice, one of blue flame, the hottest part—she would have known both the blue planets in me. My shut mouth. My cold blue lips pressed together. She would have explained me to myself. She would have had an ease in the world.

"She's gone," I said to Clarissa coming back with an old robe and a blanket from somewhere. "I'm cold, Clarissa." She wrapped me up. The water finished draining and left viscous ribbons around my feet, like paint.

"I HAVE THE RIGHT TO BEAR ARMS," Mave said.

I drove.

"Where'd that gun come from?" asked Nan. "Were you going to shoot me?"

"You always infringe," Mave said to me. "Lord over."

"Were we going to rob a place?" Nan studied the mirror, eye encircled in yellow. Some fierce dark still along her left eyebrow.

"Perforation," said Mave. "A little breathing help."

Nan knew what the gun was for, she was only trying to lighten the mood. I steadied on the road and watched the lines, a Jeep bumper, the blank median. I disregarded what state we were in, I pushed it from my mind, all sense of location and compass.

"It was only for protection," I said, "but Mave's bad news with a gun. One time she shot my cousin Belinda's dog in a fight with a groundhog. Took aim at the groundhog after it had already run off—it was a good hundred feet away from Brownie."

"That was a twelve gauge," Mave said. "Buckshot radiates out. It's like shrapnel. This was my Browning, very precise. And expensive."

"One time she made me turn my pet wild bird loose. I'd found it hit by a car, she deemed it rehabilitated, and a hawk got it. She shot the hawk. Thought I'd feel better."

"You did feel better."

"Once she shot a skunk under my house and the smell soaked into everything, all the rooms and curtains, all my clothes, in my hair. You could smell it on my skin. She made me bathe in tomato juice."

"God, you hold a grudge. I apologized for that."

"You never apologized for anything."

"It was rabid. That skunk." Mave watched the world zoom by. I wanted her to face me.

"You never apologized. You gave me prints of paintings torn from Ruth's books. For the skunk, you gave me a Klimt—Judith holding the head of Holofernes after she'd decapitated him. She wore that glamorous gold dog collar."

Mave didn't face me. No reply.

"Those gold moons on her unfastened coat. She had one boob sticking out."

She sucked extra air, talked at her window. "Judith's look is incredible. It's his best painting."

"Why couldn't you just talk to me?" I said.

Nothing. Nothing when there's something to really say. There can be acres of bitterness and sadness in one person, words lost to briers and quicksand. The truth is, Ruth, I knew she had saved me. She was my savior, she was my everything. Her boots stepping onto the porch were my heartbeat. But I did not believe she loved me. She'd used up all her love on you.

The Oldsmobile glided on, our indifferent vessel. We moved closer to what? Farther away from what else? I sped up, passed the Jeep, three others, a semi. We got closer to a place that was nothing we knew. That's all we cared about. The non-humid air, no denseness or swamp, dry wind through a screenless window, no fruit flies. I remembered then—we were in Tennessee with the skinny hot trees too much like ours. I wanted extreme siltstone and shale. I wanted the canyon—to body forth what was inside me in its craggy gash. And Mave? Mave imagined a gun's report against the canyon wall, and I couldn't bear it. I inhaled deeply and knew she could not do the same as she sat there drowning.

Abruptly I said, "We'll take a couple of days out here, see the desert sights, then get you home and back into treatment. That's what we're going to do." I rolled down my window to the interstate noise.

"Little Gypsy," Mave said to her window, "I was going to knock off a few convenience stores. Just petty stuff, when the money ran out."

I heard a rustle of pages. Nan had the atlas back there. She spoke too quietly to hear over the wind.

"What?" I said.

"You could talk to her now," she said, not to me. Yellow-hounded eyes looked to Mave, who stared resolutely out the window. "It's not like you don't have time. And the radio's broke." Nan studied me. "But you don't have all the time in the world, Crazy."

In her eyes, an acceptance I refused. She accepted the gun's intent, the purpose of this trip. I shook my head at her. I heard one heartbeat, two, one bootstep, two. I pressed on the gas and passed a stream of steel and color and tires and fumes.

"By the scale, looks like two hundred miles to Memphis," Nan said. "I've never been to Memphis."

I was sick of Tennessee, but Mave had asked for Memphis. She'd given me an article about Sun Studio before we'd left, another about the Lorraine Motel wreathed and memorialized for Dr. King. She was silent. She fiddled with the cotton ball and tube over her left ear.

Nan asked, "Did you know we're going to cross the Mississippi?"

"Wondrous," said Mave.

"Okay. Tell Frankie something you never told anyone else. The car is sacrosanct."

"My dress size?" said Mave.

Nan offered no retort, she was quiet, I was quiet. The car filled strangely with waiting. I didn't look at Mave but she held her small oxygen tank in my periphery, in front of her with both hands, as if about to address it. Only road wind for some long minutes, a brief flapping of ears from Ellis waking. I figured Mave would deflect, or fall asleep.

Then she said, "First time I saw the ocean was with this girl Evie. We were thirteen, and her mother took us. We loved the boardwalk and there was a shop crammed floor to ceiling with airbrushed T-shirts and flip-flops and license plate key chains. All kinds of dresses Evie tried on. I of course remained in my jean cutoffs, but she begged until I put on a white beach dress with thin straps and a bunchy skirt. I looked at myself and cracked up, but Evie didn't. The shopkeeper was a woman from Israel who had landed in Ocean City. Her accent was thick, she asked me, 'Are you afraid of looking like a woman?' I told her no and kept the dress on. Evie put a ribbon around my head—my hair was short, in a pageboy cut—the Israeli woman brushed rouge on my cheeks from the compact in her purse. I didn't believe that girl in the mirror was me until I waved and the reflection waved back."

I drove steady, keen. Had she told you this story, Ruth? Had she told you everything and thus had little left over for me, or had this been held back in reserve? My eyes stung, the road blurred.

"I took it all off and hopped the railing over to the sand and the water. Evie followed and bought watermelon from a vendor. She was wearing three boys' names on her forehead when she caught up with me. That game, you know, sticking seeds to your forehead and naming them for boys you might marry, though she wouldn't marry any of them, she married a different boy, in the Army, five years later. We stripped to swimsuits and waded into the Atlantic no farther than where we could touch, even though we were strong swimmers." Mave paused, breathed.

"You were afraid of sharks," said Nan, coaxing out the story.

"No. It was the bigness of it. What we knew was a swimming hole with a limestone shelf to swim to. Evie said, 'There's nothing to mark our turnaround out here, except the coast of Morocco.' We hid that we were scared mountain girls. We went in up to our chests, in our ugly pilled swimsuits, and dunked our heads. Then we went back to a quilt her mother had spread on the sand, where her mother was asleep. We pulled on our cutoffs that showed the wet at our crotches. We didn't towel off or anything and our hair dripped. When Evie spoke I kept seeing my rouged cheeks in the mirror. She stuck her hands in her wet back pockets, with her elbows out in chicken wings, and beyond her head I saw the day moon—I still see that as clearly as yesterday—and Evie threw her head back to laugh and there went everything. Her chest mounded under her green suit, her neck was so free, she was a flower on a curved stalk of green." Mave stopped again, sucked air, rubbed the label of the tank.

"Did you touch her?" asked Nan.

"No. But she was my first. I wanted to die. We went back to our houses in Caudell. The humid swamp air filled my room and folded me in, like a raisin in sweet bread. I suffocated all summer. I listened to records, I found Miranda's compact and put rouge on my cheeks in private, I read about marine life and mariners and Morocco. I saw Evie some but I couldn't tell her."

"You couldn't tell her you loved her." Nan's whisper.

"I remember our last day at the beach we looked for shells, but we could find only those dried-out horseshoe crabs with the spiky tails filed thin by stones. I wrapped one in a towel to keep. It stank up my room at home with dead seaweed smell. I would press the spike to my lips till it hurt."

"Did you know about Evie, Frankie?" Nan touched my shoulder, as if pressing a stamp on a letter.

"I never knew, no. She never told me that before." What could I do but give myself to it, Ruth? Hear the waves and smell the sea. I had been so small in the shelter of her, and now—now I knew her as small, and wanting. And what did I want right then? I wanted Mave's steel toes kicked off so she could put her feet in. I wanted to start everything over from the beginning.

"I could have kissed her and died," said Mave.

"I get that," said Nan. "Oh yeah." Nan's face dreamy and absorbed and sad.

Mave coughed, not harshly, adjusted the nostril fixture of the tubes of air. I heard the air—no, it was the interstate wind. She needed to replenish the air evacuated by talk. "This right here is a closed economy," she said to the tubing and put her head back. "I'm not going back, Frankie. You know that."

Mave shut her eyes. I drove. The weight of sorrow was delayed, it hovered then hit. Her gray cropped hair matted at her hot temple. This present, squarish body tall beside me all my life in men's shirts. Bootstep, bootstep. But it was a young girl's hand I reached for.

For the first time in our lives, I held Mave's hand.

THE ROTOTILLER, THE HOE, THE SMOOTH RED BEAN SEED. I bent from the waist for the bush bean hills and sweet corn. I squatted with minor pain to sew the carrots, like ashes, and the zinnias at the perimeter. My body held its miscarriage ache for two weeks, my groin throbbing. I had bled black for a few days, skin pallid. I slept in the afternoons in Clay's bed—Lottie and me, invalids in the afternoons. But before dawn, I put on the same cutoffs daily, with the folded painting print I never took out of the back pocket, and Clay's flannel, and drove to my house. Dark and dew burned off to white sky then the deep blue of late spring, the colors strong. There was Mave's house through the fencerow bushed up with wild rose, as if time had gone backward: she in her house, I in mine, linear time exposed as mere illusion. I lost hours in the garden, I bent, I squatted, until I got tired. Soon, the corn would shoot up, and I'd thin five stalks to three to give room for the stoutest. I'd stake the tomatoes and pull the suckers. The rest of May, all of June. Each dawn.

I lifted the five-gallon bucket to water pepper plants, the plastic handle worn down to its cutting wire. I pulled on leather work gloves and remembered when Mave had gloved me to keep me from scratching out my eyes. I didn't feel the wire, I felt the inner glove, my fingers feeling around like moles in burrows feeling with their faces. How it might have felt inside an udder dried of milk, each slack but toughened teat.

The blood browned and sometimes overflowed the pads. I went in for onion sets at Matlick Feed and saw the Ellafritz girls who nursed each other's boys, though the boys were nearly weaned now. Girls who moved like each other's shadows. Faces always made up, in clothes of teen boys or men, just like me, oversized T-shirts and their belts with a foot of surplus tongue. One of them was going with the towheaded clerk, I guessed. They swung a son up to their hip in a stream of motherspeak—hands off that, like I told you, come ere, come on, slap mama's leg one more time and I'll, stop that, come ere. Out in the truck, I saw a spot of blood on my seat. I lifted my flannel to see it blooming down the cutoffs' inseam.

Clay, for his part, mourned our child by turning mother. He took time off work. Each day, when I came back late morning covered in garden muck and sweat and stink, he had grilled cheese or fried bologna sandwiches waiting for me. He tended Lottie morning and afternoon without complaint. Conversation was beyond us both, but he started reading to me aloud at the table from the *Caudell Journal*, stories at random, and I would grow sleepy. Before climbing the stairs to nap unshowered, I could hear in my kitchen chair what he was saying between the lines of the county news. He was saying, *I wanted it to be a girl who looked like you but who would be easy to know and understand and love.*

One morning Clarissa brought me extra foil pie pans to string up around the garden at my house. She helped me punch the holes and string the baler's twine, then we sat in the grass and drank thermos coffee.

"How many days have you worn that flannel?" she said.

"All of them," I said.

She told me Tess was taking summer courses in Cleveland and her drawing class had a nude model, a man. Clarissa slid out a drawing from a large envelope. Tess had drawn him hairy, frontal, loose sacks hidden in fur. He was thin, or she'd drawn him thin, feminine in the face and tilt of head. Clarissa blushed with secretive awe. We squinted at the cock from the sun hitting the pans.

"Never saw one that beautiful," I said, and she laughed.

"Life drawing," she said, her fingertips padding the womanish face on the paper. "Darrell is sick," she said. "He's being a baby about it, I can't stay long."

"Did he see this?"

"What do you think?"

"Hey." I caught her hand. Some bruises at the wrist.

"It's fine."

"I thought that was over."

"It is over. He's sick, been having dizzy spells and it makes him mad at the world. He just made a mistake." Small hands always in her lap like small birds, they held the naked man gently in their beaks. "What about you?"

"What about me?"

"And Clay?"

"This is as far as I can get," waving my dirty palm in front of my face, as if in front of someone in a trance. "Right here, up close, and here in the garden. I don't much stray beyond the immediate." Stale metal-coffee taste. "My hands move on their own. Clay's been kind, taking care of things. Grieving in his own way, I guess."

"Try with him, Frankie. You're lucky he tries." Her hair pieced into her eye. She brushed it back, another bruise on that wrist, very blue.

I nudged up my body enough to pull the folded painting from my back pocket. I unfolded it. A page torn from your book of Georgia O'Keeffe prints. I showed her the cattle skull.

Clarissa understood. "Mave's sympathy card?"

It was *Ram's Head, Blue Morning Glory*. Obliterated nose bone but strong, sinuous horns intact. That morning glory floating like a star. I'd stared at it when Mave had brought it at night. A skull once draped with hide and studded with humanlike eyes. Neither Mave nor I had cried.

But the next night she came again to Clay's, a vagabond at the kitchen door, and found me in my nightgown at the stove. I wore one of Lottie's diapers then. She gave me another torn-out page. A photograph of O'Keeffe, her sun-browned hands holding a cow skull as if it were a baby.

"Did she even bleach it?" Mave asked. "All the maggots. Look how one finger slips into the jagged nether space of tooth."

No, not like a newborn, but like a lover's head. As if she could drink from it, drink all its fluids into the body, if there had been any to drink.

Mave said, "Everything she painted was dream and object at once. That is really the skull. That is really the bone mouth, but it's also something else. Later on, when she advanced and her abstract work got twisted by the interpreters who were supposed to be so well versed in paint, her message got garbled, she didn't like what they had to say. So, she stuck to the cow skull. Uninterpreted." Mave had rarely been in that neat kitchen. It made her look extra ragged and out of place.

I nodded, I bled, I sat at the table in the hard blue chair, but she kept standing, about to go.

"You, with the big life in you," she said, another attempt. I didn't know whether she was talking to the skull or the painter or me—or you, it seemed always she really addressed you—whether she was voicing O'Keefe or her own graying, unraveling self. She nodded, I nodded. It was two days after I'd miscarried and Clarissa had stayed with me in the hospital and Mave had lurked in the waiting room. Wouldn't sit down, Clarissa said.

That page with the photo I handed back to Mave. "You keep it," I said. "So we both have one."

I WROTE ON LOOSE LEAF IN THE EVENINGS. I wrote every feeling and flick of ear and bird purchase, blade of grass, blade of anything, and then, empty, kept writing nonsense, words like dry heaving. They might have been letters, to a dead you or to my dead former self or to my dead mother. Probably to you but it was babble, and I threw pages away as I wrote them. Over time, when I was able to sleep less, I spent the afternoons with Lottie. Clay went back to work part time, swapped hours so he could be with her all the mornings I was gone. Noon, I came in earthy, but I cleaned up and clocked in as caregiver as he clocked out and headed to the day's paving site. I wiped her mouth and sometimes sponge-bathed her, baked something, lotioned her purple feet. My favorite part was unfurling her hair as I'd always wanted to. It was thinned to cobwebs, so fine but still long. I brushed and rebraided it. She was in a place of gray whispering, difficult to hear. I took Murphy Oil Soap to every wood surface so the astringent clarifying fumes kept us both in this world. She held her braid and whispered. Ellis was offended by the fumes but trailed me anyway, always underfoot. When I remembered the baby bird he'd chomped that once, helpless in the grip of instinct, I shoved him away with my foot, not hard, his eyes watery in bafflement. It's okay, I said to him, but I needed a radius of air to cushion from his big mouth and wet nose and aliveness.

The doctor said it was Lottie's heart, but it was mostly the mysterious ailment of old age. I entered the kitchen with a cutting of the late leaf lettuce one day in early June, and Clay was flustered, said she didn't know him for a minute. Her face and eyes had gone blank. That night, he wanted to try again. Please. I said okay because his mother was dying, because he'd been so kind. My breasts were struck dumb but he gently worked them, like dough, and I vaguely realized that he had grown more experienced with me, less mechanical. The oak headboard was a stubborn thing I pressed my hands to, his fingers thick but not fumbling, I supine, and he finished with a cry I did not recognize as his. I could not read his grief, it was written in a tongue different from mine. But I knew I owed it to him to try, as Clarissa had said, to translate and interpret.

"I'm moving band practice back here," he said.

"Okay."

"In the basement, so we're not too loud."

"Okay."

He didn't want to leave me or Lottie to the mercy of evenings. The Good News Boys would set up between the deep freeze and washer and dryer. I could barely remember the former time, when I would have quickened at Stew's lanky body in the doorway.

Saturday, in the greening night-haze of June, they loaded in, the trucks in their usual tilted line at the road. Soon, the tsst tsst of the high hat. I sat at the kitchen table and put my ear to it, as if to a seashell to hear ocean. I could not lift my head. Ear suctioned to table, as if to a tomb wall for all the silence that drowned out the rhythm guitar. Tell me why, Dead Buried Ones in this tomb, I thought, with your arms crossed caging your heart, how have I slipped this far into my life and it is a stranger's life?

The phone rang. Clay wouldn't hear it and I would have to pick up. But I let it ring. Silence, then, a few minutes later, it rang again.

I knew before she started in that it was Belinda with her whiny injury voice turned on, the voice that says: Where have you been, why are you not witnessing my turned-upside-down life over here in Jack's ranch house with my new son, and also you're worrying me. I'd never told her about the baby that was and then wasn't. It's true I'd not seen her for a month, since her shower in the community center. She said last Sunday she and Jack picked up his great-aunt Virginia at Heartland Nursing Home in Monroeville to take her to church at the Crossing—they picked up new people each week, she said brightly. I knew Virginia from my childhood in the pews. Virginia was now their small powdery package to deliver, and Belinda said the aides had her nails painted red and her hair permed.

On the phone line, I heard the newborn's cry, like a rifle report.

She chattered on, my head full of gauze. She said on the drive back to Heartland, Virginia wept when she saw her old trailer and put her hand up to the car window. I knew that trailer. It sat near an access road and a culvert over Heather Run—it looked like a demolition derby car.

I said, "You should've taken Route 9 back instead, it probably killed her to have to see her empty place."

"That's the long way," Belinda said, "and Jack had golf on ESPN. Anyway, come see me. Come see Roger. I think he favors Daddy in the face."

We hung up. Somewhere in my chest, the specter of Virginia lodged—she still wept her ineffectual tears as she situated herself on her strange narrow nursing home bed, frayed and bony as a hungry rabbit. The gauze tore in me then, somewhere within my brain, I could barely feel it, but I felt it. Virginia who'd had her nails done. Why take her out of there when she would only have to feel the shock of internment again? I laid my head back down on the tabletop tomb wall, I listened again for silence, but a hand pried me up, each of its fingernails Revlon Red. I felt a pulse of strength in places grown foreign, in my mouth, in my groin.

My husband rhymed *Christ* in the cement-floor basement. Tell me, Virginia—I said in my skull—if I pass my decrepit home on a drive back to my one-day rabbit hole, will I weep out of longing for it?

THE DAY CLARISSA'S DARRELL DIED, the Army came for my cousin Ron, one of Rex and Miranda's twins. 1990. June. He'd quit the flagger job at the Division of Highways and enlisted, maybe because he was the slender, stuttering, brooding one, in the shadow of his brother Benji's bright athletic build and aptitude. Ron's duffle was packed, but when the recruiter pulled up, Ron locked himself in the bathroom. I was with Mave when Miranda called crying—Rex was not there, had left for Weston that morning for a load of fertilizer, having already said his goodbyes. Miranda had tried talking to Ron through the bathroom door. The recruiter was getting impatient.

"Fuckers," Mave said. We drove my truck over. "Napalmers, goddamn babies with guns," a string of pacifist froth. We pulled up as the recruiter took a stance on the porch as if he were commandeering the house, Ron's duffle beside him, and Miranda beside the duffle, curved and slight in sweatpants and a long T-shirt.

Mave said nothing. She gave a mocking salute, tromped across the porch in her heavy boots, and went inside. I got out but stood beside the truck. We all stood waiting. The primrose alert, the paint peeling on the house that had aged like Miranda, the geraniums top-heavy in antique milk-pail planters. I felt time, like a presence, taking things from us.

Out came Mave, Ron's arm around her shoulder as if wounded in war, feet draggy, all in army green and brown. Always a lean, unsure boy with feathered hair, now in a fresh buzz cut. They walked off the other side of the porch into the grass toward the pasture, toward the Guernseys all bearing stolid witness, soft strewn sentences from Mave's lips I couldn't hear. I felt a childish pang of jealousy. They disappeared before anybody spoke. The recruiter vouched for the caliber of his usual recruit, who had what it took. He left.

I didn't know where Mave was taking my cousin so adamantly, so tenderly, a boy she hardly knew, really, since Rex had always kept her at a safe distance from the kids. Miranda and I stood for a while in the strange wake of it, I by the truck and she on the porch, feeling in our bodies a helplessness. She sank to the porch steps. I joined her. She wasn't aware of the miscarriage, or maybe she was. Maybe Mave had told her.

"I don't know my boys anymore," she said. "I don't know why he ever enlisted. I'd expect Tuffie to enlist before him."

"Tuff's too wild for the military to handle."

Miranda smiled, smoothed her sweatpants as she would her usual pressed housedress. Her hair had not been combed; it seemed the recruiter had ambushed them. She asked after Lottie.

"Slipping," I answered. My hair felt heavy and I lifted it from my neck, and as naturally as anything, Miranda, shifting one step above mine, gathered my hair into her hands in a horse tail and kept gathering, which made me cry.

I asked, "Do you remember how Dillon wanted to enlist in the Air Force to fly jets but he didn't have the eyesight?"

"I do." She kept gathering—my hair so endlessly outspread and in need of gathering. Mave's tenderness toward the boy, Miranda's toward me, and Dillon's toward whomever. "You still think about him, Frankie?"

Oh—I thought his thoughts, I heard his fingers through my hair with hers, I felt the taut skin of his belly as I lay my ear on it under the branches on the banks of Heather Run.

"I just wonder about him sometimes."

Darrell died that evening in a deep gray dusk withholding rain.

His complaints of dizzy spells and blurred sight had turned out to be minor strokes preceding the final major one. He'd gone out to run the combine and hadn't returned for dinner. Clarissa found him in the little pilot car of the mammoth machine, followed its final crooked swath where he'd gone off course, his head down on the control board as if napping.

Clarissa held the wake at the house, in the old way. The living room stuffed with flower arrangements, the kitchen laden with casseroles and potato salad. Our friend Liza and her mother assigned potluck dishes, Liza practiced in widowhood.

Tess came home from summer classes. She had somehow fastened her ropy hair in a stylish pile atop her head under a scarf like Rayletta wore. She hovered near her mother like an older sister and held her hand. I watched their hands, and the other hands holding Dixie paper cups or a fork, or an elbow, or a blinking toy. I stood with Clay, whose one hand carried our assigned cornbread and whose other hand pressed the small of my back where the dress waist bunched, as if to say, Don't let me lose you in the crowd, people are being lost, people gone like pale streaks in the sky. I wore a mint-green dress. I carried a paint box that I'd found for Clarissa at Mave's. It had been yours, of course, Ruth, tucked into a closet with books that hadn't fit on her makeshift shelves, the font on each miniature paint bottle gold and antiquated, *ochre*, *cobalt*.

Mave was nowhere, perhaps still with Ron in his camouflage and Army-issued boots, bivouacked on the outskirts of town.

Would Clarissa design the plate of his headstone at LaFaber? She designed everyone else's. I wondered, after all the hardness from him, what she truly felt in her supple body about his pale-streak goneness. I remembered all the times she had come to me after a beating, her hair always falling in pieces across her face. Eventually we came around her with a restraining order, he repented, he would change, and he did, the bruises slight after that, but his drawled dark voice—Tess told me—held an invisible hand at Clarissa's throat. His demands swarmed her, pressed her, but she would not leave him. She made her tiny paintings on tiny dried gourd slabs in secret, she made toys from old beads, Tess gave her oil pastels and she closed her eyes and drew the contour of their alfalfa field under stormy sky, drew it blind, drew it by feel.

I watched Clarissa standing near his open casket, his hands folded on the chest of his light blue suit. Her womanhood was stark, her wifeliness. An insistent memory disrupted this vision of her: once, during a LaFaber League game, Clarissa had gone for a half-court shot right before the buzzer sounded. Too feminine to really feel the court and move with it, she always shot air balls, but that game I saw her wind up her whole body and spring load and heft the ball off the tips of her fingers with gruesome force. She missed wildly, but she actually overshot. The few seconds after, she stood disbelieving her own strength, still standing on the toes of her Hi Tops, her breasts springing lightly in the jersey and an O on her red lips.

Now a woman planted beside her dead husband, now the stream of faces and hands. Miranda, diminished but changed out of those sweats into a lavender dress, herded Belinda's two, held the third, the newborn boy, Roger, as Belinda spoke to Clarissa and Tess. Tuffie was there, in all black, Rayletta and Hope from the co-op with their husbands, Jennie without Stew, the large extended Tide family, and the Snyder's Crossing pastor, who was perhaps bothered that he had not been involved in the wake. I stood with Clay by the burgundy armchair and the lilies bursting from their vases on the floor like hands trying to grab a rope. I gradually moved away from him, into the receiving line, with the paint box.

You understand, Ruth, I was not quite myself. I was still hidden, in a way, still clawing out the gauze. Voices swelled mildly on the front porch, in greeting, someone not seen in a while. I couldn't discern the welcoming voices, or the welcomed. Only footsteps scraping and a shuffle of bodies. I watched the front screen door open.

He ducked in as if the door were low. He peeled off his ball cap from back to front in one quick, deferential motion, threaded his thick hair, black like mine. Sharp nose and narrow face like mine. Some beard, some crosshatch on the skin and redness, darker skin around his eyes. His old Army jacket, the full oncoming streak of him.

"Dillon," someone said and shook his hand and he smiled. Then others.

I stood near the casket, near the mute blue dead. Across the room Dillon smiled at someone else. He erupted through time, a spike punched through the gauze into the blank expanse of the days of my life as I lived it then. How many years? Twelve? Fifteen? He did not see me. My chest shrank in asthmatic constriction, my breaths shortened, and I touched all parts of the paint box which was unlidded, more like a paint tray with a handle in the center, like a shoe shine kit. I touched the jars of acrylic, ochre cobalt sienna goldenrod smoke, their names so touchable, Ruth. A slot on one side held two wood-handled horsehair brushes you had carefully used once or twice, which I had rinsed and softened. It was for Clarissa, but I set the paints at Darrell's feet inside the coffin, in a panic, and I weaved through the crowd with what breath I still had. Through the kitchen, out the door to the side yard where no bodies congregated.

From the glove box of my truck, I grabbed the paper bag always stowed there, put it to my mouth. The truck was blocked in. I stumbled toward the field, in out, in out, the wheeze not deep yet but frantic to find its tunnel to my lungs, in out, in out. Bugs rose to small storms, disturbed from their feeding by my legs and by the gale of loose mint dress when I ran, once I could breathe. I ran through Darrell's half-uncut alfalfa into the woods, into the swamp mallow and skunk cabbage—suffocating and too familiar, but I wanted it then—the marsh slopping black onto my shins and calves. The suck of the ground and slap of low leaves reduced me to girlhood.

Thicker into the woods the air went dense. I breathed into the bag again and closed my eyes. A thrush mourned, another answered incongruously with a trill of joy. I walked, eyes closed, letting branches snag my hair. I walked all the way to the spring source of Heather Run where the moss seeped. I calmed and believed I would walk back to Clarissa when I could, I was glad Tess was there, I would go back. She needed me. I did not go back, though. I knew where I was going. I walked to the Train Cave.

I'd always loved how you could feel more than see the cool outstretched limestone. The hush deepened into the ground, ancient and transgressive and moldy. Several yards in, I stood just shy of where the dark swallowed everything and let my eyes adjust. I heard the mutter of water. I breathed. Beer cans peeked into my settling vision, the foil of chip bags, crumpled blankets hiding condoms I didn't need to look for. The Train Cave where high school kids still drank and fucked. As I had once. I was the twenty-something aching for a Dillon absent even as he was inside me, then I was the adolescent, and then even younger, when Dillon and Clarissa and I had played cards as kids, packing in RC Cola and flashlights. Then—there in the cave like a hologram—the boy who tied a string in my thick hair, who salved and shared the solitary in me.

From the evening light washing through the cave mouth into the small anteroom, I made out a battery Coleman lantern someone had left behind. I turned it on and held it up, the shine dim. Tusks of stalactite, stalagmite, words I loved to say, rustle of bats, pools of the eternal wet. Lichen sleeved a flat rock, and I sat. A little cache of Coors right behind it, and animal-raided snacks, shreds of dollar-store bag. My dress and underwear instantly soaked through. I was cold.

I turned to the cave wall to scan the old graffiti. But the graffiti was not old. It looked new. I stood and touched it—not even dry. Bold colors like the ochre and cobalt in the paint box, brush painted, I guessed, not the feathery traces of aerosol.

I held up the faint Coleman to strange hoofed things. A tricolored sheep with a missing face. A rowboat unmanned and pretty. A woman, also faceless, arms reaching out in mid-movement, long hair a streak. Hollyhocks. Things that had taken time. And also suggestive, lewd pictures. A cock erect and blue. Another. Vulva and spread legs, breasts cupped by six multicolored hands. More flowers that grew more small splayed bodies. I held the lantern closer to the beautiful flesh, touched it again and, yes, the paint was new. Strange fecund bodies that did not stop or separate, their rivers would not dry, each limb a folded-back petal. No high school kid had done this. There was a tenderness, there was skill, and also sadness.

Only one face was painted, all the other bodies left faceless. The face painted red on a blue body with green hair. I couldn't say if it was sad or happy, but the eyes looked real as if seeking me out, as if living. How could I not think of your hieroglyphs, Ruth, your desert cave walls where bird and body and bread sounded out the story? I backed up to take in the whole of it, nearly a mural, the right-hand side ending in rushed sketches, the painter had had to go. It was baffling and it moved me to think of it wasted on darkness. I switched off the lantern.

"Ellis stinks," said Nan. "He needs a bath."

The light had shifted in the Tennessee sky, autumnal and slanting though it was barely noon. Vague cloud cover. It felt like Mave's dining room with its dusk of dead flies bowled in the light fixture. In the front seats of the Olds, Mave and I had settled back into our separate bodies. We didn't comment.

"Well, you don't have to cozy up with him," said Nan as if we'd defended the dog's clean-enough state.

I'd wanted the light to be opaque sometimes in that house. A blackout. The translucence was sometimes too hopeful and confusing, like her words caught in midsentence and about to mean something.

"We should go for a swim." Nan rustled the confiscated atlas. Crunch of pork rind, flip of pages. "Scoot." She shoved the offending hound, who whined. "Let's go for a swim, buddy. You're a garbage dump. You're a dirtbag. What highway are we on? Forty?"

"Look up pawn shops on the map," Mave said. "Guns and gold, those kinds of places."

I felt her eyes on me. My body balked with rightness but lost conviction. My limbs felt slack again, hands loose atop the wheel. We should have been farther than Tennessee by now and we would have been, had the plan held—to bask under the desert sky then beat it back to resume treatment, resume life. But now? Now the urgency had bled out, the direction gone fuzzy. I knew now she wouldn't make it all the way. We were cut loose and floating in the rusted tonnage of the car.

"We're close to a park with a blue splotch. Let's go swimming, Frankie. The exit might be coming up."

"We buy gold, we sell ammo, that kind of thing. Let's take that exit."

"Come on, please. It'll feel good."

"It's too cold," I said.

"No, it's not. It's called Natchez Trace State Park, coming up. The brown sign for it was back a bit. Maybe this exit then." Nan's voice was guiding and gentle.

"We've only been going an hour and a half," I said.

"Natchez Trace," Mave said. "Fine to kill Indians as long as you name a state park after them."

"It's a reservoir or a lake or something."

"You want to?" I asked Mave, who shrugged, said she could work on her tan, said she could hold silence for the tribe. Said, "I'm keener on Memphis."

"You don't even need a bathing suit." Nan poked her head between our seats, then sat back. "I have that bikini, but I'll skinny-dip in solidarity." She poked Ellis's head and thick body up between us with great effort. "Am I right? Like a garbage pit."

Ellis looked at me, sorry. Paw to my shoulder in general protest.

I exited and we wound around skinny roads looking for the blue splotch. It was only October cold, Nan explained, the water would be warmer than the air, and the lake would probably be empty this time of year so we could swim naked in private. I said not a chance.

We saw a sign for Cub Lake with an etched stick-swimmer beside the arrow. I turned in. The small sandy beach was indeed empty. A boat skidded on the surface a good distance out, gone in a moment into a cove, and then it was only us. Nan didn't wait and didn't leash Ellis as he spilled from the car behind her. He stopped short of the sand and she held out a pork rind, bait he snubbed. She took his collar and lugged him toward the water, his paws dug in and legs out straight. She dragged him with both hands, gathering his loose neck folds into an accordion. At the edge she eased, he sniffed the lapping water, drank, and headed back to the car.

"No, you don't—help me, Frankie!" Nan yelled, grabbing his collar again and slipping off her shoes. I pictured the goose flesh rising up her legs. She got Ellis in a headlock. She was in up to mid-calf.

"Semiotics of the body," Mave said, head cocked. She opened the car door, oxygen squeezed in armpit, got the leash from the backseat and carried it to the water's edge for Nan. They spoke, they wrangled Ellis, I couldn't hear them. The dead-fly shadowed light cracked to some real sun rays, shining as if upon them. Nan was so pretty in bare feet and new cheap dress with no bra, a slip of ease and skin and great bushy head. Mave stretched her stiff back. Ellis tested the water with his front paws and didn't pull away this time.

Then Mave removed the tubes, the plastic hooking around her ears, the cotton, the nostril fittings. Like a clump of cooked spaghetti in her palm. From her back pocket she pulled a napkin, probably from the motel lobby, unfolded it on the sand and lay her tubing and tank in a pile. Her back was to me, T-shirt tucked in, jeans, belt with mother of pearl buckle, boots. In one yank, she took off her shirt.

Mave's back so broad and pale, the flesh-colored compression bandage barely visible, barely not flesh by this time in her life. Light shone on Nan, and somehow shone out from Nan, her wild hair radiating, her face unbruising. My looking shifted—it was the kind of looking you do so you will remember. Any lingering urgency ebbed from the car and I got out, put my elbow up on the roof watching your Mave unwind the wrap so tenderly, as you might have done it, Ruth, and watching Nan waste no time, in one swift fling, off with her dress, her black panties, and into the water with Ellis, yelling and barking from the cold like a seal. Mave stripped jeans and men's briefs and took her time at the lake edge, allowing for this new variety of light to make her seeable, to let her body speak and mean the way words can't. The mysterious language of her lungs remained indecipherable, but I could read and hear the language of the rest of her, the way you hear better near a body of water.

She eased in, stiffened with the cold at first, as it neared her crotch, then she crouched and half-dove forward, an arc of flat butt, then gone. When her head surfaced above water she was facing me, all that wire-gray cropped hair swept back from her naked face. So rarely now did I see her plain face, no tubing, no deflection, no shadow, an open page.

Nan splashed the bobbing hound, stood up in the shallow, "See, it's not even deep, Frankie, come on," and the water reached her mid-thigh. Her breasts pointed their small bulk. I thought briefly of a longhorn skull, the womb shape memorialized in oils, but this one, superimposed on Nan, did not deteriorate down at the bone snout, but ended in a promising nest of wet hair. A long distinct scar just under Nan's ribs too, speaking. Other vague reddish tissue murmured across her taut belly.

I remember once entering Mave's house thinking she'd shot herself. I'd heard the shot go off closer to Clarissa and Darrell's, probably Darrell shooting groundhogs, but I had run to her house sure she'd finally done it. It was before Clay, it was evening, I still had the film of squash vines on my hands, I remember my skin itchy with it.

The dining room light was on, the dead flies ever hushing the light. I breathed as though I were standing in a closet of old coats. Your books bowed the boards that were all propped haphazardly and makeshift with bricks, as always, and the always-detritus raised alarm only because it was unshaped, it orbited around nothing—old papers and plastic bags and rotted philodendrons and rotted TV guides and a Halloween wolf mask that was a joke once and food uneaten. I choked with intense missing, not with a fresh grief, but one years old, dulled.

"In here—out soon," Mave had said from the bathroom. "That you, Frankie?" I remember leaving without answering her. I remember not wanting to see her body emerge in the midst of feelings so forceful.

At Cub Lake, grief solidified like a hard bone in my throat with that similar rockflint of missing, though she was right there before me, so nakedly there. Almost small and knowable in the water.

I left the keys on the seat and followed them. The sun was still warm and the dry coolness in the fall air didn't threaten. I unbuttoned my blouse, unhooked my bra, felt the air reach for me. I shed my jeans and underwear in a cotton pile next to the black lace peeking from under Nan's inside-out dress and winced from the water and they watched. The lake was clear, the sand and pebbles shifted under my feet. My skin opened, nipples hard, I considered tying back my hair but left it alone to soak slowly as I waded in.

"Not bad, right?" Nan like a child. "Look how funny Ellis swims."

Once I was in, he paddled cheerfully toward me, swam oddly, yes, with his back legs hanging, using only his front.

"Look at his legs limp like his dick," Nan said, her fondness for him evident. "Little useless thing."

He was more spry and alive in the lake, gulping the water into his black mouth at intervals. My nearness gave him leave to take off swimming for the center of the lake and I swam out to steer him back. He hugged over to the shallows, then, in the cattails, and stirred the mud. I rolled to my back, my hair spread into a heavy fan. I rose and watched Mave near me. She went under, came up eyes closed and skin smoothed. I had never before seen her fully naked.

"Why nobody after Ruth?" Nan asked. "You weren't old." She was closer to both of us suddenly, treading water, the roots of her hair a darker color unnoticeable when the webbed curly mass was dry. She had gone from stowaway to navigator. She had taken on the role of soother, too, soothsayer, truth-seeker. "Why didn't you move on? Sleep with some other woman?"

I had never dared ask Mave that. I watched Ellis panic-paddle toward a water bird that flitted from the weeds.

"There was no after Ruth," said Mave. Shut her eyes, sank under, bubbles rose above her face and she stayed under longer.

Nan was silent. I was silent, ears under water.

Mave's face emerged. She wiped lake from her eyes, started moving for the shallows and her body rose from the water like a creature out of the bog, sun remaking the skin as it oxidized. The broad shoulders, the indentations of the wrap, the small of her back.

"Why?" Nan asked.

"Because," said Mave toward the shore where Ellis was now shaking off, "if you study my geologic strata, split the stone, you find all the rich ores there, in only that Ruth layer."

The admission hurt me—that the dead dull years were her and me, and she saw no richness there, but I didn't say anything. I knew that's how it was for me and my rock layer of Dillon. Still. Ellis rolled in the sand, probably in the remains of old fish.

"You all swim on. I'll sunbathe upon the lakeshore. Need my metal lung." She was fully formed and bright on the sand, breasts purpled and wrung. She reinstalled nostril and ear fittings and dressed, and she stood a few beats letting the tanked air do its work. But Nan wasn't satisfied.

"Why?" she asked again. "You can't just seal up and quit your life."

"Leave it, Nan," I said.

"She told me the same thing, Little Gypsy." Mave sat in the sand, knees up to pull on her socks and boots. "When Ruth was dying, I brought her home to Aldrich Street and set up her bed downstairs in a room we left empty except for this elaborate tapestry hanging and a record player on the floor. She used to dance around in that room in private because of her limp. She was vain, you know. When I carried her from the car to the hospital bed, she was weightless, just bone and wing. She was a wisp, my mighty Ruth. But not her voice—her voice was still that bold full sound I'd first heard in a lecture hall, and she lectured me still. She said, 'Bury me like the pharaohs with all my jewels and favorite foods and flowers for the next world, and you move on. You stay out of the tomb.' I said okay and put on a Sarah Vaughan record. I had to be careful because the pain was in her back and neck mostly, but she was so light, I picked her up like you do a kid—well, maybe like you do a kid, I wouldn't know—and danced with her all wrapped in these rough Bedouin blankets she loved, without her feet touching the floor." Mave stood again. "A lot of days, Nannette, I can feel that scratchy blanket on my cheek still. I feel us in a slow spin. Barely moving." She walked toward the car as Nan and I treaded water.

A red pickup turned into the gravel lot with a crunch, pulled up next to the Oldsmobile near Mave and the hound, who had trotted over and now sat back on his haunches. A man got out and scanned the sand where our sloughed clothes lay piled. He and Mave spoke but I couldn't hear them.

"Shit," said Nan, "wish he was cuter." An attempt to ease the sadness that surrounded our naked selves as completely as lake water.

He was older than Mave and dumpy in his fishing hat. He pulled at its brim several times as though a wind were trying to take it. He remained about ten feet from her, shook his head, looked out at us. Nan waved and I couldn't help but smile at the situation. He got back in the truck and took off and Mave turned toward us, clearly amused, her body so square yet gaunt at the neck.

Nan and I quickly got out, Nan making herself laugh, and we rummaged in the trunk for T-shirts to dry off with before someone else could show up.

"What did you say to him?" Nan asked Mave, who was drying her head as if it itched.

"I asked him if he had a gun. Said I'd trade him the dog, but he said no, then I said I'd trade you, Gypsy."

"Oh, fuck off, Crazy," still laughing and glad for the banter.

"He gave it good consideration."

"No doubt he did."

Dressed, my raw skin stung with clarity and freshness. I started the car and tried to figure out the heater for the first time until I saw the heater had gone the way of the radio. They got in but Ellis had wandered off lakeside again, vigorous in his rolling around, grainy with sand now and happy like a pup. "Come on, Flop," I said out my window. He grudged up and left behind what was, in fact, a fish skeleton knotted with weeds.

"In you go, boy," said Mave. "Let's head to Memphis." He steadied then accomplished his practiced jump into the backseat, immediately going for Nan's lap.

"Oh god, he smells worse than before!" she said. "Get off! God."

We kept the windows down, freezing, and Mave moved her head out into the air current and her short hair dried pressed back like that, so her face looked like it was just breaking the surface of the water.

Two days after Darrell's burial, Clarissa and I crossed the Ohio River in my pickup, her body nervous, as if it were her first transatlantic. She lifted her feet as we hit the bridge, canvas shoes, her best jumper ending just above her ankle socks. I should have dressed in better than jeans, but I'd scrubbed all Lottie's floors, thorough and long, steadying. I still smelled of Murphy Oil. Tess had left the very day of the burial to prepare her first art show in Cleveland, and she'd asked me to bring Clarissa for the opening.

What we did not say in the truck cab: *Dillon is back. Who will design the LaFaber plate for Darrell's marker? Who are we, really, anymore?* I remembered the bronze plate she'd brought me one day, with a lily of the valley etched on it, and the date, for my dead child's nonexistent grave.

What Clarissa did say, once her feet settled onto the floor mat again: "Want some zucchini bread?" Unfolding the Saran Wrap. "I put black walnuts in it." I took a chunk. "I never put black walnuts in his quick breads," she said. "They overpower, like licorice, he never liked them."

The building in Cleveland to which Tess had written us directions was squat and cylindrical and stylish in the evening light, simple on the outside, and, inside, air conditioned and elegant. The small gallery space sat just inside the door, to the left. Spotlights angled toward the center and shone on the walls. Tess sat in the middle of a crowd on a tall stool, hands in her lap like her mom, but Tess's was a lap of military pants with a cowboy belt. A red handkerchief held up and out her ropy dreaded hair, and a black tank top exposed more than she ever exposed at home: a tattoo as pretty insect crawling above her heart.

She would have impressed you, Ruth. Me, on the other hand, in my Murphy Oil drench and jeans—I don't know. I like to think you'd have glimpsed some kind of life inside the life, whatever you had seen in my letters at one time.

Clarissa hovered near the door. Someone asked Tess something and she answered and those folded hands flapped with a sureness as she spoke. Clarissa had a clutch of jumper in one hand, stood very still. Barrettes held back her pieced horse-mane hair on each side. People soon noticed us, and then so did Tess.

Clarissa looked elsewhere from her girl to the art hanging on the walls. There were charcoal drawings first, and it was clear to me they were drawings of Clarissa. Some others were red pastel and, in some, I could hardly make her out, but she was there, even in abstract, one in blue ink with a gold streak like a scar of light, some mixed media, according to the card beside the frame—gelatin print, bone, paper, gouache, collage with an old photo of Clarissa painting her gourds on a backyard table I knew very well—I'd found her the plywood at Rex's to put up on sawhorses. The bone crushed and sprinkled onto glue like road-dirty snow. A tiny bit of lace at the edge. I didn't know the right words for this. One was a field, with a flowing section of Heather Run—I somehow knew it was Heather Run and its laurel and moss, appearing clipped from the marsh like a lock of hair, and even this was Clarissa portrayed. It was her body, blue and black and lace.

"Gouache." I said the word quietly, but Clarissa heard me. She said nothing. A speechless widow in her best jumper.

"I want to talk about my body of work," Tess said. All faces in the room rearranged themselves in her direction. A man in a dark jacket, older, probably her teacher, put a hand on her back as though he were going to first introduce her, but she stood and gave him her stool and she started speaking from the oak of herself, discussing each method and medium, needing no introduction to the world except the one she got when she slipped out of Clarissa. I want to talk about my body of work, she said, and she did. It was a body you could handle and bathe and sniff up and down, in its creases, a body to nurse and nurse from, a body you soap up and take a bed pan out from under and hurt and heal and salvage and raise up. I could make out other bodies then, in the strokes of gouache—could summon Lottie, could summon you, Ruth, the limpidness of Clay, the shock of Dillon, could summon the living and the never-got-to-live. She said all this without saying it that way. The man in the jacket, all the women and men, nodded and admired. I was in awe of her.

Clarissa's face so hot and so unbruised and so seen. Tess crossed the gallery and kissed her.

After an hour or so, when we left to drive back across the Ohio, with the dash lit like the city at night, it started to rain. We would get home late. I thought how, despite the time of night, I would pour new Murphy Oil and new hot water and do the boards tongued and grooved in my own house. I wanted to do that and nothing else, to arch over those boards and think about the bone-lace evocation of my friend's body and all bodies. And I knew, too, that, newly alone and afloat in her house, Clarissa would get out the paint box I'd given her, the ochre and the horsehair brushes, and clear the dining room table because at last she could take up all the space she wanted. I pictured her in the New Mexico light in O'Keeffe's roofless room, the box of parsley, the still life skulls and hollyhock, the vision of feeling coming out in oils. The rain dousing the canvas so the colors clarified.

As if seeing what I saw, knowing what I knew, she said, "I think I do my best work when it rains."

In the morning, I brought Mave a bud in a vase and a sprig of sumac. I told her about the art show.

"You smell like the janitor you used to be." She studied the vase I'd set on the TV tray. Bathrobe over a dirty white V-neck, unlaced boots. She said, "A bud cannot be forced but will give, in time, and will be the color you did not expect."

"I've befriended the paper bag again."

"I heard who showed up for Darrell's wake."

"Miranda tell you?"

"Is it reasonable to mourn yourself before you're dead?"

"It's not even ten," I said. "How much have you had?"

"How much is left, you mean. Enough for a quarter pint each." Mave touched the sumac as if it were poisonous. "You pour."

"No."

"Then light up so I can get a whiff," she said.

"Miranda told me Dillon's dropping gypsy moth spray around here. I didn't even see the webbing in the trees, but if you look around."

Mave carefully moved a few books that were open to black-and-white photos of ornate buildings onto a book pile already started on the floor and gestured that I sit in the chair covered in peeling contact paper.

"Miranda said he's married," I said. I did not sit. "They're staying at his grandmother's. It's been so many years. He could have written. Or called."

We both stood among the ruins of her dining room until she went to the kitchen for what beer was left. She would drink the half pint herself.

THEN LOTTIE. Only a couple of months later, in late August, she was part of what became our thick fog of funerals. Right after Tess's art show, I had handled Lottie with greater care and focus, absorbing myself with her, partly hiding from Dillon, but that wasn't all of it. I felt her lean against me when I helped her walk. She would lay her head on me when I escorted her to the toilet, press into my neck just above my shoulder joint. I somehow pictured clearly the joint free of skin tissue and cartilage, saw both of us as bones, brief and calm, until I'd lower her to the commode and hold up her nightgown for her and we'd both fully flesh out again at the sound of her peeing.

She died when I wasn't there, only a few minutes before I walked into the house. The kitchen was still, sealed, one of the blue chairs overturned. I righted the chair and pulled old bananas from the freezer to thaw for bread. I saw Ellis stretched into a heap near his bowl full of uneaten food. Then I went to her room. The aide shuttered Lottie's eyes as I entered, and Clay, sitting bedside, held his hand out and up on the bed, a hand useless and unencumbered. Since Lottie had needed twenty-four-hour care, Clay had hired Home Health to help us at the end.

I felt intensely in that room that I did not belong, not without Lottie's presence. Not without the wifeliness and tenderness that she enabled in me toward him. But I went to Clay and took his aimless hand and he cried. I held his back, strong and soft. Lottie's long gray braid did not lie across her chest but out to the right, shooting off like a horse tail when a horse runs. I did not remember where I'd been before entering the house, perhaps just outside to get some air. A numbness spread to my body so that I held Clay more tightly.

"Thank you, Anne," he said as I held him. The aide named Anne continued her ministrations, crisscrossed Lottie's hands on her chest with a kindness that must be innate to those who routinely handle the dying and the dead.

"Thank you," I echoed. I longed to be as kind as she was.

Clay wept silently, trembling, making one coarse noise at an intake of breath. He turned his face into my standing body and wept into my belly, pressing in. Anne's seahorse scrubs were simple and her clean ponytail made me look feral, my hair unwashed and unfastened and my clothes not clean but smelling of cleaning chemical, but he breathed in whatever scent I had on me. "It's okay," I said. Anne left the room. Clay reached his hands under my shirt and placed them on either side of my bare stomach, the way you make a tent for your eyes looking into a window, but his face stayed outside the jersey fabric. My T-shirt dampened.

Time unfixed itself. I watched Lottie's familiar head become a skull. I wanted to rewrite our story from the beginning as something different, something dense with love, and it seemed to me terrifying and also liberating, the idea of making it up from scratch on an unlined tablet. I pulled my hair back from my face then let it fall toward him. My neck lowered, and I held his head.

At the funeral, which Clay wanted to be at the Crossing, within its nondescript white-paneled walls and with all its window light washing out the storied pictures of Christ, I fixated on the possibility of kindness in me, like someone witching for water. Aquifer beneath the shale. Clay and the Good News Boys played beautiful old hymns. Dillon did not come and I had not seen him, so I both hoped and dreaded that maybe he had loaded all his emptied canisters of killing spray and taken his rumored wife and gone.

After the service, Ray touched my arm. Could we have a co-op gathering the next week, at the start of September, she asked, would that help? Yes, I said, and touched my high-neck dress, my long-sleeved dress, a dress that did not fit. I had bush beans and a good carrot crop I could trade, I told her. She said she would host but I said no, I wanted to prepare my old cavernous house to have something to do. Ray didn't protest. She understood that I was now an untethered caregiver.

I stood near Lottie's casket. Clay was no longer singing hymns, and I didn't know where he was. I saw she wore blue as Darrell had worn blue, as the irises near the tub where I'd bled out had been blue—and my bronchial chamber, so often restricted, rent itself, like a pressure valve opening and stuttering steam, or like a deep, simple breath. I took a deep breath. I very naturally reached behind me seeking Clay's hand and found it. My eyes were wet, my mind softened. It was no drilled well to an aquifer, but it was something.

Mave said she'd bring Jameson and some decoy ducks she'd mail-ordered. But when cars drove up to my house at six, Mave didn't show and her lights were off and I knew she wasn't coming. What I didn't know was that pains in her chest had put her in bed early and convinced her she'd be there long enough to need a stack of books and her TV unplugged and moved, with great effort, to her bedroom. Neither of us knew, in this confluence of deaths and eruptions, what pale-headed cells had long been forming in the secret of her lungs.

Gathered goods were plentiful in early September. Belinda brought her new son to suck under a nursing shield with smiling starfish printed on it. Liza and Clarissa and Hope were there, Delores and Tuffie came late—Tuffie was more often than not high on something those days, looking haggard. Rayletta with buns and pulled pork in a crock pot. Clarissa wore a green scarf, pretty at her neck. The room had a color of life and warmth.

Ray took a beer from Tuffie's usual offering and brought up Jesus. She said some African women saw Christ as the good mother, with his hands in the sick bed. "God was a mother like them," she said. "Jesus fluttered like an old granny. And cried out like one, and maybe he'd carried water jugs like one. Would you all believe in a woman God?"

"I think it makes sense," said Hope, "but you'll never get it passed."

"What—like a bill in the Senate?"

"I just mean it's too dangerous an idea."

"For who?"

Belinda said, "Too weird." Rearranged her baby under his stars.

"For men," said Liza.

"Maybe Mave would take to a woman God," Ray said to me, and I laughed and said I planned to propose it the next morning. I would take her sobering coffee and revel with her in blasphemy.

The forward-looking thought, the hopeful idea of the next morning walking under the black walnut trees, through the overgrown break in the fence, took me in hand, a great big holding hand. It held up my accumulated years of life next to the life I lived in the present, as though I might be able, now, to continue. I could make this work with Clay. I could start again. Up through the fog that had settled on me for how long now, how many weeks or months, a pulse sounded, or a foghorn even. I laughed with real lightness. So brief.

Then—the irreversible moment when the meat turns and the maggots hatch and the bone snaps in two.

Headlights traveled the bare mantel through the window, then extinguished. Everyone was already present, except Mave, but she wouldn't drive over, she'd walk, or stumble, in her unlaced steel toes. I stood and handed the strung-out Tuffie my half-empty Coors; I threaded back my hair so I could see into the kitchen, through the screen door to the black gravel dark beyond it. A figure formed itself on the porch. I'd forgotten to turn on the porch light, so it formed from the subtler light of the kitchen. A woman with huge hair stood with a hand at her belly.

"Is this the get-together?" the woman called into the kitchen, and in she came, her dress straining with its freight. Her Army jacket too big. Onto the table she spilled the beet crop that I'd worried was a dead baby.

"My god," I said at her dress.

"Thought maybe I could join you all?" she said. "I have these to trade." She told me her name. That looseness in her stance, in her legs, in her joints, so sultry. The combination of her radiating sexy youth and the beet stains on her hands and up her arms immediately called to mind the paintings I'd seen that day of Darrell's wake. I somehow knew she had painted the walls of the Train Cave, which I'd told no one about. The bright violent orgy of lines, bodies, rivers I had thought stunning. How? How could that be? "I heard there was a get-together." And I knew, of course, though she did not tell me, that she was Dillon's wife. "Looks like you got beer?"

Belinda and her nursing boy appeared beside me, Clarissa in the lovely scarf. They didn't know who Nan was, and Clarissa said, "Sure, come on in. Those beets are huge, gosh. I'm Clarissa, this is Belinda and little Roger, and this is Frankie."

Nan locked her gaze on me, drank me in, my heavy hanging hair, my old jeans, my mouth shut tight hiding a black-coated throat. That brief, fragile lightness I'd felt all dissipated as this woman sucked me back down. How had she heard of the co-op, from whom had she stolen the beets, how had her hands painted the limestone so beautifully and strangely? I said nothing as Clarissa and Belinda reentered the living room and Nan took steps to follow. I looked at her as though in her dress she had in fact hauled in a dead thing. She came close, a couple of feet from me; she smelled of paint thinner or diesel or something aerosol.

"So you're Frankie," she said quietly. "You're the one." Her gaze was open, and that starved look marked her even then as she measured me against any and all of the stories Dillon had told her. And what had he said? Who had he told her I was? His second self? His shadow?

In my thick jealousy, I dismissed her hunger pangs, and the question of her, and simply watched her snake-body walk into the living room with the others, where God was a woman keening and healing the sick, drawing up water from the well to carry, the deepest water, the deepest well.

"What's the worst thing you ever did?" Nan remained enamored with truth-telling in the car. She had erected a boundary of bag and floormat between her and Ellis. "And what's the best thing?"

"Nannette," said Mave, "you are a veritable font. Sometimes quiet is welcome." She looked tired from the lake detour and the over-spilling of truth, and, by her voice, I could tell she'd taken some codeine.

"And what if it's the same thing?" said Nan. "Like someone says, who do you hate the most and who do you love the most, and often it's the same person. I think that's often true."

"Are we sure this radio doesn't work?" Mave twisted the knobs.

"For me it's one and the same. The worst and the best. Have you ever been in an abortion clinic? There's no windows. And there's a machine sucking sound you don't get out of your head." Her voice was steady and intent on its mission to get everything out. Looking at her young face in the rearview, I even admired her for taking on this mantle. Mave moved her hands over the radio in hocus pocus, willing it fixed.

"They suck you clean. But if I hadn't? What then? I had no way to feed myself. My kid would have ended up like me." Up came Nan's head between the seats facing Mave. "Scared to live." Nan receded like ocean. "I did it out of love, but it was the worst thing I ever did." She was quiet and then there was only road hum, since neither Mave nor I responded in kind. The discount store tractor trailer we passed treaded out its brief roar. "She knows it was love," Nan said. "Or he. Wherever my kid is."

In a few miles, at a gas station outside of Memphis, Mave needed the bathroom. Nan and I stayed in the car as Mave assembled her network and got out. She looked at me through the window rolled halfway down, said, "I was just thinking, you should make sure everything is dated in the book. People will wonder who said what when. And with what inflection—inflection is everything. That will be the hard part. I need to take a shit so don't worry if I'm in there awhile. You can leave that out of the book. Up to you though." She headed for the station glow.

"What book is she talking about?" said Nan. "Are you really writing a book?"

"It's just our joke. There's no book."

Some silence then, and Nan forgot the quarantine and I heard her scratch Ellis's ears and his groan of gladness. Then she said, "I bet you could write one. You're smart, you're always thinking. You're lucky to have a crazy aunt like her, just to push your mind."

"Maybe," I said. "Push me to the brink."

"We were World Wide Church of God growing up. My mom died when I was fourteen, not sure what from, probably appendicitis. I lived on with my dad and my sister for a while in Virginia. He didn't let Mom go to the hospital. And he had a fear of snow. He was a wacko—the bad kind. Wouldn't let us drive or cut our hair, never let me date. Never raised his voice, but mean. He abandoned us once because Mom borrowed money for a car she couldn't drive but wanted anyway, and borrowing was unbiblical. But he came back. He was into vitamin therapies, natural food, making your own yogurt. I didn't leave till I was seventeen. My sister took after him. I don't know if they're alive or dead. Maybe leaving home was my worst thing. Or could have been my best. Weird, right? How you can't tell sometimes?"

"I don't think my worst is my best." I thought about marrying Clay, my gray slate of heart. "You never heard from him? Your dad?"

"No. I sent him a postcard once, around his birthday. But he didn't celebrate birthdays."

"Where did you learn to draw and paint like you do?"

"Oh, it's nothing really. Fooling around."

"No, I've seen it, Nan. Some of the sketches you hide. And remember the painting you did in the cave in the summer, when you first came to Caudell? We always called it the Train Cave."

She wrinkled her brow, touched her hair. "I never knew you saw that."

"I never told anyone. I thought it was beautiful. I remember the full colors and the sure strokes of thick paint forming the bodies. You'd left your lantern there."

"I never knew you saw that," she repeated, shaking her head in disbelief.

"That cave was the first place Dillon and I made love. In our twenties." Then quiet again, both of us too exposed now.

After a while, Nan said, "Sometimes it felt like you were the one he still wanted."

Too much for me, too slippery, that notion. I could not find purchase on it.

"I'm sorry he's..." The words wouldn't leave my throat. I gestured to her eye, the skin clearing. "He wasn't always like that. I wish you'd known him as a boy." The talkative Nan only looked out at the Shell sign. "Want to see something?"

She said sure. I reached into my back pocket and pulled out the Georgia O'Keeffe I still had, after all this time, the page folded in fourths, the ram skull with morning glory torn from your book and handed to me in condolence, the way someone would tear from a loaf of bread and give it out.

Nan looked at it awhile. It was tattered from riding so long in a back pocket. "O'Keeffe," she said. "So horrifying and beautiful at the same time."

I told her how O'Keeffe came to love the desert, how she met it first in the panhandle of Texas when she would hop a hay wagon to get to Palo Duro Canyon and paint the light on the red rocks, or paint the feeling the light pulled out of her chest. My voice sounded like Mave's.

"Where is that canyon?" Nan asked. "We go through the top bit of Texas, I think." She flipped the road atlas pages.

"Near Amarillo."

She found it with the index. "Yeah, we go through Amarillo on the way to New Mexico. Forty runs right through it. We should go there, to Palo Duro."

"Mave probably can't."

"Mave would want to." She leaned up closer to my seat, propping her head on the back of the empty passenger side. Looking at me as if to say, You're going to have to be honest with yourself about what Mave wants.

"It feels strange, doesn't it?" I said. "Just driving west."

"But it feels good." She smiled. Her lovely young face. Her bared woundedness.

When Mave had talked about heading to the desert, after the first and last round of chemo, she'd said we would make mats and baskets from bear grass, or stick dolls from cholla cactus, and sell them for food. I'd said we'd visit the chapel at Chimayó where there's a hole of healing dirt. We could reach into the hole where the reputed crucifix had been found in the desert sand. I'd heard there was a whole room of canes abandoned by the healed. She said, "Sure—mix it as a mud salve on my chest like Vicks VapoRub. Voilà."

I told Nan, there in the Shell parking lot, "It feels like we're fugitives running from our own lives."

"She would like Palo Duro," Nan said.

I'd wanted to bring the dying Mave out to the desert, but then what, Ruth? On the paths studded with claret cup cactus, the prickly pear the bears can eat with their tough tongues and rough mouths, what then?

I did want to take her to the canyon. But we were in Memphis. Or just east of it.

Mave headed back toward us carrying a large obnoxious soda and more pork rinds, mini powdered donuts already snowing up her mouth.

In late afternoon on Sunday, the famous Beale Street was of course dead, signs gaudy and blank. Not much traffic, no one walking around. The building façades were sad.

"I've been looking forward to Memphis," was all Mave said.

We found the Lorraine Motel on Mulberry, saw the white wreath on the door of the room where Martin Luther King Jr. had been shot by a sniper from a window across the street. A new Civil Rights Museum had just broken ground and the sign said it would open next year, so we sat mournful in the car, gazing up at the closed pale green door. Then we looked for Sun Studio but couldn't find it. Johnny Cash, B.B. King, Rosco Gordon, all the people Sam Phillips pioneered. Records she'd pulled out at home even though she had no record player and had, I guess, decided not to take the one from Aldrich Street on which she'd played Sarah Vaughan and danced with you as you were disappearing.

"We can stay till something opens," I said.

"Doesn't matter, it's a tourist attraction now anyway. Shadow of its heyday." Mave took a long suck of cola. "Let's go. I'm done with Tennessee. What I want is the wide plains and the New Mexico sky."

Maybe it was never Memphis but the Mississippi River that we'd wanted to mark. Before we crossed the Mississippi, I pulled over and we got out to look at it. None of us had ever crossed it, had ever gone this far west. It would be new territory hereafter. We carelessly left Ellis off leash, but he sat somber, gnawing a secret piece of trash. I poured some water into his Country Crock water bowl.

"God, it looks like the ocean," Nan whispered.

"Not really," said Mave. She watched a barge a long way out, scanned the vast river up and down. "But jump in, you'll end up in the bayou."

"Bye-you. I like that word." Nan kept at a reverent whisper.

So now? Now we would head to points further west, into Arkansas, into Oklahoma. We could have turned back. This could have been far enough.

Mave sat down cross-legged on the grass, as if to say, Yeah, far enough. Unwound her tubing and looked at the great river barefaced. A few trucks passed on the freeway and blew our hair around. I sat too, couldn't help but breathe deeply when I heard her shallow breaths. It was a reflex I felt guilty for. I hugged my knees and tried to constrict my airways. I knew the asthmatic constriction well, but I tried to feel her brand of it. I tightened my chest. She would think this stupid. She had said razors scraped within her chest, she had said it was like tar spreading, she had said lungs could turn hateful.

I let out a gasp and inhaled after several long seconds.

"Jump in, you can feel everybody's pain," said Mave. "People throw it in there with their old boots and rubbers." As if she knew I was outside her pain trying to get in. And as if she knew pain was the old story and everybody would get their chapter, some long, some short. Nan was over there thinking of her crackpot father, her dead babies, her mother with the split side, her Dillon gone bad, her faceless paintings seeking a face. The wide river bore its mud along and I conjured my own mother's dying, my father's, my and Clay's child all tissue and cells, my version of Dillon on the night he left—a version I knew was long gone, replaced by a man I did not long for.

Once, Mave had said she understood what it felt like, when Dillon left. She had lost you, Ruth—she drew on the loss of you. Stood in the doorway aloof but near, trying her best, shifting her gaze around.

"Yeah?"

"Yeah," she said. "It feels like when Rex is having a lambing."

"Feels like that on the inside," I said.

"Positioned backwards with the legs all tucked." She stayed in the doorway, obligated. "That's how they come out breech. Hurts like hell."

THE URGENT IDEA OF STEEL WOOL got me out of bed at four a.m. Tank top, underwear, the house a dark meat locker. This was a few mornings after Nan had crashed the September co-op and had pulled me back underground. I took steel wool to all Lottie's copper-bottom pots and pans. It was cool but I didn't fully dress. Clay still slept. He slept in on Saturdays. A lingering scent of skunk infused the dew. Out the kitchen window, I knew the poplar leaves were starting to yellow, and I imagined shivering birds in need of stouter plumage for the coming months. I scrubbed my hands into a heat.

It must have been around seven when my cousin Tuffie knocked on the kitchen's screen door frame and stared at me.

"You forget to get dressed? It's chilly, you know. It's like autumn."

"Are you strung out, Tuff?"

"A little. I'm on an errand for Mom. She sent me with a half bushel of Romney peaches and some wine saps for you to can."

"You look like death with that eyeliner."

"You look like hell too. Mom's got her hands full with Belinda."

"What's wrong with Belinda?"

"She says Dillon's new wife was flirting with Jack at the Shop 'n Save yesterday."

"Nan? Does Dillon know?"

"How should I know? But I'm guessing it's not the first time. Come help me carry."

I entered Lottie's old room, where the clothes hamper overflowed. The metal rail on the bed useless and bright. I pulled dirty jeans from the hamper and a so-so long john shirt. I walked with Tuffie to her landfill car. I carried the crate of peaches and Tuffie hefted the apples on her bony hip. She was eight years younger than I, still no chest at twenty-eight, a filthy mouth, black lipstick, black clothes, stringy hair dyed black, always on some kind of drug now. I itched everywhere, did not scratch. Something in my head muted sound. Her gossip had planted in me the sudden desire to stop hiding and just go see Dillon.

But when Tuffie left, I lingered in the familiar grooves of work. I scalded the peels off the peaches, and the kitchen walls began to sweat. I halved them and lay the halves down into Ball jars, cupping them tightly to each other, like spooning lovers, and I poured in the hot syrup. I lowered each jar into the boil bath canner and flushed at the steam, pushed up my long john sleeves. The rolling boil cast a gentle sound, steaming the room looser with the scent of hot furless peach.

I showered and put on the mint dress I'd worn to Darrell's wake, then changed into jeans and a red blouse. Afterward, I pulled out the warm jars, halfmoons in syrup floating upward to each lid. Late morning. I would take a quart to Dillon, wait at his grandmother's until he landed his pesticide plane. I didn't know what I'd do or say if Nan was there. I wrapped the hot jar in a towel so I could set it on the truck's bench seat, but the phone rang just before I pushed out the screen door.

"You ever have an ache that calls for its phantom limb?" asked Mave.

"No," I said. "Where have you been?" I hadn't followed up after the co-op and felt the guilt sting.

"I think you should come over," she said.

"I'm busy. And it's early for a drink, isn't it?"

"Just come."

So I took the hot jar of peaches and drove to Mave's, and decided I would seek Dillon after.

The hydrangea off the left side of her junked-up porch still had one blossom. The near-noon light struck it, like a bell, and so the living room was more noticeably dark and dismal when I entered. No Mave, only your storehouse of books, Ruth, with their grayed tongues sticking out, places she'd marked for passages that had spoken her life into being. She had bedded me down in that living room once, on couch cushions on the floor, when she'd first moved back—remarkably, it had been the cleanest room in the house. I lay that night wrapped in a wool blanket pulled from a chest of camphor blankets and afghans, a kid in a cocoon, papers scattered under the cushions—Leave them, it's okay, she'd said. There were places in the books that would utter me, too, though I hadn't known that then. But lying in my cocoon, I'd heard the books' murmur and had scratched my ears for the tickle. I'd heard the chaos and the anthem.

Jar of peaches in hand, I smelled an odor like diesel. The same old circulars and plastics and wilting philodendrons lay scattered around my feet, TV guides and a Matlick Feed ball cap and empty pretzel bags.

"I have an ache that calls for its phantom limb," she said from the kitchen. I followed her voice.

"Brought you some peaches," I said.

"A drink?"

"Is that why you called me?" Having worked myself up to finally see Dillon, I couldn't mask my irritation.

She wore her ratty robe, her gray hair a spritz around her head. Nothing underneath the robe, it seemed. Some cleavage, no compression, some softness. I looked away by reflex. She picked at the lid rim on the unringed jar I'd set before her. One robe sleeve was pushed up. I saw she wore an X of white tape at her inner elbow, a cotton ball. As if blood had been drawn.

"My pipes are no good," Mave said.

"Rex will look at them. Probably a dead squirrel in the line again. I told you to put that screen on the intake at the spring."

"These pipes." She patted her chest. She put her hand out to say sit. I sat.

Ruth—what parts would you want to know? Those that are unreal because too real? Those you'd prefer without detail? Without diagnosis?

"I had a peculiar pain," she said, "so I got it checked out."

"Who took you?" I swiped at a moth stuck in liquid on the table.

"AWOL took me."

"Ron?"

"During his lunch. He's back working for the State now."

"Yeah, Clay told me."

"Highway flagger again. Slow, Stop, Slow, Stop. He won't tell Miranda on me."

"Tell her what?"

"Otherwise I'd be lambasted for waiting too long."

"Tell Miranda what?"

"That I have stage four lung cancer."

In my skull a great sudden pressure, like a tamping down. I said nothing. She studied the peaches. I felt as though the pressure would spill me out at my edges, so I rubbed my arms, containing myself.

Strangely, I could not feel her near, though she was right there across the table. Her robe fell a bit more open to almost bare her abused left breast.

She said, "I love words with two contexts that metaphorically mirror. Think about *trough*—a trough of a wave that follows the crest, and a trough for slopping hogs. You work those toward sameness." With a spoon, she gently popped the newly sealed lid from the quart jar and scooped out peach halves onto two soiled plates. I put my head down on my forearm on the table. I felt her sweep pieces of my clean hair away from my plate.

Once, Ruth, as a teen, I'd told her I found my life disappointing.

"Your life?" she'd said. "What's yours about it? The ham hock legs sticking out of your shorts?" I asked her whose it was then, but she never said.

DID YOU EVER WANT TO EMPTY YOURSELF LIKE A BOOT with small rocks in it—shake it out and start over? Did you ever want a new name? Hydrangea. Hibiscus. Horse. Horsehair. Did you ever want to be less alone and more like the Ellafritz girls who nurse each other's sons? Well, you never knew the Ellafritz girls, so probably not. I want aloneness and also to be less alone—that fat, divergent greed. When you traversed the Sinai, did the desert scrub take away the confused wanting, or intensify it? Where the stars are clarified and the water more secret. The air unhumid and undense and unswampy, breath coming in like wind through a screenless window, carrying neither wasp nor fruit fly.

We didn't leave Interstate 40 through Arkansas, as though the state's territory was somehow off-limits. It was hairy around Little Rock, but the rest was a mindless four hours. The trees did finally thin. This was the first time we'd really driven as though we had only our destination in mind and the blue Olds was nothing but a means to an end. Let's just get there already, said our slouching bodies, said Mave's covert surveillance of her tank's oxygen gauge, said Nan's periodic sniffing of nail polish remover to drown out the dog stench, said the dog's low whine.

At one point Mave confirmed the sensibility, said, "I'm ready to see the roofless room and see the rocks immortal, the New Mexico daylight." She coughed lightly. "Get our turquoise rings in Abiquiú. Did you know about O'Keeffe's macular degeneration, Nannette? Did you know she went blind holding her palette knives, calling up color from memory in her studio along the Rio Chama where the cotton of the cottonwoods snowed down—like radioactive fallout—upon the adobe ruins?" She coughed again. Nan uncapped the polish remover and sniffed.

"You can quote me on that in the book. That's quotable." Mave surreptitiously fished out a codeine from her brown sack in the door pocket. She took it skillfully without a drink, after surveying the empty cups crushed at her feet and in the console holes. She winced. I said I thought it was time we stop for the night.

It was late when we got to Fort Smith, which, Nan reported from her study of the atlas, was all the way on the western edge of the state, "like smack dab on the line of Oklahoma." I pulled into the Super 8 lot where a street lamp dropped a wall-less wardrobe of blank light upon us.

"I don't want to sleep," said Mave.

"You're tired," I said. "We're all tired. We're sleeping."

"Can you really ask about a pool this time?" said Nan. "I'm throwing Stinko in." Stinko stirred to life, aspiring to a long pee or a snack.

"I'm not sleeping. I refuse." The slur of the pill. "I'm ready for that red Oklahoma dirt."

"Fine," I said. "I'm sleeping and I'm taking these keys."

Mave squinted at me, or at the light too bright. "I don't want to miss this. Shh. Listen." She pointed out her still-rolled-down window. The freeway was close, we heard only the revving whomp of semis.

"Your codeine is speaking to you," I said.

"If we have to stop then fuck the Super 8," Mave said. "Let's camp out in the dry scrub. Let's get a whiff of the Ozarks that lie to the north."

"Unh-unh, I don't camp," said Nan.

"Sleep in the car then, Gypsy. Which are you afraid of? The rattlers and coyotes? Or the women that turned into hairy spiders?"

"I'm afraid of you, wacko."

Mave cracked up.

"I'll get us a room."

I was weary and heavy-footed crossing the lot. I heard Mave say to Nan, "Lay me with the multi-eyed tarantulas. They jump, you know, they jumped when they were women. They'll take me bite by bite and scurry up my legs, a furry foot where this tube runs right here to my nose holes. Then feed the rest of me to javelinas." The car door opened. Ellis trailed me, lifted his leg on the lamppost.

"Pool," yelled Nan.

A hollyhock lived, stick-straight in a half barrel of dark dirt outside the lobby door, surprising in its beauty. Smoking or non-smoking: smoking. The man demanded a pet fee since Ellis followed all the way to the glass door and smooshed his nose on it, waiting to be let in.

I pulled around to Room 131, popped the trunk as if it were routine.

"Seems like we ought to put one foot in Oklahoma, at least." Mave pointed out my window. "I can see it over there. Traversed by Apache, Kiowa, Comanche, and Cheyenne. We're close to Comanche territory."

We loaded into the room. I filled Ellis's Country Crock water bowl and he was wild with thirst. "Sorry, Flop," I said. His kibble was dwindling more than it should have been, so I gave him a few of the lingering pork rinds.

Mave started stripping the comforter from one of the beds, tank armpit-tucked. Threw the blanket on the floor and ripped off the top sheet in one impressively forceful motion.

"Mave," I said.

"Frankie," she said. Balled up the sheet and carried it, and one of the two table chairs, out to the parking lot, to a far spot where there was little light.

"I would like you to shave my head," Mave called.

"No," I said. "Please bring the sheet back."

"I want Little Gypsy to do it."

Nan came out of the bathroom. "Do what?"

"She wants you to shave her head."

Mave sat out in the parking lot facing the small dark hills, barber bed sheet draped around her. Nan and I closed the door. She claimed the Super 8 notepad. I pulled the table up to the bed so I could sit down at a surface, Nan scooted the chair into the other side and drew. She'd noticed the hollyhock too, and in lip liner she sketched a bed of them. She got up after about ten minutes and looked between the slatted blinds.

"She's still sitting there. What a nut. She's not coming in."

"She will when the drugs wear off."

"You know she has only a dozen of those pills left."

"You checked?"

"Yeah." She opened the door, yelled, "Come inside, Crazy." Silence from Mave. "Why do you want a shaved head?" Silence from the parking lot. "I don't have any clippers. No scissors, even."

"Trade your body for some," Mave said, face to the hills.

"Fuck off."

But after another few minutes, Nan said to me, "What the hell. I'll be back." She'd stripped to her black slip, now pulled on her striped dress and ballet shoes. Ellis whimpered after her at the closed door.

Through the blinds, I watched her walk to a room across the courtyard where a Ford F150 was parked, which I thought was a bad idea. She knocked and the door opened, so I opened our door and stood in it so the shirtless man who opened knew there was a witness. Mave glanced toward Nan, then back to the hills away from me, a silhouette mostly. Stoic. Contemplative. You should have seen her—like a stubborn kid.

Nan returned with a black plastic case. "He had clippers," she said. "And nice arms."

"Focus, Nannette," called Mave.

Nan took an end table and towel out to where Mave waited, opened the case and assembled the attachments in the half light. "They're battery powered," she said, and hummed the clippers on then off.

"Ready," said Mave.

I approached their backs and said, "You sure? Why do you want a bald head?" When I reached them, I saw she had removed her tubing and closed her eyes and bit her lip, which lightly bled. Somehow, this silenced me.

Nan said to me, "If she wants it, then—" and she took a slow swipe right down the center of Mave's gray head, the short thin hair at first collecting and covering Nan's hand like a glove and then dropping to the asphalt in a clump.

"Oh my god," Nan said, "it's so easy. Doesn't hurt, right?"

"Right."

Another stripe of hair, of fur, of concealment. My first thought was—You look like a cancer patient. Then I thought monk, desert hermit. Then I didn't think. My head emptied. I said out loud, "Want me to order pizza?"

When I came back from making the call, her scalp was bare and Nan brushed hairs from the sheet with the hand towel from the room. The scalp looked cool and eggshell-like: I could picture it hatching a mind if the air had been warm enough, but it was not warm. It had gotten cold without me noticing. I saw Mave shivering, palming her head. She reinserted the fixtures of her outer lung.

"Write about this in the book," Mave said quietly, closing her eyes again as Nan toweled residual hairs off her face. "And don't have me grow old in it. I'm out like a firework. The potassium nitrate oxidizes violet and pink, lithium will give the burst some red." She shot her hands out in a mock burst.

I told her I liked the new look. She said to spell lithium right in the book. She said to keep the title simple. Call it Horses. Call it Hibiscus. Call it The Hundred Years' War.

I told her I was not writing a book, I never had been. She said, "You've been writing it from birth."

So then we slept, full of pepperoni pizza. We were not camped out with feet pointing to the Ozarks. We were in Room 131, having returned the battery-powered clippers and shaken out the sheet. Mave had finally been knocked out by the pills, her bald head eerie beside me on her pillow, like a desert person leaving behind her trappings. All three of us desert people maybe, hermits together, not renegades but runaways. The terminally ill and her two sidekicks, both looking for something they could not name.

Nan whispered, "Tell me what the book is. What it's really called."

"The world doesn't need another book," I whispered back, turning toward her on my side, her young pretty face lonely across the aisle. "Who would read it?"

"I would read it," she said. Big-eyed. Quieter, she said, "Mave was shaking, you know. She's near the end."

I CUT A STEM OF BITTERSWEET and pictured the tiny head, the exploding-star heart. My ungloved hands on the woody twig and the rust-bright berries would have liked to have held the child's head, to feel it anxious or happy. So many times the baby I'd lost swelled into my mind. I've not told even you of all the many times.

The bittersweet was for Mave's table. I couldn't find a clean jar in her house, so I washed one, filled it with water, and set it on top of the eternal rubble. Between a crust of blue mold and a plate of mystery food, possibly pudding.

I don't know how much of the chemo narrative to describe to you. It's what you would expect from that unrelenting linearity of story. It was late September. There was the deep burning, the lifted arms and hurling interior body which I could witness from her external body, hurling while stationary—the puking upon the bed. The IV bruising its way in and her discussion about the TV tuned in to inane game shows. "Fucking *Wheel of Fortune*," she said. "Black humor, these oncology girls." When they changed it to PBS, an elephant baby was getting a bath. Mave turned on her side, the gown showed her flat butt. I stayed the night on a cot in the room and woke up at some point to eat the egg salad sandwiches Miranda had brought.

At home, I helped her affix the foreign tubing that irritated her ears but did help. The friendship was fraught but not one she was going to give up. She even cradled the portable tank with affection.

"That's the first round," I said.

"That's the last round," Mave said. "Get me some kind of cushion for the rubber on my ear."

"What do you mean?"

"Like toilet paper, or a cotton ball."

"What do you mean 'last round'? You just started this. It's not optional."

"Everything is optional. I'm gone. Out of town tomorrow."

"Sure. Okay."

"Get me a book."

"You'll die then. Which one."

"I'm blowing town. Any one."

There was the tall stack of art books unshelved and piled and unpiled, O'Keeffe on top. *Art and Letters.* The long thick one you'd clearly loved, with its many dog-eared pages, the pastels arching their backs on the cover, *Music—Pink and Blue II.* I brought it to her bed. She nestled the small tank beside her and took the book.

She said, "Do you remember the plan we made for our Mediterranean veranda, all that white stone and the whitewashed cottage?"

"No."

"Well, something you could call a cottage eventually. It would be abandoned, but we'd fix it up because we have pretty good hands, you and I. You could be handier, honestly, but we could make it work. Just trust me."

"A good view of the sea?" I said.

"Pretty decent. Some obnoxious condos off to the left, but from certain windows they won't interfere with the blue line. And then of course we'd head south, across the sea, to the deserts and the pyramids. Yeah." She opened the long book, vertically long, to the prints in the middle. There were those couple she had torn out, only jagged edges, the ones we still had stowed in the pockets of our jeans, but there remained *Red Hills and White Flower*, *Red and Pink Rocks and Teeth*, *Red Hills and Bones*. There was still *From the Faraway Nearby*—that skull with multipronged antlers, and the poppies and poppies and iris and nudes. We looked at them all until we got to the text of the letters. My head near hers, hearing her breath as something no longer her own. No longer guaranteed.

"It would never work," she said. "A transatlantic flight, even stowing away on a cargo ship. A road trip is all I can manage, I think. Somewhere we can get to in a few days. I want to go west. Like all the young bucks."

Give me her *Evening Star*, or one of her Blues. *Sky above Clouds.* I'll take *My Last Door.* The horrible black square. I heard Mave's aided breath. "That dream thing" O'Keeffe called it, whatever it was. *Abstraction Blue.*

"I don't think we should do that," I said. "What will we tell Miranda?"

"Gone fishing. Be back tomorrow." She perused the letters written by O'Keeffe in reply to letters not collected in the book, a one-way conversation. "'To Maria,'" Mave read, "'I have left the good country—I must get myself ready for the other kind of life with the dawn.' Let's go to her desert, where it's less peopled, Frankie. We'll mud up a house and thatch a roof. No, no need." She turned the page. "We'll find her roofless room in Abiquiú. I've always wanted to see that. I want to see her roofless room."

"Want to sleep for a while?"

"Good idea. You go shop for provisions. We'll pack tonight."

"Mave."

"Frankie." She flipped back to the prints. "Look at this one. This one of Pedernal, the view heading out of Ghost Ranch. Tell me you don't want to see the mesas. And this, *Red Landscape*. When she first saw red it was in Texas. Look at her heart in that sky above Palo Duro Canyon, how the white gypsum and red claystone made her feel. The yellow ochre mudstone. Tell me you don't want to see that."

"I don't want to see that."

"Bullshit."

"I want you to rest."

"Start packing. Say your goodbyes. Fucking Dillon—sayonara. Should have done that long ago. Clay, he'll understand. I'll come up with a roof if you're afraid it will rain. But the rain will be rare." The first out-of-breath gasp, the love affair with the tubes and tank beginning. I stared back at the stem of bittersweet, away from her, how it was framed by the bedroom door, like a picture, and I thought, *red ochre*. When I looked back at her, she'd flipped forward in the book again, to the letters. "'To Carl,'" she read, "'Tonight I will sleep in some of our barest country.'"

Somehow, eventually, she convinced me to leave soon, at the start of October, and in some compartment of myself I knew from the beginning it was her suicide mission, but how could I say I didn't want to go? And, really, was she going for me more than for herself? Didn't she know I needed to go? Of course she knew. She always knew.

I'm cold, she said. I want the scarcest river, she said, the Chama, she said, I want the clarity.

I DID SEE DILLON BEFORE WE LEFT—not in his grandmother's house, but in the Shop 'n Save one evening with Clay, the evening before the trip, near the paper towels because I remember the word *Bounty* off to my left. But first I saw more of Nan's paintings. I knew they were hers, the same signature style from the Train Cave graffiti, this time on the brick retaining wall at the four-way stop near the Shop 'n Save. She must have painted in the middle of the night, some kind of desperation move—lilies, which seemed pretty, seemed innocent and childlike, until you looked harder. And Clay—how could I have not written more here about Clay?—Clay contentedly set his forearm on his driver side door, window down despite the bite of cool October air. Shirt sleeve rolled up. Such a solid arm. Strong hand upon the door.

"Clay," I said.

"Yeah," he said.

I almost told him I'd be heading west in the morning. "Nothing." We got out and got our cart as husband and wife, trolled the aisles. It was so strange to be there in the Shop 'n Save getting supplies, Clay unaware that they were road trip supplies—tampons and breakfast bars and donuts. I should have been more strategic about getting Mave's favorite things.

Then there he was. In all the force of his decade-aged body. In the paper goods. Clay beside me, he knew Dillon too, and of course what Dillon had been to me. Dillon's black hair exactly the same, beautiful and smuggled under a forest service ball cap with white netting on the back half, which I saw before he turned my way. Hollower now at the cheekbones. Narrow-waisted still, a T-shirt, blue I think it was, with an animal on it, the hem of it pestering and teasing around the top of his belt. Perhaps Clay understood the privacy needed, the gravity and gruesomeness in the moment, but he didn't leave my side, simply stood there with our cart, both hands on the handle.

I saw no boy in Dillon then, I knew he was a husband and he flew planes and dropped killing spray. I knew very little else about him anymore. At one time, he was my mirror and his silence I'd taken for understanding. You're the one, his wife Nan had said to me at the co-op gathering that night. The one that what? Was I the one he meant to marry, or was I the one that drove him off, closed him out? His eyes under the cap's visor revealed nothing. I wanted to say I was sorry, and I wanted to say I hoped he was sorry, and I wanted to tell Clay goodbye, all things at once, unceremoniously, in aisle six, be done with everything. I wanted to say, I'm going west. I only half believed it.

What I said was: "How are you, Dillon?" Fumbling for my jeans pocket.

"Doing okay. Good to see you, Frankie. I've been meaning to come by. Sorry about your mom." Speaking then to Clay.

"Thank you. She's in a better place."

The useless talk like hands at my throat, menacing. "Right," said Dillon. He held tissues, or maybe toilet paper or paper plates—they are also in that aisle. My hands at my sides, big weights.

It was fitting really, to see them both at once, and in so anticlimactic a setting. I wanted to say to them I somehow had yet to begin my life. If Nan had been there, cleaving to his side. If she had looked at me out of her bat face then, I could not have managed to stay standing.

"I'm in Athens, Georgia, now, just spraying for moth around here for a while."

A few other selves came out, in a layup in league shorts, in cutoffs with his hand down them, in a dress, and one of those Frankies ankle-deep in Heather Run before falling. What is the word, Ruth, for that kind of falling?

"We heard that," I said. "We should go, Clay." And we went—just like that—the longer way to the checkout than the way that would have taken us past Dillon's body.

Back at Lottie's—I still called the house and blue chairs and kitchen *Lottie's*—I said to Clay, "I'll stay with Mave tonight. She should have someone to watch her. I'll see you in the morning." I kissed him, oddly, on the forehead because he was seated, as you'd kiss a young boy. Holding my overnight bag small enough for one night but packed full and quickly.

At the truck, Ellis jumped up when I opened the door and put his front paws on the running board. He could never make that jump himself with his barrel body. I lifted him to hug him goodbye, but found myself setting him down on the bench seat, watching his body breathe as I turned the key fast like a match striking.

IN THE OCTOBER MORNING, I packed the black Ford pickup, which had run just fine the evening before, while Mave sat, patient and lordly, on her porch beside the broken butter churn. She drank coffee and set the mug on one of the TVs at intervals. I had told only Clarissa, who had promised us a sandwich lunch. The lights were on in Mave's kitchen and bedroom.

"Want me to get your lights?"

"No, it'll throw them off," as if we were about to begin our real careers as fugitives. She wore her best flannel, jeans, boots. She had combed her hair wet, her head was probably cold in the early fall air. I made myself not help her step up into the truck.

"What's with the hound dog?"

"I don't know, he followed me."

"You sure about this, buddy?" she asked Ellis, who licked her nose and its accompanying tubes.

I turned the key with great transgression. Nothing. Only the buzz of battery. It wouldn't start.

"You're kidding me," said Mave. "Sabotage."

"It's not sabotage. Hold on." I unlatched the hood and wrestled it up, selectively viewing the wires I'd viewed at some point before, to see which one looked different, out of place. Then of course the blue Oldsmobile Royale drove up my gravel drive. The pretty waif got out, ran onto my porch, then saw us in our predicament in front of Mave's house. Here she came through the fence break, ten years younger than I, many times more lithe, so striking. I saw she'd been struck. The blackened eye and blued arm.

"Please help me," with that pleading, ravenous look.

I calmly thought how odd it was that, twice now, I'd seen Nan's paintings just before I'd seen Nan. Those calla lilies near the Shop 'n Save a kind of lewd sign, in the semiotics of the lost.

Tonight I will sleep in some of our barest country. I believed in bareness more than I believed in filigreed fields and forests or the drench of bog. I don't know why. Maybe you could tell me why the desert people went to the desert and walked out of their lives, or into their real lives.

We rose early without agreeing to. We rose fateful. Baby-bald Mave looked out the window at the Super 8 sign and said, "Take me to the scrublands," as though she'd been waiting to say such a thing. Until now, she'd been careful to hide the compression socks the color of sand dune. Now she stood in them, her legs bare up to her boxers. She rubbed her hairless head, remembering it.

The truth is, I helped Mave get dressed that morning. The day was different and my throat threatened constriction but did not constrict. Nan not speaking, Nan the one loose with all words and body—Nan whose easy fountain of voice I envied—was quiet and somber and put Mave's thick wool socks on for her, over the compression socks, and then her boots, saying only, "This one. Now this one," as if readying a kid for the school bus Mave had once driven.

Nan leashed Ellis and took him out as I packed up. We were practiced now at cohabitation.

The night before, eating pizza, Nan had given her pepperoni to Ellis and said, "Let's get one of those Airstream trailers, the little silver compact houses. We could live out here, you know."

Mave had said, "And one for Elijah, and one for Moses."

I'd laughed despite myself.

That night, after I'd told Nan there was no book and she'd said Mave is near the end, after another little while—I didn't write this before—Nan had asked me, "Did you ever meet Ruth?"

I'd said no. And I'd said, "But I know she is the only one Mave ever loved."

"What about you? She loves you."

And I'd said nothing.

In the car, Mave said, "It's early. We'll get many skies today, undented by buildings or roofs. We're in the plains now." Long breath refill. "Or maybe unpunctured. I'm unsure how much give the sky has."

"Good. Her drugs are working. I'm fucking hungry," said Nan, mustering.

"Thank you for your thoughtful contribution, Gypsy."

I pulled into the Arby's drive-through with the clear if unarticulated idea that we didn't want to waste time getting out.

Oklahoma started with oil rigs pumping like huge thirsty birds. There were more trees than I expected. The wind pushed hard at the car, I kept two hands on the wheel.

What I will tell you, Ruth, is that we were in the car about seven hours and they were bad hours. Stopping only for bathroom breaks, and there was no longer any pretense about shouldering Mave into the stall, walking her like the war wounded, as she'd walked my tender cousin Ron that day he stammered out his refusal to report to his post. I remember at one stop, near Oklahoma City, right before we passed the interchange to I-44, Nan and I were walking Mave to the restrooms at the back of a service station packed full of Western décor. Rodeo shirts and outlandish belt buckles and beaded medicine bags, turquoise everything. And Mave stopped us in front of a shelf of cow skulls, not bleached out like O'Keeffe's but lacquered, the horns wrapped with tacky fake leather. "We're getting close," Mave said before we stumbled on to pee.

I counted nine pain pills left, all the other medication of course flushed before we'd started, and then a confession that made me livid when I asked Mave if she was ready to switch out tanks, said maybe that would help.

"I brought empties," she said.

"Empty oxygen tanks? Are you nuts? Are you really crazy now?" My anger melded with panic. "We're finding a hospital."

"No hospital. Drive, Frankie."

"Why? Why are we doing this? This is suicide."

"Into the desert."

"We will not make it."

"We only need to make it far enough."

"Where is that?"

What I will tell you is that Nan and I both begged her, finally, to go to a hospital, but Nan relented before I did. "I'm the one driving, I decide," I said weakly, but somehow I kept heading west, on Interstate 40, as fast as I could, idiotically, blindly, the wind bullying us.

"That's it, drive," Mave rasped.

"Insane," said Nan, but she said nothing more about stopping.

WE CROSSED THE TEXAS LINE, into the panhandle, a rusted blue bullet racing a couple of parallel trains. Mave said O'Keeffe's spiritual home was always Texas, so maybe it would do. She stuck her hand out the window, as if to test the air. "The wind feels different, Frankie. It's a dusty desert wind. You got me out of the bog. It will do."

"Will do for what?" I said.

She said it wasn't what we'd planned, but maybe it was even better. The red canyons churning, the sun on the rocks. "Little Gypsy, don't paint the canyon. Paint what the canyon makes you feel."

"What do you think you're going to do, jump from a canyon ledge?" I still protested, though not with conviction. "You couldn't even get up there. You're too weak to get up there and kill yourself."

"Would be a lot easier if you hadn't tossed the gun." She pulled her paper bag of nine pills from the door slot and held them toward the backseat. "Help me with these, Nan."

"No you don't," I begged.

"Go," said Mave. "Be like the bighorn sheep. Be like your desert mothers. They're your mothers, not mine. I was born of a toad. They are your better mothers, I was a lousy mother."

"Spare me."

"I've always spared you."

"You did your best."

"I spoke to you as if to Ruth. I didn't respect you were small and hurtable, with more years ahead than behind." Big awful inhale.

"I'm not doing this," I said.

"I tried to count on your years behind you catching you like an old mattress. But nothing pillowed your fall."

"You don't know that."

"I know you fell," she said.

A long quiet. I heard atlas pages, I heard snout nosing limb, I heard the mighty Texas wind, the barer country, you could call it *windswept.*

Then Mave said, "I remember going to one of your games and you didn't know I was there. I was with Ruth then, wrapped up in her, home to see the twin boys when they were born. I didn't stay long. Rex was sworn off me, but Miranda wanted me to see the boys. I drove down and drove right back, but I went to your goddamn game. You fell, you hurt your hip that time. It's been like that with me and you."

"I don't remember that game."

"I was there but I was never there."

I shook my head, firm despite tears coming. "You were always there."

It was not long in Texas—what, two hours maybe?—before we started to see the brown signs outside of Amarillo for Palo Duro Canyon State Park.

"Get off the goddamn interstate," she said.

"No, it's the quickest way."

"To where? We don't need it. Where I'm going, I can go on horseback. I want to check out a horse."

"It's not a library book."

"Rent it. Rent me a horse. A palomino mare."

Can you ever forgive me, Ruth, can I ever forgive myself for seeing also a blue square sign with an H and choosing not to exit for the hospital though Mave was there dying in the passenger seat, her pale cells fading, her wrong molecules gelling like fish eggs, the network of tubes now unfettering her face? "Palomino"—she loved the word and repeated it, the name, the word rooted in resemblance to a dove. Would you condemn me for following signs for Palo Duro, Palo Duro meaning hardwood? Because of the shrubs and trees fighting to live in such a place—the yucca, mesquite, and juniper, cottonwood, willow, and salt cedar. All these were fighting upward through the rock.

The turns were few: just a hair to the south, on the outskirts of the town of Canyon where I knew O'Keeffe, young and heedless, had rented a room with many windows, as much sun as she could stand.

"Do you read the prophets, Nannette?" said Mave.

Nan was at a loss.

"Me neither. Except that place where the prophet says the desert will break into crocuses. All the way out here, the whole point is desertscape, and I think, yeah, I do want the crocuses goddamn Miranda planted for me in the yard without asking my permission." Her face unto the road showing lines of pain, sweat at her temples, on her whiskery lip. She was soaking wet. "Not just the desperate yellow rose of the prickly pear, either, that bulges like a boil with pus. The black bear eats the prickly pear, and when the bear finds the crocus—voilà—the wet cup for bees, he eats it and tastes a memory of being in a fertile place, of when he was under seawater in darkness. The only place a crocus matters is where it ought not to be."

Her mouth tender and harsh, her mothering of me a coaxing, a crocus, a strange set of smoke signals speaking from her house to mine through a break in the fence.

"Stop here," Mave said.

"No," I said.

"Now you're the one who doesn't want to stop."

"I'm not stopping." I shook my head wildly.

But I stopped, the sand and gravel crunching under our tires. Old West Stables stenciled in yellow on the sign. A small dusty office and a set of paddocks, one holding a dozen or so horses. I turned off the ignition, we sat like fools in our blue steel vessel. We were a mile or so from Palo Duro, the rocks cropped up in the distance, the carved claystone we'd driven all the way out here to see. "The ancient life is buzzing," said Mave. "You hear that buzzing? Is it my tinnitus?"

She did not get out of the car. About this time, I was weeping like a rock cracked open for thirsty wayward people.

She looked at me, held out the pills. "Help me, Frankie. I'm ready. I want to ride a palomino horse down into the canyon. I wish to be small atop a large beast that knows how to take care of everything."

It was Nan that got out, letting Ellis take off to be alarmed by the horses stirred up. She opened Mave's door. I didn't move, no way. Nan squatted down, took the bag from Mave's hand, and emptied the white pills into her palm and clasped them. She asked me gently for the cola cup in my door's cup holder. I gave it to her and she helped Mave take the pills two at a time, with deep swallows. Then she hefted Mave at the arm, but Mave softly shrugged her off, struggled alone to her feet and walked on, almost bowlegged, to be funny or simply aching through her lower body. Her head glared.

Nan stood there solid and able, not a waify, hungry thing, though she wore the same apricot dress she'd showed up in. I saw her somehow bleached clean by the Texas sun, her acceptance of Mave's choice, of the limits of the body, much braver than my obstinacy. I knew she would be able to paint the skeletons heaped up by desert drought, stare them down and expose what the skulls made her feel.

What on earth did Mave tell the man inside the stable office, with her bald head and scant air and whitened wet face, that convinced him to let her emerge from the building wearing his cowboy hat with a feather in it, and off he went to saddle something. What kind of man would take one look at her and not call an ambulance?

He was tall. He escorted her to a fence post which she leaned all her weight on, about to fall. Nan and I were both out of the car now.

"What did you say to him?" I reached to touch the hat brim.

"I promised him a night with you, Gypsy," she said. "Don't be mad."

"Fuck off," whispered Nan, tenderly.

The man brought out a horse saddled, bridled, deep brown with a black mane. It put its nose to Mave's shoulder. "Steady, boy, whoa, Nellie," said Mave. "I think his name is Spirit."

"Leroy," the man said.

"Okay, Leroy."

The man didn't really smile, but he had a knowing kind of hand, handing her the reins and helping her walk alongside Leroy's baleful, living bulk, each of his heaving breaths taking one of Mave's away as the excess of drug moved through her stomach lining and out into her coursing blood. Her breaths almost countable now. Can you feel this happening, Ruth? Can you feel my heart breaking? The heart that has doubted love as a thing I'm fit for, but I see, of course I see now, it is the only option. Can you picture the tall dream-like man setting out the stepstool for Mave, then hoisting her, like a windless sack with legs, to sit astride the horse, where she looked like a little girl, her hat, his, cocked until she righted it, wiping her face as though thinking the tubes were still netting her? He took the reins, he walked big Leroy toward a ring enclosed with fence where Ellis had his front paws up on a bottom rung, taut barrel body panting.

"Is it a palomino?" Nan asked me.

"I don't know," I said. All things blurred.

"They're lighter colored than that maybe," she said.

He led Mave on Leroy around the red-dusty circle, a little girl on a show horse, and she was as tall as she could be in her ever-present flannel, like a semaphore flag she'd spoken with, saying: I'm here. Learn to canter, learn to be boss, Little Thing; learn to turn in your heels for the steep canyon trails all slated up into white sky. You ride into the desert sun and you sense the scarce river where the river carves in, you go on, I'll be okay, I'll live, here in this world.

And when I gathered her in, almost on her final breath, when I held her like that, and the man let me, steadied the horse, and I brought her down slowly from the saddle and caught her whole body soft as a baby, what kind of love would you call that? That's what I'm writing now to ask you, you who know all the living words. What word? What name? Tell me, what kind of name does it have?

I AM GRATEFUL TO *Black and Grey Magazine,* which published the material on pages 81-82, in an earlier form, as the prose piece "Swine."

I would like to thank West Virginia Wesleyan College for the Faculty Innovation Grant that offered me time and space to work on this manuscript, along with the Writing Workshops in Greece that offered me the same. I would also like to thank Richard Schmitt, William Schneider, my agent Michael Snell, and Dzanc editor Michelle Dotter for reading earlier versions of the manuscript and helping to bring this novel into being.